THE HELLION IS TAMED

#4 LEAGUE OF LORDS

TRACY SUMNER

THE HELLION IS TAMED

Copyright © 2021 by Tracy Sumner

All rights reserved.

Edited by Elizabeth J. Connor, www.marginatrix.com

PROLOGUE

THE PAST

1802, An Unappealing Public House on the Thames Wapping, London Borough of Tower Hamlets

*H*er smile told lies. Made promises. Worked an angle.

Simon Alexander recognized the angle even at twenty candlelit, smoke-filled paces, because he'd worked it so many times himself.

Out of desperation, then later, when he no longer had to hustle, out of self-preservation and a low threshold for boredom. Thief, liar, swindler. All parts of the pathetic boy he'd supposedly left in the slums. When in actuality, he'd taken the despicable pieces with him, dusted them up with fine clothing and a fancy education. Society had no clue a renowned pickpocket, legendary on the filthy avenues of St Giles for sleight of hand unlike any the city had ever known, wandered their ballrooms and danced with their daughters.

A legend no one wanted to be—engulfed in a life no one wanted to *live*.

Until his rescue, he'd spent his boyhood in a wretched locale a mere twenty-minute carriage ride from the dreary public house he currently found himself in. Streets he'd vacated when a viscount with expertise in the occult, and a calling to save those afflicted, heard about a gifted pickpocket who spoke to the dead and came to retrieve him.

A starving, neglected urchin, Simon wouldn't have made it out alive without his adopted brother, Julian. The man who'd created his narrative of being a deceased viscount's byblow.

He wouldn't have survived without Finn. Humphrey. Piper. The Duke of Ashcroft.

In the early days, he'd stolen from them, rejected every kindness, snubbed every offer. Until the morning his view of the world changed. Shifted on its axis. He remembered the exact moment it hit him, sunlight streaming through his opulent bedchamber window and tumbling across a silk counterpane that cost more than any one item he'd ever owned. His heart cracking open like a locked trunk, emotion spilling free.

No one was abandoning him.

He'd finally understood that, unlike his abusive mother and his mislaid father, his new family wasn't going *anywhere*.

Like he wasn't going anywhere until he retrieved the Soul Catcher, the mystical gem the hellion sitting across the crowded den from him had stolen from the League, Julian's faction of supernatural misfits. She'd lifted it right out of the Duke of Ashcroft's pocket all those years ago, her image like a faded daguerreotype. He'd been unable to touch her, could only beg her with his eyes.

And she'd left anyway. Gone back to her time, never to return.

Consequently, he'd followed her into the past the moment—after ten years of study—he'd figured out how to do it.

He laughed beneath his breath and took a lazy sip of truly rotgut whiskey. He was going against his instincts on multiple fronts—but still, here he was. Fighting battles for the League, a group he'd resisted joining in the first place. But love led a man where it led a man, and he loved his brother. Hence, Julian's objective was becoming, in part, Simon's own, the lines dissecting life blurring, as they did the longer one walked this earth, he supposed. Layer upon layer of inconsistencies, contradictions. Until you didn't know who you were anymore.

The woman he'd tracked eighty years into the past had no idea what he'd done to reach her. Left his home, his cherished gaming hell. Walked through a portal he'd spent years researching when he had no way to return. Chasing a woman he'd never spoken to but who'd haunted him since he was a boy. Not his usual type of ghost, either. A daring girl who'd stepped in and out of his existence, a wordless, yearning presence, like his haunts. Yet so very alive when he was surrounded by death.

Then, one day, as if she didn't need him anymore, she was gone for good.

Much like his mother.

Simon dug his boot heel into the pitted plank and swallowed the rest of the whiskey *and* his resentment. He'd gotten over the slight long ago. Forgotten all about her.

Although, believing he'd found his person when she was not his person at all had been as devastating as watching his mother willingly step in front of a cart to her death.

Today, his goal was straightforward and didn't involve benevolence, deviation, or mooning over the past. The girl had filched something that belonged to the League—something he was going to reclaim or die trying. If he witnessed a stray spark of remembrance in her bloody blue eyes, for him or what he'd thought she felt for him, then he'd take that curious nugget back to 1882 and feel damned good about it, like a winning hand or fortuitous roll of the dice.

Unmistakably rotten luck, since he was thinking about luck, when his was usually good, that his time travel had landed him in the correct year, the correct month, but in the middle of a dank pub, his target surrounded by cutthroats, during a game of hazard she actually looked to be winning. *Fucking luck,* Simon thought with a grim laugh he wisely kept to himself.

The girl was reckless.

The type of hazardous distraction that Emmaline Breslin would expire from in two years, knife wound to the chest in a tavern two streets over, if she didn't travel back to 1882 with him.

This knowledge that he'd lied to himself all along about why he'd come swirling through his mind and his belly, twisting both, Simon squinted through the hazy candlelight at the girl he'd once loved.

His greatest fear wasn't facing Emma again.

Or the mission he'd sent himself upon.

It was his inability to state with utter assurance that he didn't still love her.

The next concern, reasonably significant, being his return to 1882. He didn't think he could travel back *without* his troublesome time traveler—and when she'd last left him ten years ago, he and Emma hadn't been on good terms. Her leaving and never coming back, that is.

So, he couldn't guarantee she'd escort him home. Or that he'd be able to convince her.

Of anything.

Blowing a breath through his teeth, Simon curled his hand into a fist in his trouser pocket and slapped his glass on the window ledge at his side.

If only she hadn't grown up to be so beautiful.

An unsightly woman would have significantly assisted his cause.

Not ugly, this one. The flames a dazzling amber wash over her, bringing forth streaks of auburn in her dark hair, highlighting the gentle curve of her flushed cheek. A face carved from marble, a stubbornly gorgeous face one wouldn't forget. Couldn't forget. Unrelenting shadows and a raucous crowd encircled the threadbare table before which she sat, some men in rags, others in more suitable attire the likes of which Simon had only seen in aged paintings hanging on gallery walls. All stinking drunk, their curses and ominous portent charging the air, the clamor mingling abrasively with the sound of waves cuffing the Wapping docks. The bitter hint of London's brume, familiar when nothing else about this time was, riding a velvety fog and pushing an element of despair into the room.

With a shiver, Simon glanced around in joyless uncertainty.

He'd learned to limit contact with ghosts in his time, but in the past, in *her* time, they swarmed him, their eyes bloodshot, their hands grasping. What he imagined was their hot breath striking his cheek. He couldn't provide the reprieve from misery they sought.

To save himself, he'd discovered he must, at times,

5

care for his deliverance above theirs.

Simon straightened from his casual repose as the man seated across the table from his prey took her wrist between his meaty fingers and gave it a punishing squeeze.

Simon fingered the knife in his ragged coat pocket, taking a swift step across the uneven plank floor. The shabbiest piece of clothing he'd worn in years, a calculated effort to blend into the environs. All part of protecting the girl, and hence, protecting his family. Retrieving the damned stone. He wasn't above killing, should anyone stand in his way.

Although he wasn't planning to have to kill *her*. He hadn't spent years exploring how to travel back in time and locate the one woman who'd haunted him, only to lose her now.

Emma. He whispered her name, his voice as unbending as the blade in his hand.

Emma.

He would never let her mean anything to him again. But he *would* save her.

"You think to twist this game of hazard, darlin'?" The ruffian wrenched Emma's arm, which she allowed. However, Simon noted the tensing of her lips, the leach of color from her cheeks. "Ramsey don't like bein' tricked. Even by the gel said to be the shrewdest sharper in Tower Hamlets. Dark Queen of the East End, innit it? That be a kind name, my girl." He leaned until his shadow fell across her, shrouding the vivid glints sparking her hair. "Some say you're touched. Here one day, vanishin' the next. Gallows down the way, a pirate hanged this very night, should ya be thinkin' to toss me a crooked slant of the dice. A constable on my payroll, don't ya' know. He has no tolerance for mystics." Ramsey reached, trailing his knuckle down her jaw as she winced. "Don't frown so, gel. I reckon even queens ever so often meet their match."

Emma inched away until her back hit the chair slats, the abused wood creaking. Lifting a chipped glass to her lips, she tossed back the contents, then wrenched her arm from her captor's hold with a ferocity Simon had been expecting to see…but was a little afraid to.

Giving a jaunty salute with the glass that made Simon's stomach clench, she laughed. A sensual vibration that lifted the hair on the nape of his neck. The first sound he'd ever heard from her, as she'd been silent in his dreams. Trapped in a soundless world during her visits to his time, they'd only communicated with their gazes. He remembered the feelings she'd aroused in him as he'd watched her lips, stained from mulled wine, curl in a knowing smirk any man would be compelled to destroy with a kiss.

What would she taste like? Simon wondered in absolute insanity.

What would this impossible woman he'd once thought of as his *taste* like?

Ramsey leaned back in his chair, hard-edged and without humor. Flinging the dice across the table, he gestured with a fierce jab of the smoldering cheroot in his hand. "You goin' to get this game rollin' or wot? Lots with a bit of blunt jus' waiting, gel. For the queen. My lady, she's waitin', too. Her naughty bits prefer a full pocket, if you catch my meanin. Swivin's always better when things are full."

Emma tilted her glass into the candlelight, lifted one shoulder in a languid shrug as she gazed through it. "Handsome swell such as yerself? Full pocket, empty pocket. What's the difference?"

"That an invitation?" Ramsey asked and pressed his barrel belly into the pitted wood, rocking the table on its spindly legs. "I heard tell the queen never extends 'em. Not to nobody. Touches no knobs, no sir."

Emma took the dice in hand, pursed her lips and blew across them. Not an answer to the question of how many knobs she touched, but a challenge, moving her a step closer to catastrophe, which she seemed to wildly welcome.

Simon opened his knife with a deft move and tucked it in his sleeve, crossing the room until he stood within reach two paces behind her.

Because she was careless. Encouraging notice—when he'd learned to hide. At some point, everyone with a supernatural talent learned to hide in the shadows. Control the situation—every situation—by being *in* control. The preternaturally gifted didn't have the benefit of attracting attention.

How had she survived this long if she'd *not* learned this?

When he could see she hadn't.

She rolled the dice, the pinkie on her left hand twitching as she flipped them in her favor. Blood pounded in Simon's temples as black edged his vision. He would have slammed his hand over hers to hide the tell if he could have. He owned a gaming hell and could spot even the most discrete tic, blink, stutter. This wasn't good; Emma wasn't as clever as she thought she was. He could smell the piquant edge of fear sliding into his nostrils.

His and hers.

A man who'd acquired his morals from cutpurses and lightskirts, thieves and degenerates, Simon Alexander knew trouble.

Emma Breslin, Dark Queen of the East End, was trouble.

More than he'd encountered in his twenty-seven

years.

Nevertheless, he decided, repositioning his knife for better access. He was going to fucking save her. Save the woman who'd visited him for a year when he was fifteen, then cruelly stolen his heart, his family's treasure, and left him to his haunts and his solitude.

"Guv, can anyone join this game?" Simon asked, slurring his words as he stepped into the low-lit circle, giving the shaky table an intentional bump that sent glasses tumbling to the floor. He let the knife slide into his hand with the disruption, bringing it by his side in a move he knew no one noticed.

Because he still had the fleetest touch in England. 1802 or 1882.

He didn't duck his head as Emma gasped, turning at the sound of his voice. Her eyes were as blue as he remembered, a heartbreaking shimmer in the candlelight. The startling color of blustery skies and bottomless oceans. Places one didn't want to inhabit. His heart gave a fierce thump, unwelcome desire for a woman he was determined to liberate only because she had something he *wanted* tolling through him like St George the Martyr's bell.

He had to remember that she'd never come back for him.

"Simon," she whispered, the last vestiges of color draining from her cheeks. The dice she held slipping from her fingers to roll across the table.

His pulse danced as her gaze did a sluggish survey from his head to his feet. But he held himself steady, warning her with a fierce look once she tracked back, to follow his lead.

"Out of here, guttersnipe," Ramsey snarled and vaulted to his feet, the legs of his chair scraping across the planks and bringing conversation in the fetid space to a halt. He crushed his cheroot beneath his boot with a vicious stomp. "This be a private game, a private *club*." Skirting the table, he grasped Emma's wrist and yanked her from her chair. "I can see in yer' face what you come for. And no one's gettin' to the queen before me. I've played the long game me whole life."

Simon felt the corner of his mouth kick up. *Guttersnipe*. True, he'd been that very thing.

Rocking back on his heels, the pounding in his temples picked up speed as Ramsey tugged Emma against his hip, a possessive move that should've mattered little when one was only liberating. An undeniable risk to show he had a weapon, but Simon nonetheless decided to, using his knife's pointed blade to scratch his cheek. "Care to wager for 'er? I'm willing. To stick my neck out, that is." He tilted his head, ran his tongue over his teeth. "For a queen and all."

Ramsey's fingers tightened around Emma's wrist, his knuckles paling as she winced. "You're bleedin' mad, is that it? Loose in the napper? A stranger threatenin' me in me own place? You must be. Maybe this is my night's entertainment." He jacked his thumb over his shoulder, in the direction of the river. "I own the docks; I own it *all*. You shoulda never stepped into this tavern, my friend."

Emma's gaze caught his, her lips forming a silent plea. *Stop*.

She'd betrayed him, but Simon would kill for her.

Because she was one of them, a member of the League, even if she didn't know it. He tipped his chin just enough to let her see he wasn't backing down. Not now, not ever. Confrontation and diversion were, he'd decided, the way to get them out of this mess. He was used to blending into any space he inhabited—a tactical gift—but he also knew when this strategy was doomed.

"You with me?" he asked, a muted whisper he hoped only she heard.

She shook her head, mouthed *no*.

He held up three fingers. *On the count of...*

Her pupils widened, hair spilling forward to roll over her worn bodice, the slopes of her breasts. "You're going to get us killed," she ground out between clenched teeth.

Seeking validation of her statement, Simon glanced around the barroom. The crowd had closed in, circling like ravenous wolves, the air throbbing with the expectation of violence. The alley entrance was close, twenty feet, give or take. He wasn't sure if they could make it there before the pack was on them.

His focus found its way back to Emma, the grin twisting his lips only partly contrived. He was cracked for thinking it, but this brewing battle felt *good*. His body thrumming, his mind balanced on the edge of a cliff. He hadn't felt alive in years, centuries. Addictive, the rush. All the things his brothers were afraid still lurked inside him. "Emma, queen of the slums, thief of mystical objects, you know who I am, and you know what I'm looking for." Bloody hell, no need to whisper if they were going down. He pointed the knife at her. "Do you have it?"

Her gaze betrayed her, shooting low. Coat pocket.

"You can get us out? 1882. London. Or where you showed up before. Oxfordshire. Either will do."

She swallowed tightly, pressed her lips together, nodded.

His fingers curled around the knife. She could've come back at any time but had simply chosen not to. "Then, my dark darling, we're in business."

Before Ramsey would interpret the words they'd spoken, Simon took a swing, connecting with the brute's jaw. His years of training with the Duke of Ashcroft had prepared him for this skirmish. Had prepared him for *battle*.

But giants never went down easily.

Ramsey staggered into the table with a roar, turning it over, sending glasses and candles flying. He went to his knees, hung his head for a belabored breath, then shoved to his feet. But, as Simon had hoped, the horde was more interested in warfare than him. A stranger they'd never seen, cared nothing about. Ramsey, they likely had problems with. So, they played into Simon's hand, turning to each other, inebriated fools determined to prove their mettle.

As the tavern erupted in shouts and the sound of breaking glass, Simon jammed his knife in his waist-band and reached through the crowd. Her hand fell into his, seeking, and he hauled her across the bar, elbowing bodies aside, stepping over crystal shards and broken chairs, bodies and disorder.

Someone gave Emma a hard shove that propelled her into his back, and they stumbled through the doorway and into the alley, moonlight a dreary spill over them. The scent of burning rubbish and coal rode heavy, the air foul and thick. Simon took a breath of it and turned to her. She seemed stunned, her gaze locked on their linked fingers. Chest rising and falling, bringing generous breasts he didn't want to imagine filling his hands against the neckline of her ragged gown. Her eyes lifted to his, and for a brief moment, the sounds of chaos—shouts from the docks, carriage wheels hitting pitted cobblestones, terse conversation and cruel calamity—faded until they were the only two people in the world.

Like they had been before.

Emma. The girl who'd visited him when he'd been a lonely, confused adolescent, she the beautiful creature who'd stepped out of his dreams and into his time. But never fully. Never where he could do more than look. And *yearn*. The only person who'd ever arrived in his world from another who wasn't dead.

Not a ghost, but not someone he could touch, either. This moment was the first for that.

She looked the same, standing there in the silvery, fog-shrouded light. Hair as ginger-sullied as he remembered. Indigo eyes, lashes so long they grazed the hollows beneath. Tall, the top of her head coming nearly to his shoulder.

And those lips.

Inviting exploration, inviting blind fascination.

Which, at one time, he'd allowed.

Been sucked into in breathless captivation. However, his yearning had perished lifetimes ago.

Along with his naïve view of love.

As if she could read his thoughts, those gorgeous lips parted, releasing a misty gasp into the night. Her breath stole into his lungs, the scent of cinnamon and cloves a delicious tickle. An awareness as tangible as her finger trailing down the nape of his neck and past the open collar of his shirt.

Awakening feelings long dormant. Unwelcome and uninvited.

Because the boy who'd loved her was gone.

"Where is it?" he asked and wrenched his hand from hers, letting their arms drop. He rolled his fingers into a fist to stop the tingling in his palm and brought his arm against his chest to keep from reaching for her.

At his stark tone, she took a lurching step into the alley's rough brick. Her gaze plunged to his boots and worked its way up, the most excruciating inspection of his life. Exhaling deeply, she patted the pocket of a threadbare coat that had seen better days years prior. "Here. It's right here. I never once, not ever, let your swish bauble escape my sight." When she could see her admission didn't sway him, she whispered, "Honest to heaven, I needed it more. I skipped in an' outta time, no control 'til I found it mentioned in a book about the spectral and arcane. I never meant to bother anyone, only get what I needed to survive. I can read, you know. My ma taught me, before"—she swallowed deeply and looked away—"she passed. Was a wonder I made it ta' you those times, seeing as my control ain't the best. I've been able to mostly stay in my own time now thanks to that hunk of—"

"Fluorite," Simon finished for her, refusing to let her plea soften his heart. *Refusing*. "It's called the Soul Catcher, and we have people who desperately need it. You're wrong about no one but *you* needing it. Children growing up with supernatural abilities who have no control, either. In truth, we have a brethren of souls seeking solace only that stone can give." He jerked his head toward the tavern with a curse. "And the Dark Queen of the East End can obviously take care of herself."

Jamming her hand in her pocket, Emma yanked the Soul Catcher free. A gem the size of a walnut, the stone glittered in the moonlight, casting crimson facets like stardust at their feet. Shoving it toward him, she snapped, "Take it, then. Your all-powerful rock. Take it and be gone with ye'. Fancy toff such as yerself. In the wrong place. The wrong *time*." At his measured silence, her smile grew, her teeth a flash of pearly brilliance in the night. "You can't go wifout' me. Ah, blimey, is that it?"

Snatching the Soul Catcher from her hand, Simon let the wave of contentment at touching the gem

14

slide like sunlight through him, pushing aside the raw feeling of touching *her*. "Honest to heaven, to use your verbiage, what if I can't?"

She huffed, her smile slipping at his mocking. "You'd risk this for me? Come here and not know 'bout gettin' back?"

Simon tipped his head back and laughed, the sound as jagged as the slivers of glass beneath his boot. Glancing down at her, he shoved the gem in his waistcoat pocket with a careless shrug. A gesture he hoped concealed the storm of emotion he experienced when he looked at her. "No, my dark queen, I risk it for my *family*."

Her chest rose and fell, another call to lose himself in the creamy swells of her breasts, dive into the warmth he could feel radiating from her body. Never to resurface. Lost. "I couldn't step out then, when I came to you before. I didn't know how until I stole yer blessed stone. Stuck in a box, walls holding me in. I would've. Maybe. Maybe later, I even tried. But you—"

The tavern door burst back on its hinges as two brawlers stumbled into the alley, falling in a tangle to the grimy cobblestones, their grunts and punches echoing through the night.

Simon grasped her hand, dragging her away from the bedlam. The knife in his waistband and the pistol in his boot considerable reminders of the protection he could provide. But he didn't want to kill anyone. Not tonight. "We have to go."

She halted, jerking against his hold. "I'm not goin' nowhere with you, mister."

The Soul Catcher heated until it glowed like a piece of the sun from the depths of his pocket. The haunts circled and edged, their breath hot, rank. He wondered if Emma could feel their presence. If she had any idea why he was trying to save her. He'd promised Julian and Finn he wouldn't tell her, because it broke the rules. But how could he *not* tell her? "You can't stay," he finally whispered, the apprehensive tone painting his words unmistakable. At least to him.

She gave another yank of her arm that he controlled by pulling her flush against his chest.

Her heartbeat danced through the thin layer of her pathetic coat and right into his chest, like an arrow jammed in deep. Until his matched hers, a frantic call. "You *can't* stay," he repeated, his strident pronouncement echoing off the alley's walls.

She blinked, her face sliding into a brooding countenance Simon would have loved to capture on paper if he'd the skill, which he did not. He could only speak to the dead and steal. "How long do I have? If I stay?"

The uproar from the tavern intensified, and Simon glanced over his shoulder to see another set of combatants tumble out the door. Turning without comment, he hauled Emma down the alley and onto Wapping Wall Street. They could lose themselves in the warehouses leaning like beaten guardsmen along the river if need be.

Until he could convince her to go to 1882 with him.

A fine mist had begun to fall, coating them in the slick, stinking moisture only London could bring. Crossing the congested lane, Simon dodged carts, sedan chairs and hackneys, stepping over excrement and discarded rubbish, the night pitch without the gas lamps he was used to, the cobblestones greasy beneath his boot.

"I'm just down on Milk Yard," she panted, struggling to keep up with his long-legged stride.

"Headin' into the docks at midnight ain't wise for—"

"Isn't wise," Simon whispered and pulled her into a concealed nook next to a freight warehouse's open doors. Men swarmed in and out of the structure like ants, shouldering scuffed crates and dripping barrels of ale, tossing the couple lingering in the shadowed alcove nary a glance as they passed them.

Giving Simon a weak shove when he released her, Emma glared at him, her eyes matching the cobalt shimmering through the darkness and making his heart stutter. "Headin' into the docks at night *isn't* wise. Not for a posh man like you. The shabby clothes ain't enough to prove you belong here. They know, these tough rookery blokes, the minute they lay sight on you that you don't. The accent, too, polished like the queen's silver, it is."

The man came out of nowhere, his silver blade slashing through the corner of Simon's vision.

Simon hurdled into a mindless protective mode, insanely thankful the Duke of Ashcroft had forced lessons in self-defense upon him since he was in short pants. Shoving Emma behind his back, he kicked low, connecting with the assailant's shin and sending him to his belly on the cobblestones. Going down on his knee, Simon wrenched the knife from the man's hand and twisted his arm until one more rotation would have it breaking. When the ruffian looked over his shoulder, gaze wide with fear, Simon spun the weapon on his palm like a card he was sharping. "The package isn't always what it appears, my friend. A lesson for you, free of charge."

"Oh, for the love a' God, let me handle this if you're only goin' to tease him," Emma muttered and was suddenly down there with him, her ragged skirt crumpled about her ankles. She grabbed the knife from Simon's hand and pressed the glittering blade against the man's neck without another breath passing from her gorgeous lips. "Jonesy, you know better than ta' welcome a visitor to our fine neighborhood in such a manner. And a friend of mine, too. A real good one, for all ya' know." Hooking the blade until a dribble of blood oozed into the tattered collar of Jonesy's shirt, she laughed. "You are one right fool. After we had a discussion the last time you snuck up on me. Dicked in the nob, you are."

Simon frowned, bracing his hand on the slick stone. "Dicked in the *what*?"

"You don't speak our language, posh man," Emma whispered with a smile that broke through London's haze to light him up inside. "Crazy. He's crazy ta' chase me down again like this. Not the first time I've forced a cutting edge to his throat."

Simon rocked back on his heels in horrific comprehension. Jealous, possessive certitude. "Is there more to this story than I'm seeing laid out before me, my dark queen?"

"As if you'd know what life be like down here, you toady toff," Jonesy mumbled from his twist on the cobblestones.

Simon jerked the knife from Emma's grip, tossed it aside and yanked Jonesy to his feet as if he weighed less than a sack of grain. *Another grateful nod to the duke's training*, Simon thought with a torrent of unsolicited fury. Shoving the man two steps away, he straightened his cuffs in an effort to gather his wits. So like his brother Finn, he almost, *almost*, smiled. "I should point out, I grew up in St Giles, so you can keep your bloody opinions to yourself, friend. I'd find another couple to brutalize if you understand my meaning."

Emma edged behind Simon as Jonesy stumbled

away, her gaze burning into his back. Hell, he'd surprised her and himself by admitting where he'd grown up. *What was he doing?*

"I can't leave here."

Losing his fabled control, Simon turned, grabbing her by shoulders. "Is there anything holding you in this time? A family? A child?" His voice dropped to the far reaches. "A lover?"

Her cheeks shown pale in the moonlit shimmer a drifting cloud cast over them. The sounds from the warehouse, clanks and shouts and cranks, rolled over them like a wave. Simon didn't think the shine of tears in her glorious eyes was a play on his emotions. Instead, they seemed a play on hers.

Stumbling out of his hold, she glanced around, her throat clicking as she swallowed. She tucked her hair behind her ears, shifted from one worn boot to the other, delaying the decision. Finally, after a silence that he thought included her heartbeat in its rhythm, she shook her head. *No.* Nothing holding her in 1802. "What am I going to do? Learn to live another way? Like one of your society women? Fancy me up like a doll."

He snorted, imagining that. However…his mind spun as he took Emmaline Breslin in. A thorough inspection that sent a flush shooting across her face—but an inspection she allowed. Her body was magnificent, even in rags. Her face spectacular, even with dirt smudges and hollows chalked all over it from lack of food, lack of sleep. Her accent was trash, her expression criminal. Her attitude…he sighed. *Rotten.* But he'd been no better, worse maybe, and look where he'd ended up?

It wasn't the craziest plan he'd ever had.

He knocked the toe of his boot against stone,

giving her time to accept her decision. Accept his. "Do you have a portal? To get us there?"

She chewed her lip, gaze shifting from the ground to the wall to the sky before returning to his. He checked her pinkie for a sign she was lying, but it remained still. No twitches. His heart tilted in his chest, and he knew he was still much too vulnerable to her, which made him unaccountably angry.

She held out her hand, her smile frank, mixing tartly with her rotten expression. "With the swish stone, I don't need one."

Slipping the Soul Catcher from his waistcoat pocket, Simon gave it a quick spin and tumble, in and out, around and over his fingers. Partly to impress. Partly because he could.

She might be decent at sleight of hand...but he was a *legend*.

"Showy," she said with a scowl, but a rosy flush relit her cheeks, her dazzling eyes tracking his performance. Maybe she wasn't completely immune to him, after all. "So, you goin' to tell me where we need to go or play with the swish stone until dawn?"

He dropped the gem into her palm, hoping this wasn't the last he'd ever see of it. "1882. London. Or Oxfordshire, where you showed up before. April, if you can manage it."

She took his hand, her touch storming his senses. The Soul Catcher flared, golden light glowing against their skin. "Easier if I drop us in this very spot. An exact day, I can't guarantee. My travel isn't that...accurate."

Simon muttered a curse beneath his breath. *Brilliant*. "Then this spot it is."

She straightened her spine, closed her eyes and whispered something he couldn't quite catch.

Then they were gone.

CHAPTER 1

THE PRESENT

1882, A Duke's Boisterous Residence
Mayfair, London

Five days and eighty years later, all Emma could think was: *Simon Alexander's a do-gooder.* A hypocrite. A changer of lives. His bloody own, the most astounding. From rookery bugger to natty bloke. A mighty grand life he'd procured for himself.

Now, he thought to change her. Procure this life for *her*. Without even considering that she wouldn't want to be beholden, owe such a debt to his family. To him.

The daft part of the deal? She *wanted* to change. For him, without knowing him anymore, an understanding she'd stumbled over like a wrinkle in the extravagant carpet upon which she trod. She glanced around the luxurious bedchamber with a tight swallow. This life of measured sips instead of gulps, walking with your back straight as a ruler and whispering when you felt like shouting was a life she wasn't sure she wanted.

The lot of them, Simon's family, wished to file away the rough bits that made her Emmaline Breslin. They did, indeed. Every dreadful, jagged edge. The lips that opened and allowed cockney to tumble free. The hands roughened by labor and desperation. The red hair. The freckles. The scowl they said made her beautiful when turned to a smile. The curse words and the ribald jokes not suitable for a woman of *standing*.

Every chatty chit in his family had surrounded her since Simon ditched her, promptly disappearing with a duke, like a dog with a nagging wound to lick. And they hadn't shied away from telling her how wonderful he was. Selling her on an item they didn't realize wasn't for sale. Not to her. Not for a blimey second had they quit shoving his agreeable qualities before her like a dripping slice of tipsy cake.

Gentle, calm, strong.

Intelligent, handsome, witty.

As if she didn't know these things about him.

The year they'd spent together when she was fourteen and he fifteen, her popping in and out of his life, his time, had been magical. A reprieve from poverty and despair. An effort to control a mystical talent that had been nothing but a hardship from birth. Even if she couldn't find a way to destroy the barrier separating them and touch him, talk to him, she'd been enthralled. Fascinated, charmed, attracted. Boosey with him, like the time Winsome Sally had challenged her to a gin match on her birthday, and she'd promptly lost both her dinner and the wager. But it had been grand fun before the muddle.

Back then, she'd studied Simon with—

Emma scrunched up her face and searched for the word...

Diligence. She'd studied Simon Alexander with more diligence than the books her ma had borrowed from that posh family in Berkeley Square she'd worked for before she died. This months-long investigation had allowed Emma to witness his undying love for his brothers, men not in actuality his brothers at all, his struggle to deal with his magical gift and all the ghosts who surrounded him, and the distance he held himself apart. She'd desperately wanted to reach him, had wanted to change his life, too. Had wanted to be a *part* of it.

Though she belonged in his world less than a rodent in a ballroom.

But no one in this splendid Mayfair townhouse grasped her motivation back then—and *he'd* forgotten. Or convinced himself that the way they'd talked without words had been a—

Emma sighed and hunted for the phrase she'd read in the duchess's book last night, shifting from foot to foot, her new slippers pinching her toes worse than the intricate twist her maid had wound her hair into was pinching her scalp. She snapped her fingers when it came to her.

Simon had convinced himself their feelings had been a *figment of his imagination.*

He was angry with her for leaving and not coming back. When she hadn't been able to come back. Not for ages, due to pitiable circumstance and weak command of her gift, and when she had, five years ago, he'd broken her heart without knowing it. And that, friends, was that. He wasn't going to forgive her—and perhaps she couldn't forgive him. Even if she learned to speak without dropping her Rs, which she'd done quite right with on her own.

Wore exquisite gowns and prissed around like a princess. Held out her pinkie when she sipped tea. Sipped, not *slurped*, being the goal, according to the duchess.

No, Simon had dropped her like a lump of flaming coal, taken himself off to his frantic city life, ignored her all week after thrusting her into a situation that pinched more than the slippers.

The boy she'd left behind had turned into a full-fledged man. His soulful brown eyes were the same. His hair was a shade darker, now the color of dying sunlight, curling around his face just so. Made a woman want to push the strands aside, give them a neat tuck behind his ear.

But everything else, *changed*.

When he'd brandished that knife like no sharper she'd ever seen, his long body bent over Jonesy, she'd been reminded of a fighter she'd seen once in a Shoreditch market, muscles in his arm bulging, broad shoulders tensing beneath a shirt made to look ragged when it was tailored sleek as a cat to his form.

Simon Alexander fought like no posh toff should, that's for sure. Skills she didn't imagine he got to use often in Mayfair.

Emma glanced around her assigned bedchamber with a frown, her gaze snagging on the velvet curtains, the silk counterpane in shades of cream and violet, the gaudy rug that was worth more than anything she owned or would ever own. It was, without a doubt, the most fetching chamber she'd ever seen, much less stepped into. Or been given.

Given by Simon. Saint Simon.

While spouting off about his many fine qualities, his family hadn't mentioned his astonishing skill with a blade. His bloodthirsty bent when he heard the call to bring the sentiment forth. His fast flashes of temper, what her ma would have called getting his breeches in a twist.

But there weren't breeches in this modern world, only trousers. Oh, they'd told her that, too.

"*Restez immobile.* Stand still," Madame Herbert, the modiste whispered, her French accent muscling her suggestion into an authoritarian area Emma both admired and feared. "You need contemporary clothing, and you need it *today*. I'm going to jab you if you keep moving. You'll bleed, and then where will we be with this exceptional linen I had my assistant retrieve right off the ship this morning?"

Emma fidgeted as Madame Herbert yanked a needle from the pincushion attached to her wrist and slid the metal sliver into the material she'd bunched at Emma's waist.

Glancing back at Delaney Tremont, the Duchess of Ashcroft, Emma sent a pleading look across the room. "Duchess, how many do I need? This is the fifth gown we've altered, and I only had two day dresses before. How am I to pay you back if you keep ordering more items than I can ever pay you back for?"

"Proper address is 'Your Grace'," the modiste supplied, giving her hip a little squeeze.

"Call me Delaney, please. And these clothes are my gift to Simon, darling time traveler. And to *you*. If you hadn't stepped in front of my horse that day ten years ago, a stunning apparition, and caused me to land on my rump, my duke might have waited years to realize he loved me," the duchess murmured from her sprawl on the chaise lounge, her hand covering her rounded belly, her eyes closed in near-slumber. She was expecting her third child and seemed to sleep most of the day away.

Poor thing, had been Emma's first thought.

Until she'd seen the duke's lovesick expression when he looked at his wife and changed that to, *lucky girl*.

"Rags, what you had before," Madame Herbert muttered around the needle she'd thrust between her sharp teeth. "And your shape is quite lovely. *Quite*. Curvaceous, but not too. Too many curves ruin the contour. Deserving of my talent, this figure. But showcased by tatters such as the ones you arrived in will not serve." She tucked and pinned, mumbling beneath her breath, pinching harder than necessary to gather the pleat. "Men will drop at your feet, a blind spiral, when they see you in my creation. With that scarlet hair, ah, la, and those sapphire eyes, the colors I've chosen, it will be a triumph like none London has ever seen."

"I'm done to a cow's thumb," Emma said, dread growing like ragweed through stone in her belly. Simon and his band of mystics wanted to pass her off as a distant relation of the Duke of Ashcroft, the duke such a close friend that Simon had immediately dropped her at Ashcroft House upon their arrival in 1882. Like he would a dog they were watching while he traveled. All the while, telling her she would soon be a valued member of this League he kept mentioning, as if she cared about the occult.

She hated her gift, hated being extraordinary more than she hated being poor.

They thought the solution to her problem was to create a fresh history for her. She plucked at a stray bit of fabric with a frown. Maybe the magic surrounding these people was twisting their senses. Time travel had made her unafraid of living in a different era. But this? Country cousin to a duke? A backstory of isolation and modest associations allowing her to step into a life she'd neither earned nor felt comfortable accepting. Allow for the social gaffes she was sure to make at every turn.

Society, no matter what year you chanced to meet them in, was a poisonous bunch.

"Done to a cow's thumb," Madame Herbert whispered, appalled, her gaze skating over Emma then back to her task. "We can't parade you through a ballroom in one of my marvelous gowns without improvement of your speech, *chérie*. Like slapping paint on a decaying building."

"It means I'm tired, exhausted, worn plum out," Emma said, her temper flaring. Moving out of range of the modiste's questing grasp, she stalked to the window, gazing at the tumult that was the city of her birth. Chaotic, just like it'd been when she left. *If this French crow thinks to belittle me and me stand for it, she has another think coming.*

The duchess groaned and lumbered to her feet, her arm curled low to cradle her belly. "I'm a transplant here as well, Emma. A filthy American, as you can hear from my speech. Not exactly someone the *ton* wanted to filch one of their dukes. But filch him, I did." She shuffled across the room, perching her hip on the escritoire by the window, her crimson silk gown a delicate flutter around her. She appeared a duchess in every way, *except* for the accent. "I had to learn to fit in, too. It can be done. Easily. Your enunciation is very good, considering. I imagine you've been filtering out the impurities all along. Anyway, you're a member of the Duke and Duchess of Ashcroft's family. And society pays attention to anyone with even a hint of blue blood racing through their veins." Delaney tapped the windowpane and smiled. "But better yet, you have the League's support."

Emma grunted and gave the tassel wrapped

around the velvet curtain a yank. She'd heard this one before, all week long.

"Everyone in this residence is special. Did Simon tell you this?"

Infuriation swelled, emotion flooding Emma's cheeks when she thought of the way Simon had dropped her like a bag of rubbish at the duke's door. "Honest to heaven, he told me nothing."

"Such a foolish man, but then, aren't they all?" Delaney murmured, her smile growing. "Then I shall tell you, since he has not. You aren't alone. Every person we employ has a supernatural talent. From maid to footman to duke to duchess." She wrestled herself into the chair sitting before the desk, kicked a rubbish bin upside down and stacked her slippered feet on top. Elegant, though, the entire production. Bloody impressive. "Even our Madame Herbert."

Emma turned in a flurry of half-stitched linen, her mouth falling open. Madame Herbert glanced up from her sketch with a slight bow of her head, a blisteringly graceful rejoinder.

"You must learn to see past what is presented, *chérie*." With a wrinkle of her nose, her thimble floated from her reticule, drifted across the room and into her waiting hand.

Emma blinked and stumbled back, plunking her bottom on the window ledge. "Why, you have a cursed rum touch."

Delaney covered her mouth to hide the laugh that blessedly came out sounding like a cough. "A 'cursed rum touch' that made her vulnerable as a woman living alone in Lyon. As you know, our gifts do not endear us to, well, to anyone except each other. So Madame Herbert came here ten years ago to be a part of the League after hearing about protection with a supernatural group in England. She made my wedding dress. And every stitch of clothing since then."

"I don't even know what a League is," Emma grumbled, picking at a loose thread on her skirt.

"The League is a group of people with gifts, like you and me. Madame Hebert. My talent is knowledge." She tapped her temple. "I have an attic of material at my disposal, enough to fill a thousand libraries. It's been useful to us on occasion. Carrying important information to our contacts in other countries, for example. Not a letter someone could confiscate, but rather, reams of research tucked in the dark corners of my mind. I've learned to manage it, this gift. Not let it suck the marrow from my bones. That will be part of the agreement if you join us. That we research this ability you have to travel through time, then help you better control it."

Use me when you need it, Emma guessed, was also part of the deal. She scratched her shoulder, an unfinished seam pricking her skin. "I can control my skill fine enough with the swish stone in my possession. The Soul Catcher." But she reckoned that picking an *exact* day to appear when she strolled through time would be better than the random arrivals she now directed. She'd dropped herself and Simon like a stone three solid *months* past when he'd disappeared, an incident he'd said nothing about. But she could tell, aside from his noticeable relief that she'd landed them in the correct *year*, he'd not been impressed by her overcalculation. "I suppose we could barter, a swap of sorts. I might be willing to play, depending on the terms."

The duchess tilted her head in thought. "Swap?"

Emma sighed. God save her from the aristocracy. "You pick me apart like a bent timepiece, study all the bits and pieces close-up like, and I get to keep the swish stone. Until I figure out how to go along without it. It's yours, of course, the League's. I ain't" —she huffed a breath, let it go through teeth the duchess had claimed were straight and white as pillars—"I'm *not* going to steal it. And I will stay in 1882, for now." She fluttered her hand down her chest and made an X over her heart. "You have my word."

Madame Hebert snorted.

"My word is as true as a newly-minted guinea, duchess," Emma whispered, tears stinging her eyes. *It was.* And her word, her honor, was *all* she had.

The duchess groaned and rose to a shaky stand, crossing to Emma before another poignant confession could be uttered. Another dressmaker's rebuke issued. "Delaney, please. I haven't been called duchess this much since the day I married Sebastian." She took Emma's hand in both of hers and squeezed, the affection behind the gesture sending fresh tears swimming across Emma's vision. "How long has it been? Since you lost your mother?"

Emma stiffened, drew her hand away and tucked it by her side. "Did he say something?"

"Simon?" Delaney ironed her hand over her belly, amusement curling her lips. The duchess smiled more than anyone Emma had ever seen. It musta been from having running water shoot from pipes located *inside* the house. Superb plumbing was enough to make Emma smile for the rest of her *life*. "Does he know anything to tell?"

Emma lifted her hand to chew on her thumbnail. Simon had admitted the League spent years trying to find her—but had admitted little else. How much they knew, she'd no idea. Her whole bloody story, perhaps. "I don't know. Does he? Do *you*?"

Delaney nodded, pleased in some way. "If I said I helped research the gift of time travel for a young man desperate to find a young woman named Emma who'd stepped into his world and then suddenly left it, would that suffice? Until you get the tale from the person who *should* be giving it to you?"

"Looked for you until he was mad with it. *Fou d'elle,*" Madame Hebert murmured without glancing up from her sketch. "And now, the boy's lost to the charms of that obscene gaming den. Amidst the lightskirts and the—"

"Madame Hebert!" Delaney interrupted, sending her index finger in a slicing motion across her neck.

"Men be men, in any century. Shameless," Emma confirmed, wishing she could call the declaration back when Madame Hebert arched a perfectly shaped eyebrow, an explicit acknowledgment that reforming Emmaline Breslin was a waste of everyone's time.

Emma would never admit it, but the emotion pressing like a fist between her ribs wasn't one she could fib about. Not to herself, anyway. *Jealousy.* She remembered that slow burn in her chest from when she'd returned. Simon Alexander and his mob of women were nothing new to her. Boy, could she shock the ladies in this room with what she'd seen five years ago in a countess's murky bedchamber. Burned into her skin like a brand, the scene was.

Delaney twisted a ring with a diamond sizable enough to choke a horse topping it, round and round on her finger. Emma knew a blatant, nervous tell when she saw one. "Simon owns a gaming hell, true. A quite successful venture. Very respectable, comparatively, in a scandalous line of business. My husband is even an investor. As to the women, well"—she gave the ring a final spin—"boys will be boys."

"Gaming hell," Emma murmured. "So that's where he is."

31

"The Blue Moon," Madame Hebert helpfully supplied. "He and his brother, Finn, run it. Tight as thieves, those two. The boy lodges in the suite of rooms above or at the family townhome just down the lane. Or in several beds throughout the city. The gossip sheets love writing about the Alexander boys, enough indignities to bleed all the ink in London dry."

"Madame Hebert," Delaney said with an edge bending her voice and her smile. Her ring making a series of fast loops around her finger.

"Oh, *la*." The modiste tapped her pencil against her cheek, gave Emma a sweeping glance, and then looked back to her design. "Not as if our little termagant is going to race over there now that she knows where he is. Track him like a starving hound. Simon will turn up sooner or later. Women *wait* for their men. And, goodness, even a gutter rat wouldn't sneak into a betting den."

Emma laughed, the sound inviting two sets of eyes to swing warily in her direction. One, gutter rats were known to do any *number* of inadvisable things. Two, Simon was not *her* man. "I would never dream of going to some filthy gaming hell," she murmured with all the humility she could summon, crossing her fingers behind her back.

Because, when the moon arrived this very night, she'd dash into it.

The man she sought was a gambler, and she was calling in her stake.

CHAPTER 2

Simon stood on the Juliet balcony overlooking the gaming floor of his beloved hell, the clink of crystal and dice, coarse laughter and brash conversation, rising like smoke to contentedly circle him. The scent of brandy and American tobacco, perfume from the few ladies present, drifting along as well. This night presented a diverse mix of gamblers. Politicians, society gents, soldiers, even a poet of considerable renown trying his luck at *vingt et un*. Interspersed with croupiers dragging coin and dreams across dark green baize. From midnight to dawn, fortunes were won and lost at the Blue Moon, although his principled brother, Finn, read minds when he was in residence, ensuring the worst tragedies emerged in other dens. If a bloke came to the Blue Moon thinking, *my life is over if I lose this bet*, Finn made sure they didn't make it, tossing them out on their portly asses with a spot of advice about solvency thrown in.

Hence, the Brothers Alexander—Julian, Finn and Simon—were known as the least mercenary of men to own a club in the city. Julian, a viscount, was embraced by society, and his bastard brothers, Finn and

Simon, were mainly accepted, wealth and good looks paving a moderately smooth path. When in actuality, the tale of them being brothers was a ruse. A story invented by Julian, one he'd also used with Finn years prior, created to provide a legacy where there was none. The deceased Viscount Beauchamp, Julian's father, thought to have slept with half of London and sired them all—due to Julian's diplomatically indiscreet remarks at this ball, that club. Epsom. Ascot. The narrative had been bandied about for so long that Simon believed it himself most days.

Only with the occasional nightmare did the old world intrude dreadfully upon the new.

To the dismay of his family, Simon hadn't been able to leave the past behind.

The *ton* would be appalled if they knew the vile depths he'd crawled from to stand on the perimeter of their ballrooms and think, *how did I get here?* There was only one person aside from his brothers who would understand the experience of living *that* life.

And his heart had given up on Emmaline Breslin long ago.

A refined disagreement erupted by the hazard tables, a shove turning into a shout, and Simon stepped back, ready to act. Ready to *fight*. When he had men patrolling every nook of the gaming hell, brutes more vital than he prepared to handle these skirmishes. Still, he longed to 'plant a facer,' as the rookery urchin inside him would have called it. The fury of an abusive childhood was still a raging river beneath his being, never far from reach.

He felt the presence of another person before he'd had a chance to unearth who'd sneaked up on him. A rare occurrence, that. Usually, it was only the haunts who got the better of him. And less of that over the years, as he'd encouraged them to return to their own worlds.

"Steady there, little brother. Your men will take care of this." Finn leaned over the balustrade, gazing out over the club he and Simon had spent years building until it was the finest in the city. Memberships were incredibly hard to obtain but were democratically awarded to those from fishmonger to prince. A title didn't get a man into the Blue Moon. "You went down last night to break up a scuffle, and where did that land you? Why in the hell are we employing a platoon of able beasts if you run in instead of letting them handle it?"

Simon rolled his shoulders, dug a half crown from his pocket before turning to face Finn. "A fist in the face is what it got me. As you well know." He ran his knuckle lightly over the bruise on his cheek, stretching his jaw with a pop. "However, I was able to reciprocate, which felt bloody marvelous, shoving that earl's smirking face into the Axminster carpet, my favored pursuit of the week. The lessons in warfare are finally paying dividends. I cut that pompous dandy off at the knees, just like my friend the duke taught me to when I was no more than ten years old."

"I don't think that's what Ashcroft had in mind with his training sessions. More the plan to use those skills to protect yourself. And the League."

"Huh," Simon murmured, holding back a grin, the coin catching the light from the sconce as he flicked it between his fingers. He was starting to enjoy this. A loving wife and adorable children had made his older brother no fun at all. Finn wanted to run his business, then return home as promptly as possible. No blood-stained collars or bruised jaws involved. "Those lessons are not meant to give me the ability to smash an earl's face into costly carpeting? I must have misinterpreted."

"With the way you're behaving of late, I can't imagine a fight with an earl is your preferred pastime. What's on tonight's agenda? A countess? An actress? The gossip rags have you connected to both."

"You're forgetting Baroness Blithe. Been sending me notes, asking when I'd like to have *tea*." Simon laughed and dipped his head to press the sound into his sleeve. "Her version of tea? Tangled in her sheets, tea optional."

"Don't laugh, Si. That journalist was by earlier today, the snoop from the *Times*. Hargrave. Hard, nasty eyes for a writer. Heard about the earl whose charming visage you so kindly rearranged. He wanted a quote for a piece he's doing on vice and villainy in London. The Blue Moon to be featured, lucky us. Free promotion, when none is needed." Finn buffed his fist over his stubbled cheek and sank back on the desk with a groan. "I have a bad feeling. Hargrave's thoughts are unfettered when I read them. Scattered. And never, ever, about the topic he says he's writing about. He's baiting me. Talking about one subject, his thoughts racing along down another. I caught you in those thoughts, with heated emotion backing it. Then he led me in another direction."

"Don't worry," Simon said and wedged his shoulder against the column securing the balcony, a long-legged sprawl he used to hide his unease. The coin was a comfort in his hand, silver warming against his skin. Although he, too, was concerned about E.L. Hargrave's interest. Not in the Blue Moon. That they could handle. But in what he and Finn both feared, interest in the *League*. Who wanted to write about a gaming hell when one could expose a group of clandestine supernaturals living amongst society? Going so high as a duke who blew fire from his fingertips. "Someday, someone—"

"Is going to find us. We can only hide for so long." Finn pinched the bridge of his nose with a ragged exhalation. "I know this. We all know this. But now, there are children involved. Julian and Humphrey, two each. Ashcroft, four in another month or so. My three. Some inheriting gifts, some only living with the guilt of *not* inheriting. I want, with everything I am or *have*, to protect our families from a precarious future. Lucien is giving Julian fits. Asked to leave Rugby with no hope of a return. The boy will be working with us soon. Another Alexander sent to London to bedevil society."

"Like we were any better. Didn't Rugby ask you to leave a hundred or so years ago?" Simon pulled himself out of his negligent posture, closing his hand around the coin. "And can you stop reading my mind, please? I can see from your expression that you're doing it."

Finn grimaced and brought his hand to his temple, rubbing. "Sorry, the baby was up all night. I'm exhausted. I can't control it right now. And Victoria's not around to block. Your thoughts are slipping like mist through my mind. Everyone on the street, a cacophony of speeches, pleas, desires." He released a labored sigh. "It's grueling. Trust me when I say, I wish I were a normal man."

"If you quit having them, babies, that is, you'd get more sleep." Finn and Victoria had been married for ten years and had three children to show for a hideously loving union. They were devoted to each other, and the marvelous benefit for Finn, aside from a beautiful woman who loved him more than any woman should, was his wife's ability to block his gift when she was near. Block almost everyone's gift, except Simon's. The haunts paid her little mind and closed in on him with confidence. It was only with maturity that he'd been able to force them aside. Talk them home, as he called it. Reason triumphing over will. *Most* of the time.

He suddenly wondered if Victoria would be able to block Emma's ability to travel through time, keeping her locked in 1882, where Simon wanted her.

A fly in amber. Stuck until he figured out what to do with her.

Though he wasn't going to admit this desire to keep her close.

Not ever.

"I don't know if Victoria can block her. We'll have to test it and see," Finn said. "Part of Julian's plan is to do just that, and soon, as you bloody-well know. Better prepare her for an Inquisition to rival Spain's."

Slapping the coin on the desk as he passed it, Simon took a lingering stroll about the study, filched a deck from the sideboard and worked the cards between his fingers, a matchless sequence unlike any the dealers on the floor below could accomplish. Of course, he wasn't allowed in any club in London but his own, due to his particular *talent*.

"Have you been by Sebastian's this week?" Simon kept his gaze on the cards in his hand, his cheeks flushing. Goddamn it to hell. If Finn read *these* thoughts, he was going to smash his brother's face into the carpet.

"The Duke of Ashcroft's? This week?" With a lioness yawn, Finn kicked his legs out to cross them at the ankle, linking his hands over his belly and settling in for what looked like a nap. The man could sleep in the middle of a typhoon. "Now why would I—"

"*Dammit*, Finn."

Finn held up his hand and smiled with only partial humor, his legendary cerulean gaze snagging Simon's. "I bring good news *and* bad. Which would you like first?"

Simon gave the cards a furious shuffle that had the ace of hearts flipping to the top of the stack, as he'd planned. He'd had a nagging itch between his shoulder blades since he'd dumped Emma at Ashcroft's five days ago. Five days that felt like twenty. The way time slowed when he was a boy, and he wanted to do something he knew was blinking mad.

He and Emma hadn't spoken on the return to 1882, the entire journey taking perhaps a minute. But *what* a journey. Fantastic, like being awake during a dream and surrounded by every color you recognized, and some you didn't. Drunk, but not. Lucid, but not. The experience had left him so fatigued that after leaving her, he'd slept for forty hours straight.

When he'd checked with Delaney, afraid Emma was in a similar state, he'd been told she'd suffered no ill effects. Instead, awoken the following day fresh as the proverbial daisy. It scared the life from him to realize that she could travel eighty years, seemingly at will, without even the slightest tinge of a megrim.

Though she'd landed them three months later than he'd asked her to.

But she'd gotten the year right, thank God. And the country.

Thoughts of that hellion suddenly making him cross, Simon jammed the cards in his waistcoat pocket, moved to the sideboard and poured a generous measure of gin. "Start with the good," he muttered and knocked the liquor back. "By the time you make it to the bad, I'll have another drink in me, and I should be better able to acknowledge the news."

Finn cracked his knuckles, each one a dull pop, an activity set to keep him from doling out brotherly advice. "Julian and Piper arrived in town last night."

Julian's wife Piper, Viscountess Beauchamp, was the League's healer. Over the years, she'd helped Simon negotiate with his haunts and send them back where they were supposed to be, which was often not with him. The League had summoned Piper to assist Emma. Perhaps, she wouldn't arrive three months late on her next journey. Simon took a deliberate sip, wondering where this conversation with his brother was heading and how furious he was going to be when Finn got them there.

"You looked for her for ten years, Si. Researched how to find a portal to travel back and get her, until we worried you would never find it, would never forgive yourself for having to leave her to her destiny. The risk you took, you don't know the sleepless nights I had worrying about you. Now, she's here, in the Duke of Ashcroft's townhome. Another forlorn waif joining the League's ranks." Finn yanked the cuff of his pressed sleeve taut and threw Simon a quelling glance, his personal tell to straighten already pristine clothing. "You're restless, more than usual. The fights, the women, the drinking. Can't a brother worry?" Finn knocked his knuckle on the desk, three hard taps. "How's Emma going to help you? A person we don't know, aside from her visits years ago, when no one could actually speak to her. Is she going to quench the blaze inside you? *Finally*, is someone going to be able to do that, I wonder?"

Simon drained his drink and reached for the decanter to pour another. "Oh, here we go. Next, you'll start spouting off about true love. Wives extinguish blazes, is that it?"

"Or light them, in my case. Simon, this girl you were fixated on—"

"I've never been fixated on a woman in my *life*, brother. My interest is perfunctory, at best," he growled, slamming the decanter on the sideboard. "Don't make this out to be more than it is. I knew Emma was in trouble, *was* trouble, from the first moment I laid eyes on her. She couldn't step out of the bubble she was in and talk to me, but despair was splattered all over her like Julian's paint across a canvas. Despair I"—he thumped his chest with his glass —"recognized. The kind of poverty and desperation that drives you to madness. You must remember what that level of hopelessness is like. I wanted to *save* her from that world like Julian saved you and me. Give her a new life. And maybe assist our supernatural band of misfits along the way. We don't, at current, have a time traveler in our ranks. Could come in handy." Tipping his glass, he drained the contents in one swallow. "I've handed her over to the women of the League. There, my debt ends."

Although, and he hoped like hell Finn didn't read this thought, he'd started looking for her, in some obscure part of his soul, before he knew. Before he even knew her, he'd known someone was out there. Waiting for him.

A secret he planned to take to his grave.

"So," Finn theorized with another knuckle tap on the desk, "she's starting lessons meant to turn her into a society belle. A duke's charming but solitary cousin, a chit no one's ever heard of, debuting at a spring ball he's throwing in two weeks in her honor. A mad scramble to school a woman born on the streets. Rookery streets, remember those? Elocution. Literature. Watercolors. Proper cutlery placement. Dancing. I can see it now. Victoria, Delaney and

Piper, three *extremely* delightful examples of feminine decorum, guiding the way."

Simon jammed the top in the decanter with a clang. "I know it doesn't sound like the keenest plan...but it's the one I came up with."

"It sounds risky," Finn murmured. "The women you've picked to tutor your little wanderer determined harridans themselves."

"Emma only has to make enough of this experience to fit in, the League a protective buffer surrounding her. Enough comfort in life, so she doesn't want to..."

Finn hummed, smoothing his broad palm over the desk. "So she doesn't want to go back."

"No more meandering from one decade to the next," Simon whispered, speculating on the likelihood of that. Emmaline Breslin didn't seem the type to listen to anyone's counsel but her own.

"Not even local meandering? Jumping from, say, one city dwelling to another?"

Simon slowly lifted his head, remembering Finn had come bearing bad news as well as good. "Where is she?"

Finn ran his tongue over his teeth, trying, Simon could see, to hide his smile. "The spare cloakroom, the one where we keep the misplaced items. You know, we need to donate those clothes. The rag and bone man was by last month, and no one's going to claim a pair of drawers they lost in a linen closet whilst swiving."

"*Finn,*" Simon ground out between clenched teeth.

Finn held up a hand in apology. "She's shoved herself between a frock of some scratchy material, I'd guess wool, and a velvet dinner jacket reeking of bergamot. Planning to wait out the close of the establishment, then find you. You *owe* her, I believe she said. Nonverbally, of course. What, exactly, you owe, I haven't been able to detect."

As a calming gesture, Simon yanked the cards back out of his pocket and began to shuffle. "You've been reading her mind all this time, knew she was here, and you're just getting around to telling me?"

Finn shrugged a broad shoulder. "You picked good news first."

The cards fell still in Simon's hands, the six of diamonds floating to the Aubusson carpet. "She just showed up, is what you're telling me? Not through a door? When we had a deal?" With a curse and a rising temper, he bent to retrieve the card. It wasn't often one escaped his charge. That's how much this chit was affecting him. "Did you check if they let her in the main entrance? What about the alley door?"

Finn picked a piece of nonexistent lint from his sleeve, a typical ploy when he was assembling either his words or his expression. "She didn't come through one of the Blue Moon's doors. Or a window. This, I have confirmed. I've had a guard posted in the alley every *second* since my darling wife showed up the two times when we were, well, um, courting. It doesn't pay to let a woman surprise you." One of Finn's devilish smiles split his face, thickening Simon's ire. "Unless it's, say, a *naked* surprise."

Simon tossed the cards on the sideboard. "This woman is going to be the death of me."

Finn gave another loose shrug. "A time traveler will travel, now, won't she? And you didn't even leave her with the Soul Catcher." He tilted his head in thought, his eyes sparkling. "She's pretty good without it. Imagine what she could do *with*."

Exasperated, Simon crossed the room and took the stairs to the main floor at a run. He hadn't trekked to every library in England, Scotland and

Wales, made one trip to Germany and two to France, researching each notation regarding time travel or a portal to the past to let this female fiend slip through his fingers.

Although, he'd no *clue* what to do with her now that he'd found her.

Shouldering through the throng hovering around the hazard and *vingt et un* tables like London's impenetrable fog, Simon ignored the shouts of patrons deep in their cups, the grasping hands of mistresses men liked to have by their side while they squandered their time and, often, their birthright. He disregarded the impulse to steal, then sighed and paused to swipe a half sovereign resting on the baize before a boozy baron who had his hand tucked inside his paramour's bodice. Sliding the coin beneath his sleeve, he waved off his guards with a rigid shake of his head that said, *I have this*. Like he'd handled the episode last night, though this time, he wasn't expecting a fist to his face for his trouble.

But a fist to the heart was possible.

Emmaline Breslin was, like it or not, *his* problem.

She had been from the moment she'd stepped into his life, hushed presence before a lonely boy or not.

He forced aside the pinch of emotion in his gut, ignoring the emphasis he'd unintentionally placed on the very possessive *his*.

Halting before the cloakroom door, Simon glanced over his shoulder at the haunt who'd followed him down the stairs. An older gent, Henry, who seemed to want nothing more than someone to talk to occasionally. "*No*," he whispered, "not now. *Later.*" Henry blinked his watery green eyes once, gave a sharp salute, then continued down the unlit hallway and out of sight. Simon snicked open the door and stuck his head inside, immediately spotting the toes of the grubby boots Emma had traveled to 1882 in peeking from beneath a puddled mound of wool and linen.

Clever time traveler, yes; able spy, no.

As he closed the door gently behind him, the air shifted, the faintest hint of rosemary and lemon capturing the dimly lit space, shoving aside the baser fragrances of brandy, sweat and cigar smoke that had come in from the hall with him.

Halting two paces from the coat rack, Simon dragged a rickety stool over with the heel of his boot and sprawled on it. Braced his elbow on his bent knee, took a silver cufflink he'd lifted from a baron two hours ago from his trouser pocket and began to rotate it between his fingers, gaslight from the sconce above his shoulder winking off the tarnished metal. Releasing a shallow breath he cared little if Emma heard him release, he settled in. Just him, the Dark Queen of the East End and a thousand glinting dust motes. She had no idea, Miss Breslin, but *he* was the patient Alexander. The brother with the fiercest temper perhaps…but also the one who could *wait*.

He'd gladly sit all night in this stinky little room if that's what it took to break her.

Luckily, he didn't have to wait long.

With a scrunch of wool and linen, her head gradually emerged from amidst the rack of coats, her muffled complaint echoing off the walls. The cufflink fell still in his hand. Her hair was a marvel, a wondrous surprise every time he got a look at it. Unbound and flowing across her shoulders, gaslight sparked off the auburn tresses, hints of ginger like the inside of a chestnut, an unforeseen blaze in the darkness. Adding to the allure, those cobalt eyes traveling the length of him, leaving fiery eruptions in their wake.

She stepped out with an impatient huff and unladylike shake of her skirts, ultimately giving up her ruse. She gave a bashful tuck to her hair, placing the loose strands hanging in her face neatly behind her ears. Simon rocked back on the stool, his breath stuttering. Beneath her shabby brown cloak was a gown he'd never seen. New, created for an evening event, unfinished, the ragged hem trailing along the warped floorboards, the bustle yet to be added, the final piece of the alteration process. A plunging neckline, which he didn't need to make his life or his cock harder at the moment. The curve of her hip highlighted as she stepped forward, her long legs enchanting beneath clinging silk.

He felt the surge. Lust, umbrage, sympathy. A crushing trifecta for any man.

Silly to feel resentment when the gown was everything current style dictated. In a glorious shade he would have pegged as plum or eggplant, so opaque it was almost black, a flash of violet in the murky light.

But it wasn't the color, although that was a dazzling choice with her creamy skin and vibrant tresses.

It was the *fit*.

The rags he'd seen her in had been hiding a delicious body. He longed to strip that threadbare cloak from her shoulders and slide her gown in a deliberate exhibition to her feet. Then watch her step out of the puddle of material as she crossed to him.

Caught outside his fantasy, she smoothed her palm shyly down the bodice, her glorious lips curling in what could only be construed as delight. So, she liked the new clothing. Even if she protested, which Delaney had told him she'd done. Mightily.

They stared for a long moment before recognizing the pointlessness of such an endeavor. His shaft hardened a notch further, causing him to shift slightly to hide the reaction. Her eyes were wide, so damn blue, and amazingly easy to read. Layers of pain and sorrow, and like icing topping a cake, garnished with a glimmer of hope. His heart thumped once in his chest, his erection withering.

He'd never held someone's happiness this close—or been truly responsible.

In a way, he wasn't sure he wanted to *be* responsible.

Compelling him, she stared. Right at him, right *through* him. He hoped like hell he'd cloaked the thoughts racing through his mind before they showed on his face. He hadn't done well hiding what being this close to her had done to his body.

Then with a daring glance, she stepped out of the shadows and into his space. Into his life. Unapologetic, fearless Emmaline. And Simon realized with a surge of some deeply held emotion that she wasn't meant to be tamed.

Not this girl.

She would run free until a man just as formidable was courageous enough to seize her.

CHAPTER 3

Simon looked like a tiger lying in wait for his prey.

Relaxing in a masculine sprawl on a dented stool that was struggling to hold his long, lean body. Looking like he was seconds away from pouncing. On her.

Emma didn't take the way he finessed that cufflink between his fingers as anything but a ploy to distract them both.

The faintest hint of gin, and mint, swept into her nostrils. He smelled like something very agreeable she yearned to take a sip of. A bite of. Dressed entirely in black, except for his shirt, the snowy-white collar marked by an infuriating smudge of rouge. Apart from the fetching eyes she'd seen in her dreams, as dark as the darkest tea she'd ever brewed, he looked nothing like the boy she'd left behind. He'd grown up, his cheeks full, his jaw hard. Shoulders broad. Legs long. Hair deepened to a color somewhere between fresh wheat and a dying ray of sunlight, the strands caressing the nape of his neck with each breath he took.

Against her will, her skin flushed, and she warned herself that she didn't know him. A man the old Emma would have called a *bang-up cove*. What the new and improved Emma would simply call dashing.

Discomfited, she elbowed through the coats, fumbled, finally locating her parasol and yanking it free.

Simon laughed, the glossy echo skating down her spine. He could have touched her and gotten less of a response, her body heated so quickly. "A weapon, Miss Breslin? Are you going to need one?" The cufflink flashed as he spun it between his fingers. "Maybe you will, as we shouldn't be alone like this. Your reputation would suffer greatly should we be found. Has the duchess gotten to the propriety portion yet? Meeting the owner of a gaming hell in said gaming hell is not recommended. Or are you merely ignoring every damned thing she's told you?"

Emma spun around, brandishing the parasol like a sword. "My reputation is an *asset*, Simon Alexander. And don't you ever say it isn't."

"One question before we resolve the sorrowful predicament in which you find yourself. How did you end up in *here*?" He gestured to the tight, dark space. "Although, I'm thanking the gods you didn't end up on one of the hazard tables. Or in some bloke's lap."

Emma panted an exasperated breath, a strand of silken hair that had long ago left its confinement flying high. "I was outside, standing beneath that glorious set of lamp posts. Imagine—gas lights on every street! And curbs, real curbs, not the chipped disasters of my time. Anyway, the comings and goings are entertaining enough for an evening spent watching them, but a lady can't stand on a street such as this without garnering the wrong kind of notice. I had no

49

choice but to sneak in, you see. The only way I know how. I just closed my eyes, imagined a cozy nook, a closet of sorts, and here I was, moments later. I have no trouble staying on the same day and time if the distance is short. Dropped into that pile of clothing like a boulder." She ticked off reasons on her fingers when she could see her explanation wasn't getting through. "The main entrance was guarded by two fearsome brutes, the door off the alley, another two bounders. This place is fortified like Buckingham Palace, it is."

Simon scowled and did some little trick with his hands that made the cufflink disappear. "This isn't a part of town where it's wise, even for East End queens, to linger outside a gaming hell. A spot better than it was in your time, but not much."

"Pish-posh. I'm a girl used ta' travelin' the mean streets. I have a sharp blade tucked right here"—she tapped her parasol against her boot—"if it makes you feel better." With a teasing laugh, she brushed the pointed tip across his shoulder. "And I know how to use it."

He batted the parasol away and rose to his feet, towering over her, cutting off the oxygen entering her lungs. He was a tall man, broad and uncompromising. Nothing, honestly, like the boy she remembered. "That doesn't make me feel better, Miss Breslin. A man takes that knife *from* you, he's going to be angry enough to turn it *on* you. The worst part? That you'd use your gift to get inside a gaming hell, of all places. Seems a waste of supernatural skill."

"True, it's less time travel and more walking through walls. Which may be a bit of a waste. But I can, so sometimes I *do*." She raised her hand, her index finger and thumb held an inch apart. "I lose a minute, maybe five, ten at most. I'm keen at a near distance. Still the thirteenth, right?"

Simon tunneled his hand inside his swank coat and came out with a gleaming timepiece she'd reckon cost more than food for a year for a family in the rookery. "Ten minutes before midnight, so yes. Technically."

"I did good, then. Technically. Maybe lost half an hour I didn't need anyway."

Not inclined to agree, Simon snapped the case shut and jammed the pocket watch in place. Lifting his arm, he pointed to a spot above her head. "There's a box on the shelf. Far right. You're tall enough to reach it. Something there will match your captivating but half-finished gown, I'm sure."

Emma buried the impulse to argue. She'd didn't like comments about her height because she was taller than most women and many men. But not taller than *this* one. With a cross reply muttered low enough to escape his ear, she anchored her parasol on the floor, bounced up on her toes and reached, her hand hitting the box. She felt inside, instantly recognizing what it contained. "Masks?"

"Masks. For just such a calamity as the one you've presented this eve. A woman stumbling into the Blue Moon, one I feel it best our members do not recognize. You think to prance down these hallways, where anyone could come upon you, without concealment? My family's efforts to reform you will be over the second the duke's shy, sheltered cousin is seen at a gaming hell. Alone in a dim hallway. With me. Reputation shattered like crystal upon stone. You'll have to retreat to the country for *real*."

Tugging a mask free, she faced him with a beaten sigh. "I can just pop right out once we've had our spot of discussion—"

"Oh, I know all about this spot of conversation I owe you. *Owe* being the crucial word."

"Oh, that bleeding mindreader! Did Finn Alexander look inside without asking? Of all the…" She thumped the parasol on the floor with a growl.

"What mindreader asks before nicking thoughts? Finn isn't that accommodating." He shifted, crowding her into the coat rack in a move she hadn't anticipated. Halting before he touched her, heat from his body seeping through her gown and warming hers. Awareness flowing from her breasts to her toes. She'd never been affected in this way, never felt such sensation. Desire, need, *want*. She'd ridiculed people who let such yearning trip them up when she was as weak, it seemed. "I'll ask him to give you privacy of the mind if *you* agree to no more time travel. For now."

"You don't own me, Alexander," she whispered with more bluster than she felt. "I came to 1882 because my time was doomed. I came *tonight* to find out how much ya' know. About me, about my…gift." In response, his gaze glittered in the sconce's spit of light, dark as coal and telling her nothing. "If I stay, it's because of the lamps on each and every city street. Fresh water flowing into the house directly. The fine clothes and heaps of food at every meal." When he didn't comment, she swallowed deeply, smoothing her hand over the bodice of the loveliest dress she'd ever seen, much less *worn*. "And maybe I came for the chance to finally find out who I am."

Reaching, Simon tipped her chin high. His pupils, unbelievably, had rings close to the color of her gown circling them. Something one would have to be practically touching him to see. She'd have said plum if called to describe it. And she'd always liked plums.

"There's small choice in rotten apples, darling Emmaline."

"You think ta' quote Shakespeare to me? You think I won't know." She jerked her chin from his hold. "You buffoon."

Simon blinked, stunned, then a broad smile lit his face, his mahogany eyes glowing.

What the bleeding hell is he smiling about? Emma jabbed the handle of the parasol into his chest and backed him up two steps. "Honest to heaven, I can read, ya' know! My ma taught me. And she brought home piles of books." Wedging the faux weapon beneath her arm, she fit the mask over her eyes and reached to tie the satin ribbons at the back of her head. "You must be half-sprung to be quotin' literature without a chance of anything coming back to you for your fine effort."

Simon's smile grew, nearly bursting his cheeks. "Anything coming back to me for my fine effort." Throwing his head back, he laughed, offering a weak effort at the end to cut the sound by brushing his lips over his sleeve. "I'm only a quarter-sprung, thank you very much. If sober, my effort would be more than fine. It would be grand. And I'd have a *lot* coming back to me for my fine effort."

She hissed rather than reply, her fingers slipping on the ribbons.

"Let me. You're only making a muddle of this." Brushing aside her hands and her bluster, he turned her by the shoulder until she faced away from him. "Hold the mask in place. You picked the fanciest in the box, by the way. I'm beginning to comprehend your style. Feathers, fake jewels, glitter."

"I couldn't even see which one I grabbed!" Although Emma *had* felt the smooth facets of the jewels and the silky feathers. However, her words frittered away, her pulse skipping, her heart racing until it tapped her ribs. There was nothing vulgar or overt about her reaction to his breath stealing across her cheek. His fingertips skimming her hair, brushing the nape of her neck, the sensitive spot beneath her ear. It was a feminine mystery, pure and raw, hers and hers alone.

Unless she let Simon know. Then it would be his, too, which she wasn't going to *ever* do. Not when he hadn't waited for her.

"Don't be vexed with Finn. He reads everyone's mind unless his wife is around," Simon murmured, his teasing scent drifting past her nose to twist her insides into a tighter knot than the satin ties Simon was manhandling. "Maybe I *do* owe you. I would've offered up information sooner, how I found you, everything I've learned about your gift over the years. But upon our return, I had to sleep for two days to recover from our adventure. To say traveling eighty years in minutes fatigued me would be understating the matter." In a final move, he took a strand of her hair between his fingers and gave it a gentle tug she felt like a bolt of lightning between her thighs. "Too unique, this color. The inebriated benefactors currently losing their blunt at my gaming tables would remember it. God help us if we stumble upon one of them on our way out. Often, even the back alley is congested at this hour."

Emma wiggled from his grasp, unable to endure his touch a moment longer. Glanced over her shoulder to find he'd retreated, his back resting against the door, his expression in the shadowed dim unreadable. Hands braced on his hips, an intimidating stance.

But she wasn't intimidated; she was *fascinated*. Just

like she'd been from the second she stepped into his world ten years ago.

Pulling herself away from her pointless musings, she gave the mask a nudge with her knuckle to straighten it. "I guess you make use of these often."

She hoped she didn't sound jealous when she *was* jealous. Of the women he'd taken to the apartment Madame Hebert had mentioned he kept upstairs. The carpet leading to his rooms likely worn thin from the traffic.

"A temper that never tires."

Embarrassed, sure his soft smile meant he was teasing her, she dipped her chin in question. *What did that mean?*

His smile grew, but it was subdued, his gaze dropping to his feet as he kicked one shiny boot out, scuffing the floor for no reason she could see other than it placed his gaze in a location where she was unable to study it. "Dickens." When his dark eyes found hers, drawn like a magnet, his expression one of cautious delight, she could almost imagine that, someday, he was going to forgive her for leaving him.

"Dickens," she whispered. Not one her ma had stolen much of.

His gaze fell to her hands, which she'd begun to twist around the parasol's handle. "Your gloves tucked away there somewhere? Almost October. It's getting colder at night. You'll need them."

Emma gave the parasol an obscuring tap while curling her fingers into fists. Her nails, after a long soak and vigorous buffing, looked tolerable, but her hands were chapped and worthless as consideration for being a lady, according to every maid who'd thought to touch them. "I'm afraid to wear them. If I stain the blasted things before this bloody ball where the duchess plans to parade me around, that's one more detail to fret about. She doesn't want repayment, even if I could somehow find the funds. Convinced I helped her snag her duke, she is, when I was only using her to find the Soul Catcher. You remember? She tumbled from her mount when I stepped in front of her all those years ago, practically flopping into the duke's arms. I've apologized, tried to tell her that's just not so, *my* fault, all of it. She won't listen, the stubborn chit." She traced a scratch in the floorboard with the parasol's pointed tip. "Curious, but my stealing the Soul Catcher and dumping her into the Oxfordshire dirt is now part of *her* love story."

Simon hummed the answer to a question he'd evidently only asked himself. "Delaney told me about the swap you proposed. The Soul Catcher for the League's allowance to delve deeper into your gift." Tugging a pair of kidskin gloves from his coat pocket, he extended them without a hint of mockery, which, right or wrong, would have had her tossing them in his face. "I remember that feeling. Of being indebted in a way I could never repay. When I came to live with Julian, I was very tormented. And still, to this day, I feel I owe him. And Finn. Piper. Which if I utter the sentiment, sends Julian into an indignant spiral. Only, poverty doesn't breed a desire to take things one hasn't *earned*. I know this. I understand. I stole because I had to. Now, if I'm the occasional thief, it's only because I'm bored."

She laid the parasol aside, and after a moment, took the gloves from him. They were the color of the caramel sweets sold in the market around the corner from her flat. Butter-soft. So delicate and yet, not. She resisted the impulse to bring them to her nose and inhale. He'd think she was cracked, for sure, or that she *liked* him. Tugging them on, where they bulged and hung on her slim hand but felt like sleek magic, she asked, "Trade?"

Bringing his hand to his lips—*quiet*—he opened the cloakroom door and peeked into the hallway. Then half-turning, he crooked his finger at her, beckoning. "All clear. Come. If Delaney finds you missing, we're in trouble. And that kind of trouble, I don't need."

"But—"

"No arguments. Not after my fishing you out of this stew. Another word of advice? If we come upon anyone, anyone at all, look at the ground. Those eyes of yours are about as astonishing as your hair."

A familiar sting scalded her cheeks. Her hair had always been an embarrassment, a reason for unwanted attention. Yet, Simon described it in a way that made her feel almost...*beautiful*. Taking a courageous breath, she nudged her mask high and stepped into the hall, so close to Simon, his shadow washed over her.

If she could only stay in that safe nook forever.

"What's the trade?" she whispered as she crept down the darkened hallway. Laughter and the crack of dice and crystal flowed down the passageway like a river along narrow banks. The scent of whiskey, cigar smoke and men's cologne salting the air with a piquant mix with which she was well acquainted. Not everything in the future was different. "I'm not sayin' I agree until I hear the provisions, you know."

He smothered a laugh in his fist and halted at the end of the hallway. Lifting his arm, he rapped on a scarred walnut door three times in rapid succession. Two knocks came back from the other side. Simon repeated with one knock.

"This feels very mysterious," Emma murmured, intrigued despite herself. 1882 was turning out to be more entertaining than 1802 had been. *And,* the future held Simon.

Without comment, he blindly reached for her hand and, when the door opened, tugged her through the entranceway and into the alley. The cobblestones were slick with dew and grime, the foul scent of the river and what smelled like charred meat stinging her nostrils. Pale moonlight peeking through the ashen clouds, feebly lighting their way. "For God's sake, cast your gaze to your feet," he whispered roughly and escorted her to a waiting carriage. A fine one, from the looks of it. Luxurious equipage. Nothing of the dilapidated hackney variety she was used to when any conveyance, in truth, was a luxury she'd rarely been able to afford.

A brutish sentry who'd been stationed by the alley entrance lowered the carriage step, the door open and awaiting her arrival. Emma frowned. *So, this is what the series of knocks had said without words.* A woman who needed to sneak like a rat into the night without advertisement. A frequent enough occurrence for the Blue Moon staff to have a secret code to put the plan into action.

Emma climbed the step on temper alone. Flouncing to the tufted velvet squab, she shifted her bottom and yanked her skirt from beneath her, the piercing rip she heard sending her anger bubbling. "How often do you employ this crafty dodge anyway?"

"Ofen' enough, miss," the sentry murmured with a chuckle, closing the door with a finalizing click. "Tucks 'em away in his flat right regular, he does. And we gets 'em out. A bang-up operation we run at the Blue Moon, innit? In the gaming salon *and* out back."

"Christ, Mackey, shut up," Simon growled and elbowed him aside.

Mackey gave a choked stutter, his ruddy cheeks flooding with color she could see clearly in the misty night. "Them dirty boots and the gaudy mask, oh, I thought this wasn't one of yours, Mister Simon. The viscount losing his beans at the whist table, maybe. Or that daft earl who's come in every night this week because his actress trotted off with the poet." He tipped his hat in apology. "Your ladies are quality and don't usually leave this early."

"Bloody hell," Simon muttered and motioned Mackey away from the carriage. Leaning in, he clutched the window ledge, his knuckles blanching. His chagrined expression would have had her snickering had crimson not been bleeding into the borders of her vision. His lips tilting, the bottom one tucked attractively between his straight, white teeth. As if he wanted to speak but had decided it best he not.

Invading her space with his broad body when all she could imagine were the *thousands* of women he'd had 'right regular' up there in his blasted flat. *Quality* women, which her soiled boots had revealed her not to be. She was, in fact, quality, according to rookery rules. Untouched, though she'd no doubt this would surprise most. A battle it'd been to stay that way, too, when selling herself would have paid well enough to keep her in candles most nights. Her gift of disappearing the reason she'd been able. Stepping out of dangerous situations. Consequently, she'd gained a reputation as having the touch, never a good thing.

And because of her upbringing, she knew the mechanics of the act, had seen more than any young lady of good breeding—*quality*— should have.

The thought of Simon and anyone but *her* doing *that* sizzled across her skin like a fever. Too late, the thoughts, because she had that damned vision in her head to guide her, a rotten experience she planned to never tell anyone about.

Worse than imagination when a person had the real thing to recall.

However, Madame Hebert's words flashed through her mind, the barest whiff of good feeling. Like Simon's stimulating scent drifting in the open carriage window, light but uplifting. He'd looked for her until he was *mad with it*, which must mean something.

Simon's shoulders drooped on a sigh men all through the ages had expelled, his teeth losing their hold on his bottom lip. "I'm not sure what you're so annoyed about."

It hit her then, like her ma's occasional smack across her bottom.

Emmaline Breslin, who could've snared any bloke she'd wanted in the London Borough of Tower Hamlets, even if they'd been scared to pieces of her mystical touch, wanted a man who didn't want her. In that way. He wished to *save* her, to pick apart her gift. He hadn't spent ten years tracking her down out of fondness or devotion. Same as her, at first. She'd come to the League because the gypsies who camped at the edge of town every spring told her about a group of people who aided those mystically gifted— and about a magical swish stone.

But she'd come back again and again for *him*.

His were sensible motives when her heart wasn't a sensible vessel.

"Whatever could I be irked about?" she asked, vowing right then and there in the swank carriage he used to spirit women off when he was done with them, to make herself the bleeding *toast* of London. She'd learn to speak like a countess and walk with a book on her head clear to Westminster and sip tea like blinking Victoria while wearing the most gorgeous gowns society had ever seen.

All to allow the condemned man clinging to her carriage window to feel this pain.

She'd make him so jealous he would discharge like one of the duke's poorly-made firecrackers.

She yanked his gloves off, one finger at a time. Preparing to give them back, then deciding not to. "I want the stone. While I'm learning to be a high-born lady, I want it with me. It calms me. And if your League is going to pick my...talent like a wound, make me appear here and there around this blessed city, a marionette and them holding the strings, I need it."

Simon gazed into her face so penetratingly that what her granny called look-see grooves flowed from the corners of his eyes. Adorable lines she wanted to smooth away with her fingers. Or with a tender, lingering kiss. "Take the better life," he whispered and dug in his coat pocket, his broad shoulder lifting, coming up with the Soul Catcher. A slice of weak moonlight struck it, and it glittered, casting yellow and green diamonds across the carriage's interior. A splash of an omen about the future, perhaps. "You'd be a fool not to."

"Like you did. And you're no fool. Anyone can see that."

He laughed then, a vicious sound that sent goosebumps dancing along her arms. "Darlin', I was a mudlark before turning to the more profitable and less dangerous, though completely hazardous sport of thievery. This, when I was all of eight years old. A celebrated cutpurse set to spill the last of his young blood on the cobbles of St Giles, before I was given an opportunity much the same as you're being given, to forge a new life." He rapped the window ledge once with his fist. "So, never, *ever* mistake my understanding of the circumstances you find yourself in. Or the twist in your belly when you think about accepting the offer and being indebted for life to another. It's an *exchange*, make no mistake. I'm only telling you, advice from a professional gambler if you choose to take it, that it's a profitable exchange."

Emma rocked back against the squabs, clenching her trembling hands in her lap. Mudlarking? Saints be. Only the most deplorable of circumstances lowered one to *that* profession. "Your name," she whispered from the depths of the shadows she collapsed into. "Your real name."

His arm extended into the carriage, the Soul Catcher an offer held lightly between his long, slim fingers. "MacDermot. Simon MacDermot. There might have been a middle name at one time, but I can't recall it if there was."

Emma gasped and leaned into the stray moonbeam piercing the carriage window. "*Irish*. You're Irish." She could see it now that she was looking. The faint scatter of freckles dancing across the bridge of his nose. The hair, glints of auburn, just a touch, mixed in with wheat.

"My father...he was..." His lips caught in a hard line, the skin around his mouth whitening. "I don't use the name. I'm *never* going to use it."

Shattering the charged moment, Emma snatched the swish stone from Simon before he changed his mind about loaning it to her, then patted the gem against her chest. Mostly an effort to erase the anguish from his face by turning his thoughts from his father to her. "I'm Irish, too. In County Donegal, my granny said it was Ó Breasláin." Tucking the stone in the edge of her bodice, unable to ignore the way his gaze fiercely tracked the movement, she shrugged, wishing his regard didn't light her up the way it did. That slender ring of violet around his pupils, the tawny mix in his hair, him looking so dapper standing there. Without even trying. Spit-shined, as the old Emma would have said. A body like Captain Jack, the finest pugilist in Tower Hamlets. Lean, broad, bulging muscles even clever tailoring couldn't hide.

She thought back to when Simon had jammed his boot on Jonesy's back and dug the thug's face in the dirt, protecting her.

The gesture made her warm in places it shouldn't.

She'd always taken good care of herself. It was madness to let that job fall to someone who only cared about a mystical talent that had wrecked her life. Made her an oddity when she'd wanted to fade into the background. Made her everything *but* normal.

Although, feeling nothing for him was impossible. He had this adorable dimple that winked at her when he smiled, which wasn't often. And he was handsome in every way that mattered. Like a church bell, his nearness reverberated through her, even if the noise was one she didn't wish to hear.

"Breslin. It means strife if you're wondering," she finally said when the silence had begun to chafe.

Simon yanked the curtain across the window, shutting off her view of him, then stepped back with a rough laugh. "So your name literally means trouble? Brilliant." Tapping the carriage roof, he gave the duke's address to the coachman and bid her good-night with one whispered promise that floated away on the breeze: *tomorrow.*

Though her heart reached through the window to catch the proclamation back.

As the conveyance rocked into motion, she turned, watching through the narrow window as fog settled upon her savior, a concealing mist, until she could no longer see him standing there.

But he was a beating presence in her heart. In her mind, in her *soul*, if she had one.

A presence she feared more than she feared going back to 1802—and not making it out alive.

CHAPTER 4

$\mathscr{T}$he next afternoon, Simon arrived at the Duke of Ashcroft's townhome and was escorted to what he thought of as the gruesomely green parlor, where he found Emmaline sprawled indecorously across the Axminster carpet situated before the hearth, her head pillowed on the rounded rump of one of the duke's many mutts. The mutt asleep, the girl awake. Her deliciously long legs stretched out, stockinged toes wiggling, she held a book he imagined was one of Dickens's novels he'd sent over this morning. She had the volume tucked close to her face, her mouth moving silently as she read lines of text. A charred section of the rug, fresh from the look and scent of it, lay right beside her elbow, one of the Duke of Ashcroft's attempts to send a blaze from his mind directly to the hearth.

Close, the effort. No more than a foot away. Refining his skill after years of practice.

Simon slumped against the doorjamb, crossed his legs at the ankle and took her in, this positively foreign, absolutely fascinating creature who'd beguiled her way into his life.

A woman who'd haunted him more than any ghost in existence.

She was nothing like the society chits who offered themselves to him daily. Their attraction answerable to his ownership of the Blue Moon and the skills a viscount's byblow possessed that a high-born man likely wouldn't. A jaded bunch, the lot of them, himself included, seeking entertainment and deliverance.

Glancing about the room, he came across a tidy pile stacked by the hearth. A pair of silver dancing slippers, a lilac shawl and *his* gloves. He flexed his fingers and, in a swift move for a man known for them, shoved his clenched fists deep in his trouser pockets. It seemed Emma intended to give the gloves back when he, absurdly, wanted her to keep them.

He took a step into the parlor, aware that a gentleman would have alerted a lady to his presence. But he wasn't a gentleman, and Emmaline Breslin wasn't a lady. With a soft smile, he shook his head, unsure what to call her. Termagant? Hellion?

She wore another new gown, this one a shade, perhaps two, lighter than her magnificent indigo eyes. Madame Hebert had selected jewel tones that would set her apart in a ballroom if the vivacity of her personality did not. Simon thought her raw beauty enough to make her shimmer, a diamond amongst dull, grey stones. High cheekbones, a chin that spoke of obstinacy and hasty decisions. A challenging face, sensual and stubborn. One that brought to mind tangled sheets and the pleasurable tremors that ripped through you after coming so hard you almost blacked out.

Any man's dream, aside from the abrasive accent, the rough skin, the disrespectful manner. Things that didn't matter in the least that mattered mightily to the *ton*. They'd have to change her or hide the parts they couldn't change before she'd be ready for society introductions.

He knew this because he'd done it himself.

To please him, she needed no alteration. He'd searched for her before he knew. He wondered if she realized that. Or, that'd he given up on her—and now questioned if he should have. Years too late, that decision. He'd lost himself along the way and lost her, too.

With a rousing yawn, Emma pulled Dickens closer and squinted.

Simon held back a chuckle. *Why, she needs spectacles.* He opened his mouth to tell his hellion that when two small, human projectiles rammed into the backs of his legs, forcing him to stumble awkwardly into the room.

Emma shoved to an inelegant sit, tugging her skirt over her ankles, color sweeping enticingly down her neck and bleeding into the rounded collar of her gown. Her gaze snapped to the slippers stacked hopelessly by the hearth as she gave her stockinged toes a frantic wiggle. She'd lost herself in —Simon tilted his head to read the title of the book she'd placed by her feet—*David Copperfield.*

The duke's youngest children, twins Worth and Winnie, danced in a wild circle around Simon, chanting a charming ditty he didn't know, their grubby hands tugging on his trousers and leaving what looked like specks of jam behind. He laughed and tried to brush them off. "I know you're looking for butterscotch. I didn't bring any today."

"Bother," Winnie said, flashing a gap-toothed grin, her amber eyes exact replicas of her father's. But her face, oh, her lovely face was all Delaney's. "You never forget sweets. You're the bestest for sweet giving."

Worth plopped himself on the sofa and folded his

hands in his lap, a flawless embodiment of etiquette. "I shall behave like a gentleman whilst I beg for my treat."

Winnie giggled and jammed her bottom right next to her brother's. "Me, too. A perfect lady." Then she ruined the statement by licking a spot of jam from her thumb.

Simon had to work to contain his amusement at the apprehensive look on Emma's face. "What say you, Miss Breslin?"

Emma popped her head over the back of the sofa and blinked owlishly. "About?" She wobbled precariously, struggling to put on her slippers without anyone noticing they'd been taken *off*.

Worth tilted his head. "Oh, hello, Miss Emmaline. You need to tell Uncle Si to give us the candies he always carries. He'll flip them around like a magician if you ask him nicely. Part of his gift. That and the dead ghosties. My gift is that I will someday make fire fly from my fingertips, like my father, the duke. I dream about doing it, so it must be so." He dropped his voice to a whisper. "A secret, but it means we both have gifts. It means we *all* have gifts."

Emma's gaze shot to Simon's. *Fire*, she mouthed?

Later, he said with nothing more than a shake of his head.

The League had worried that the next generation would inherit supernatural abilities, and unfortunately, it appeared to be happening. Julian's son, Lucien, touched objects and saw the past, as his father did. One of Finn's daughters seemed to be a blocker, like her mother. And Worth...Worth dreamed of fires. News that had nearly destroyed the Duke of Ashcroft when he'd first realized it. Thrown him into a depression Simon had dreaded he wouldn't recover from. The League had feared he would return to the opium dens, a place he'd frequented before his marriage, but he had not. His wife Delaney, would never let that happen.

Consequently, Simon had decided not to have children. He'd been cautious in his relationships, most of those extremely short, to ensure pregnancy did not result.

To parent a child who conversed with the deceased seemed a worse nightmare than conversing with them yourself.

Seemed like a dreadful wager from the start.

Anyway, he'd never feel that blind obsession, reckless need. Overpowering yearning.

Julian and Finn had stressed the imperative often enough. *Without love, a successful union was untenable.* He supposed it made him a romantic, but he'd seen his brother's marriages flourish, so he believed love was necessary. Furthermore, he had no title to offer. Nothing to offer except a dubious upbringing, a fictional history, an uncertain future. He was educated, thanks to Julian, and wealthy, thanks to Finn, who'd gifted him half the Blue Moon upon his majority.

His reputation, however, was in tatters. And his soul, in part, broken.

And the haunts…

Who would want to share *that* existence? At this moment, Henry, the ghost who'd been troubling him for months and who'd died in 1793, was sitting by the hearth, his wrinkled chin in his fist, viewing the unfolding scene. Simon didn't have the heart to send the aged vagabond on his way, though he knew he should.

Simon watched Emma wiggle into her other slipper, his heart taking a feeble tilt he rather wished it hadn't. She'd experienced poverty, isolation, torment. Brawled with the dregs of society to survive. Alone, without family. She needed someone with a soothing soul to rescue her from the abyss, when Simon would do nothing but plunge her deeper into it. He was a man who woke amid childhood terrors, a man who, with every room he entered, experienced the desperate urge to steal something while he strolled through it.

Simon felt a tug on his sleeve and looked down into Worth's sterling eyes. "Miss Emma makes the grandest cake in London. She showed me how to do the icing. Said she might show her little boy how to do it someday, exactly like we did. Lemon with rosemary, which sounds yucky but was terribly wonderful. Everyone in the house is raving about it, mama says. I ate two slices, then felt sick to my tummy."

Simon's gaze crawled to hers. She liked children. And baking. "Cake?"

In a gesture he was coming to understand was all Emma, her shoulders lifted in defiance and self-preservation. "I *like* to bake. The recipe has been in my family for generations. Being charitable, I gave it to the duke's cook. I'm the last of the Breslins. Lemon-rosemary loaf is lost to this world if no one else knows how to make it."

"Hmm…" Simon flopped into an armchair, the worn leather cracking, trying to imagine this virago doing something as domestic as baking a cake. Slipping his hand in his waistcoat pocket, he withdrew two butterscotch sweets and began to twirl them between his fingers. Worth and Winnie's eyes grew round as half crowns as they scooted to the edge of the sofa. The canine Emma had rested her head upon ambled over, parking himself by Simon's boot with a muffled bark. The dog had a violet satin ribbon looped about his neck, one Simon guessed had been assigned to contain Emma's wild tresses before she'd removed it.

Simon tugged at the makeshift collar, then sent Emma a glance that he realized was more than mildly flirtatious after he'd released it.

Rising to her feet, Emma lifted her hand to smooth her hair, a minuscule pleat settling between her brows. Simon didn't know if she struggled to interpret the meaning behind his enticing look. Or her reaction to it. Leaning down, she grabbed his gloves from the pile by the hearth and pulled them in close to her chest. It was as if she'd taken his hand and placed it there, just above her ribcage. He could almost feel the flutter of her heart.

They stared, lost to the moment. Until Simon freed himself, straightening in his chair, blindly handing the butterscotch to the children while debating if he was going to follow his brain's instinct to cross the room, take Emma's face in his palms and—

"Emmaline," the Duchess of Ashcroft called from the hallway. "I need to speak to you about your dance lesson."

Worth and Winnie glanced at each other before turning pitying eyes on Emma. "Good luck, lessons are a *horror*," Worth whispered around his butterscotch with all the bravery a young boy could muster, then he and his sister dashed across the room and edged into the hallway, obviously hoping to avoid their mother.

"Dance lessons," Emma whispered, her cheeks blanching. She twisted his gloves into a wrinkled wad. "What bleeding dance lessons?"

Simon sneaked a farthing from his trouser pocket, a wide grin tilting his lips. Propping his boots on the coffee table, he flipped the coin from hand to hand. "I think I'll stay a bit, after all. Dancing lessons. Sounds positively enchanting. Unless one is engaged in *taking* the lesson, that is. My tip? Don't say bleeding or step on the dance master's toes. And never, ever, think to say no to Delaney Tremont."

The very pregnant duchess practically tumbled into the room, her breath leaving her in little pants. "Oh, heavens, there you are. I worried for a second that you'd blinked and traveled to 1920 or something. You're like a butterfly I'm afraid will flit away while I'm not looking." She closed her eyes, tapped her head, then opened them again. Making a quick trip to the attic in her mind. "Did you know they call a collection of butterflies a kaleidoscope? Maybe someday we can take a trip to America, just for a day or so. I haven't been back since Sebastian took me on our honeymoon. With four children, I have no time for travel. But you're quicker than Cunard, that's for sure." Delaney patted her belly, her gaze widening when it hit him. "*Simon*. This is divine intervention. Monsieur Claude had to cancel, and we need to get moving on the waltz. The ball to introduce Emma to society is in less than two weeks." When he didn't make an immediate effort to stand, she snapped her fingers. "Get up and come along."

Simon looked to Emma, who was deciding, he could see from her strained expression, between laughing at his dilemma or being fearful of her own. He rose to his feet with a choke of laughter. "Oh, no, Delaney. I'm not your man. Finn's the one you—"

"I have *you*, the most accomplished dancer in our extended supernatural family, according to your instructor, Madame Rudolph. She said your gifts were not confined to your feet. I always wondered about that comment, which seemed odd at the time. But you're an Alexander, so maybe it's perfectly clear. I'll meet you in the ballroom." Dusting her hands, the deed done, the duchess turned on her heel and marched from the parlor, or as well as she could with an ample belly marching out before her, expecting the two stunned inhabitants to follow.

Simon tugged Emma's sleeve as she brushed past. "Delaney's joking. I was *fifteen*. Madame Rudolph meant nothing by that comment except that I'm a marginally proficient dancer." He gave the farthing an embarrassed spin. "If you must know, it came naturally. Not like growing up in St Giles gave me any advantages. Little more than bawdy houses and gin palaces. *Those* I know a great deal about."

When Emma gave him a cross glare and followed the duchess into the hallway, he shoved the coin in his pocket and trudged along behind them. *Women.*

"Can't please these chits nowadays; don't even try," Henry advised from his spot just behind Simon. He was a relatively accommodating haunt. He didn't try to get too close nor stay too long. Sooner or later, he'd disappear altogether, and Simon would feel a pang wondering what had happened to him. "Might as well go and show the young miss the waltz. Four simple steps. Nothing to it. Just remember to bow when you finish. Proper like. And wipe off that frown. Think of the advantages, sonny. No better way to get close to a girl you fancy than the waltz. A true scandal in my time. Course, just starting to be popular when I had to up and die."

"I don't fancy the girl. I'm protecting her," Simon muttered and took the circular stairs leading down into the ballroom two at a time, ignoring Henry's bark of laughter.

Delaney had tripped the gaslights, and the chandeliers glowed, casting a gilded shimmer across cream marble. The weather was gray and leaden, but in this room, the world was luminous. Emma wandered through the cascading light, her gown shifting from indigo to a shade close to the color of one of the Blue Moon's five-pound chips. They could have practiced just as well in the gallery, Simon guessed, but Delaney liked to make every event a celebration.

He wondered vaguely if her *joie de vivre* ever exhausted her husband.

Halting at the bottom of the stairs, he repressed an insane urge to steal the figurine of a hound sitting on a high table to his right. Henry clucked his tongue in dismay and drifted past, strolling to a spot along the far wall from which to observe Simon's probable thievery further.

"There's no music," Simon offered contrarily and crossed to where Emma stood, her slim body quivering like a reed as she shifted from one silver slipper to another, his gloves pressed ruinously to her bosom. She looked like she was being offered up as a human sacrifice. While Delaney, Her Grace, Duchess of Ashcroft, looked positively thrilled.

Thrilled by what, Simon had no idea.

Though, she *was* the most competitive woman he'd ever met.

"Oh, we have music," Delaney said with a smile meant to throw them off course. "In this house, we *always* have music."

Simon grimaced, looking around for something to steal. "You didn't. He wouldn't." A duke who could shoot fire from his fingertips and was, well, a *duke*, wouldn't participate in this frivolity.

Delaney snickered and curled her hand lovingly around her protruding belly. "You think I can't get the duke to do anything I'd like him to do while I'm in this delicate condition? Darling, Simon, you have yet to learn the lengths to which a man will go for the woman he loves. I only need crook my finger in his direction."

Simon blew out a breath, not bothering to look over his shoulder when he heard a familiar, resounding tread slapping marble. The duke stalked through every room he inhabited like the former soldier he was. An intentional stride, never an idle amble for this man.

Sebastian Tremont, fifth Duke of Ashcroft, halted beside the taciturn group, violin in one hand, bow in the other. "I hear a waltz is in order."

"Your Grace," Simon murmured in a brutal tone.

Sebastian tapped the bow to Simon's shoulder, knighting him king of the ballroom. "What a surprise. Young Simon, here to help prepare my dear cousin, Emmaline, for her debut." His smile grew, plumping his granite cheeks. "Or *not*," he added in a whisper for just the two of them.

Emma stepped close, *too* close, the scent of her damned rosemary cake sliding past his nose, twisting his heart and his gut. With a sigh of longing, she trailed her finger up the violin's scrolled neck. "You play, Your Grace?"

If it were possible for a duke who had most of society cowering to preen, this one did. "I do," he said and bowed ever so slightly.

Emma gently plucked a string in a manner that spoke of familiarity. "I do as well. A little. Nothing taught. My granny"—she snapped her lips shut and exhaled sharply—"my *grandmother* had an instrument. We had to sell it, eventually, to pay the rent. And it was more of a fiddle, nothing so grand as this." She trailed her knuckle along the fingerboard in a caress that had Simon's cock jerking beneath his trouser buttons.

Highlighted in the light washing over her, a detail

Simon didn't need became discernable. A tiny freckle on Emma's right cheek, an imperfection that made her *more* perfect. He suppressed a hushed, desperate yearning to press his lips to the spot—a yearning more potent than any he'd felt in his life.

"Better get that wicked lovesick expression off your face if you don't want the chit to know how loopy you are over her," Henry whispered from just behind him. "Or His and Her Grace to know how you feel. You're the kind to keep it tucked up tight, I've noticed that about you."

Simon threw out his hand in a gesture of impatience. "Are we starting the lessons, or what?"

Emma tilted her head, her blue eyes so bloody blue he was sinking in them. "Is there one around you now?"

Simon shrugged, frantic for a cufflink to steal. Button to pilfer. Coin to filch. "Henry. Bootmaker, died in 1793."

Henry gave his mustache a twirl. "Blacksmith, actually. The best in Portsmouth."

"Sorry." Simon rocked back on his heels. "Blacksmith."

"Hello, Henry," Emma said and searched the area surrounding Simon. "I'm Emma. Time traveler. Formerly of the London Borough of Tower Hamlets."

Simon halted, his breath seizing. No one had made an effort to speak to one of his haunts before, not once. Not *ever*. He must have reacted in a way Emma neglected to notice—a reaction the duke certainly *did* notice.

In a thrice, Sebastian took Emma's elbow and escorted her to his duchess while Simon's heart continued its descent to the marble floor.

CHAPTER 5

*T*he Duke of Ashcroft played better than her granny ever had, Emma decided as she half-listened to the duchess's dance instructions and the duke's meandering tune. Violin tucked against his collarbone, chin resting on the glossy wooden lip, he looked a prime piece standing there, body swaying as he moved through the song. One of those men who were big and broad but still somehow managed to look *elegant*.

A neat trick, that.

Rather like Simon and his flash of elegance.

To a degree that made her mouth water.

Simon was leaner than the duke but retained a muscular frame his fine clothing couldn't hide. Lanky, even, a new word in her vocabulary, thanks to Dickens. Restless, his hands in constant motion. Reserved, his emotions sealed. However, she wasn't fooled. He was passionate beneath that exterior he worked hard to polish smooth as glass. He'd shown his true self to her a few times. While jamming Jonesy's face into the dirt and for a flaring, hot second when she'd spontaneously spoken to his ghost. Something about that gesture had struck him deeply.

In a place she didn't think too many people had reached.

Emma peeked from the corner of her eye as the duchess gave her directions she didn't for a moment hear.

Not when she could watch *him*.

Standing before the window, hands braced on the ledge, staring out at nothing of interest that she could see. People slinking down a busy London street. Overloaded carts, posh carriages, burdened hackneys. Coachmen in liveried attire. Folks in plain dress, folks in stylish. It wasn't like it was dark, and the lane lit with those incredible streetlamps one could stare at all night. He flipped a farthing between his fingers, defying gravity, not looking down. Muscle memory, the gypsies called it. An effort to calm himself, she'd come to believe. She'd seen hawkers at carnivals who couldn't do what he could.

It made her wonder, in a mysterious little nook that lit up when she looked at Simon Alexander, what *else* he could do with those hands.

"He'll forgive you. If you're patient…and you play your cards right as women for centuries have had to. Don't feel it's dishonest; it's simply the mathematics of love."

Emma flinched and turned to the duchess, her breath catching to realize she'd been caught ogling what accounted, in a distant, supernatural family way, to this woman's *brother*. "Play my cards…"

With a groan, Delaney slid gracelessly into the chair her husband had directed a footman retrieve for her. The duke was the height of care and consideration with regard to his duchess, which Emma found a most adorable—and sickening—thing to

THE HELLION IS TAMED

watch. "He's the sensitive one in this family. Julian, Finn, Humphrey, Sebastian, none as painstakingly constructed as Simon. As guarded. Still holding on to such a substantial slice of who he was *before*. So many secrets. Too many secrets. Finn and Julian worry about his struggle, as brothers should. But I"—Delaney took a sip of tea from the cup the duke had snapped his fingers and had superciliously delivered to her—"think he'll talk to someone when he finds the right someone. What he's doing with these women, I imagine, doesn't require much talking. And is only an effort that brings more loneliness, not takes it away. But men have to figure that out for themselves, now, don't they? Uncomplicated creatures."

"Forgive me for what?" Emma asked, the snag in her voice apparent. Anger and...*understanding* flooding out. Simon was a scamp, a rogue, a bounder. And she'd been right in thinking he was upset with her. But she was upset, too. Nevertheless, if he trusted her enough to share his secrets, she'd likely be weak enough to fall right into that trap and share hers back. "What did I do?"

Delaney paused, the teacup halfway to her lips. "You *left*."

Emma glanced over her shoulder to confirm the man they were discussing hadn't moved from his contemplative spot by the window. "I couldn't come back. My mother was ill, dying. And, then, when I could, after she passed, even *with* the Soul Catcher, I messed up, over and over. Arrived once before Simon was even born. The other time, in Oxfordshire, but he was a baby in London. Once, I even ended up in Scotland in the dead of winter. Horrible. And then..." Emma glanced at his gloves, still clutched in her hands. She'd lifted them to her nose in the privacy of her bedchamber this morning and breathed his scent into her soul. He hadn't forgiven her—but he hadn't waited, either. "I made it back. Five years after I left, maybe six." She glanced into the duchess's smoke-gray eyes, the scene coming back to her, a rough pinch to her heart. "There was a woman. Older. A countess or something close to it, I figured. I stepped into a performance I shouldn't have, then stepped out as quickly as I could. Landed in the wrong year on the way back, which I fixed after a bit of experimentation."

Stepped back—but not before he'd broken her heart. What she'd always wanted to share with him, those intimate things she'd seen other couples doing in dank alleys and hidden nooks of public houses. Saved herself to share with him. An experience Simon had thrown away on one of a thousand. Just another toff getting his dangly-bits off.

She'd vowed then and there *never* to come back.

Delaney's teacup hit the table with a thunk. "You saw Simon and…" She flapped her hand in the air instead of completing the statement, her breath rushing out in a diminutive, duchess-like *whoosh*.

Emma gave his gloves a fierce twist. "I don't know how I ended up in a bedchamber. I believe it was *hers*. So much pink. Gaudy, like this brothel I stumbled into once when I happened to be delivering coal. Not time travel that one, I just walked in."

"A countess, you say?"

Emma sank her fingertips into the soft leather and tried to push the picture from her mind. "There was a tiara."

Delaney scooted forward in her chair. "A tiara?"

Emma threw his gloves on the table. "And not much else."

Delaney slumped back, her laugh rolling out too

fast for her to suppress it. *This* was the American, on full display. "I can't imagine," she whispered and popped her hand over her mouth.

"You can't imagine Simon…?"

"He's an Alexander. And a gorgeous one at that. Of *course*, I can imagine. The stories they print can't all be fake." She licked her lips, her voice dropping to a whisper, "What I mean is, I can't imagine *you*, a young girl, seeing *that*."

Emma sighed and went to her knee, deciding not to tell Delaney that fornicating couples were a common sight in the slums. *Lord, save her from naïve duchesses*. "They have a code at the Blue Moon. Three knocks, followed by two, followed by a final. This one the decider. It means a woman needs to make a shifty escape. They have so many bloody kittens traipsing in and out of there, they had to invent a cipher!"

"And you know this *how*?"

Emma rocked back and forth in slippers that pinched. "I just do, that's all."

"You just what?" Simon asked from where he'd sneaked up behind her, his long body stooped to hear better a conversation she didn't want him to hear. Aside from seeing ghosts at every turn and having the fastest hands in England, the man moved like a thief in the night.

She'd never seen him coming—a girl who *always* watched her back.

Emma swiveled on her toes, graceful herself when the situation called for it. But entirely at a disadvantage, what with him lording it over her, his body rising to his full height now that she'd turned to look up at him. His eyes flashed, those slender rings of purple visible in the gaslight. And the freckles, a piece she'd bet the countess she'd seen him tangled up with in that flaming pink bedchamber hadn't cared a whit about. "None of your business," she growled and shoved to her feet. "How 'bout that?"

"You sure about making this one into a lady?" Simon murmured and gave his coin another crazy spin. "Although it *was* my idea."

"You *cad*." Emma jammed her hands on her hips, ready to shout from the rooftops about that blemish on his person. She'd seen it up close before transporting herself back to her time. A crying, unhappy mess, landing in 1802, alone and miserable. With visions of Simon's pert, perfect, birthmarked arse forever in her mind.

Delaney sighed and lumbered to her feet. "Thank you for asking, Simon, darling. Miss Breslin would be delighted to have this dance. As the duke has continued to play, in hopes someone waltzes before dawn breaks." When they looked to her with arguments lined up on their tongues, she clapped her hands lightly. "Are you really going to argue with an expectant mother? Causing her any minor amount of undue stress? Shall I tell Sebastian that's what's occurring in his ballroom at this very minute?"

Emma dug the toe of her slipper in a crack in the marble floor, chastised. "No, ma'am."

"'Your Grace' is the proper address," Simon muttered, tucking the farthing in his waistcoat pocket with a resigned roll of his shoulders. "Are we pretending she has a dance card I initialed, Delaney, duchess dear? Bursting with signatures of the ineffectual, men sure to get their toes smashed for their earnest efforts."

Delaney cuffed him on the arm. "Simon!"

"I quit!" Emma turned, five paces away before he caught her.

His fingers circled her wrist, tugging her to a halt.

She glanced over her shoulder, the wrong moment, the exact *wrong*, bleeding moment to do it. Color had risen in his cheeks, slight but noticeable when she found she couldn't help but notice everything about him. His dark-as-oak eyes wide, his lashes, *dear heaven*, so long they brushed his skin when he blinked. A muscle in his jaw ticked, his annoying dimple pinging to life. He was handsome, plain and simple. Just a mark beyond, even. On the outer edge of pretty.

Why, oh why, had he grown up to be even more fetching than he'd been as a boy?

"I'm sorry," he said, loud enough for her to hear. But just barely. "Come, I'll help you with the waltz."

Emma wiggled her wrist from his grip, her pulse, which he'd pressed his thumb over, thumping in time with her breaths. His touch was not something she could easily endure when she'd gone years without anyone's. "Come again?"

He stepped back a feather space, his expression hardening like the marble beneath their feet. "I said I'm sorry. This was my idea, inventing a new history for you, because it's how Julian solved my problem when I was a boy. I thought to do what worked before. Bring someone into the League and construct a life for them. He lied to everyone. To this day, telling tales about us being half-brothers when we're not, forcing society to accept the falsehood. So much so that I now believe it myself. Never contemplating that they wouldn't acknowledge me because he made it so. He's very tenacious. It's endearing and infuriating." Exhaling, he dragged his fingers through his hair, leaving the strands in ferocious tufts she had to squeeze hers into fists to keep from straightening. "I'm being a miscreant. And for that, I apologize."

Her heart tumbled, an absolute roll, like a length

of carpet spilling out carelessly along polished oak. "Miscreant? Is that the same as a scoundrel?"

He laughed softly, his lips twitching as he tried to suppress a smile. "More villainous than a scoundrel. Perhaps cad is closer. When I was a ruffian at the start, this is what I honestly tell you. Julian and Finn took a rowdy, uncouth boy and made"—he swept his hand down his form with a self-deprecating shrug thrown in—"*this* of him. It's not who I would've been, but it's who I *am*. And I'm finally, much to everyone's surprise, coming to accept him."

"And you're askin' the same of me, this transformation. Emmaline Breslin, forgotten cousin of a duke made from a meager chit from Tower Hamlets."

His mahogany gaze circled the ballroom before returning to her, his face serious, solemn. His sincerity struck a chime deep within her because very few people in her life, even while telling her things she didn't want to hear, had been sincere. "Yes, I'm asking the same of you."

Say it, Emma. No reason to hold back when he knows. "Are you ever going to forgive me for leaving? Would it be easier, us working together, if you did? If I tell you I tried to come back, take it at that. Then we never speak of it. My word is good." She couldn't open her heart again, not after he'd destroyed it with that daft countess and the hundreds of others. Not waiting for her, which was a pointless bundle of feminine nonsense anyway.

But maybe they could be *friends*.

Emma would remember Simon's frank response for the rest of her days, endearing him to her in a soulful way she'd never be able to eradicate. A splinter buried so profoundly it eventually became a part of you. "I don't know, Emmaline Breslin. But I'm going to try."

She bowed her head as a shiver of awareness glided along her skin. His scent drifted to her, soap and some spice she rarely smelled in the rookery. The mint he used on his teeth. The urge to close her eyes and travel to another time was almost stronger than the urge to step into his arms and beg him to hold her. Never leave her, *take* her. But she'd left the swish stone under her pillow, and God knows where she'd end up without it. Maybe in the middle of a Scottish winter again, which had been *horrid*. This new life, the League's offer, right now, for the *moment*, she reckoned she was going to accept.

Holding out her hand in the upmarket way the duchess had shown her, Emma tipped her chin, also just so. "Thank you. I would love to dance, Mister Alexander."

Simon glanced at her hand, bare because she'd brought only *his* gloves to the parlor in hopes of returning them. Instead, she gave her fingers a wiggle, no way to change what was, the thought of dancing with him, her body tucked against him, making her jumpy. They looked to his gloves resting in a tumble on the side table, then back to each other.

Now or never.

Pausing, he tapped his boot, catching the tempo of the duke's melody. "I suggest gloves for the real thing. The waltz is intimate enough without added temptation," he whispered, then swept her into his arms.

And the world disintegrated until it was only theirs and theirs alone.

CHAPTER 6

She could dance.

Emmaline Breslin, Regency time traveler from the London Borough of Tower Hamlets, could dance. True, she'd stepped on his toes. Twice. And Simon had to keep negotiating control, a gentle squeeze of her hand to remind her, *follow, don't lead*. Too, she didn't get the four-step rhythm at first, turning as they whirled into their first rotation one way when he wanted her to go another...

But. She. Could. Move.

Dancing with her, even with the minor blunders, was effortless. She was fluid, willing to change course, direction, on a penny. She trusted him. In the ballroom, if nowhere else. There was a...*flexibility* to her form—he couldn't think of another word that worked as well—that he hadn't encountered. By the time he swept her into the fourth turn, she had the steps down, her gaze cast over his shoulder, not at her feet, her attention entirely focused.

And he was mesmerized.

The scent of rosemary and lemon drifting from her skin, mingling seductively with the floral bite from the vases lining the outer edge of the ballroom, was beginning to adversely affect his rhythm. As well, there were other distractions. That tantalizing birthmark, really more a freckle, on her cheek. Her bottom lip glazed from where she chewed on it as she concentrated on her steps. Her breasts bumping his chest with each turn he guided her through. Their thighs linked as they maneuvered the measures in a way usually reserved for horizontal bed play. Which, once he pictured Emma beneath him, even for one, hot second, he couldn't *not* consider.

The image sending his cock into the perilous situation of becoming *known*.

He wondered how she would do, letting some smitten toff handle her beneath these very chandeliers in two weeks during a fete meant to deceive society into thinking she was one of them. He'd have liked to waltz with her then, before all of London, a possessive assertion, which would never occur. Dancing with a viscount's byblow, even should the byblow be invited, which he would be, would not further her cause.

Two, he wasn't about to claim this woman ever again.

It wasn't his fault, entirely, if he imagined crawling atop her and sliding inside, nestling his body to hers without a lick of clothing between them. Without secrets and mystical gifts and betrayal between them. He couldn't help himself. Not with her unique fragrance overpowering his senses, her devastating eyes daring him in ways he dreaded and sought.

It was more memory than fantasy.

In bed. Laughing, teaching, learning. Moist skin and tangled limbs...everything he wanted to share and nothing he would. Allowing Simon MacDermot to enter the erotic dance, more destructive than a mere waltz. Cold lust, everything he'd previously experienced.

Simon Alexander was all anyone was getting.

A man for sale.

The duke's melody intensified as Simon swirled Emma through a chandelier's golden puddle, a storm having descended beyond the floor-to-ceiling windows, casting the ballroom in silhouette.

A storm had also descended in him, a bleakness he well recognized.

Emma stared as if she knew. As if she *understood*. Her indigo eyes pulling him in. Making him want. Yearn. *Hunger*. For the girl who'd stepped into his life and made him believe she was his.

When all he'd learned was, the things you hungered for were the things you *lost*.

"Is your friend with us?" she asked, breathless from the waltz. Breathless from something. "Henry?"

Lurching to a graceless halt, Simon released her and stumbled back. Snaked his hand in his pocket to grab a coin before he realized what he was doing and snaked it back out. "You've danced before," he murmured, heat sweeping his body when he got a look at the shy smile on her face. When had this untamed chit ever looked hesitant to discuss any-damned-thing?

Emma pleated her skirt between her fingers, shifting her slippered feet in time to her matchless rhythm. "Here and there. On the warped planks of shabby knotholes, no waltzes, of course. Nothing so grand as this."

Simon didn't want to ask who she'd danced with.

The thought making him walk the natural path and wonder what *else* she'd done. Which wasn't his bloody business and brought images that had the power to send his temper, lightly restrained on a sunny day, zipping off like one of those pyrotechnics the duke was so fond of. "Good thing, the prior experience. You have it. The waltz. Or close enough not to do grave damage. Practice the turns, let him lead. No more than one dance with each partner. Two in a single evening signals notice you won't wish to receive."

The duke's ballad stuttered to a wobbly close as he realized he'd lost his dancers.

Emma's head tilted as she searched his face, trying to read him. The woman concealed little of what crossed hers—and he felt a crack, a slight chasm, as emotion flowed from his heart, threatening to expose him.

No way in hell, he ruled, bowing slightly, not waiting for her curtsy, if she even knew how to deliver one.

He was out the back entrance and through the rose garden before Delaney could waddle across the ballroom and stop him. Before Emma could open her mouth and whisper a desire he wouldn't be able to ignore, or God forbid, touch him, tempt him beyond reason, something only larceny had done before.

He always got an itch between his shoulder blades when he thought of stealing.

And now, after spending years trying to kill the inclination, he also got the itch when he thought of *her*.

Bruton Street was clogged when he hit it, carriages and carts tangling for purchase, the scarce inhabitants of the boulevard sprinting along with gazes downcast to avoid the storm, bumping into him as he himself sprinted. He stepped off the curb and into a shallow puddle, certain, thanks to the modern sewer network, it no longer contained a streaming river of waste, only conventional urban grime. Henry was just behind him, avoiding the slick, as ghosts were able to do.

Simon strode in the opposite direction of the Blue Moon, following the streets as they meandered into murkier environs. Traveled through the muddled damp until he was soaked clean through to his drawers. Until his path wasn't lined with picturesque arcades, apparel shops and confectionaries, but with dilapidated structures jammed together so tightly, they looked like they were holding each other up. Gin palaces and squalid flats and ramshackle shops, one depressing dwelling after the next. Tattered clothing on hooks fluttering in the breeze, the windows he passed patched with wads of newspaper and strips of fabric.

The sounds of the lesser tier surrounded him as he crawled inside, recognition and preservation awakening his senses. Simon Alexander stepped back to allow Simon MacDermot to enter the space, the man better outfitted for the decadence that was St Giles, Shoreditch, Old Nichol. Children's shouts, hawker's bellows, the curses of blokes with nothing to lose, soared in volume as he closed in on a part of the city he could taste, breath, *feel*. Choked lanes and trapped paths and blind alleys, the gritty blend of charred meat, coal smoke and the river tainting the air. Laundry soap and ale and dung. Impoverishment and a clandestine energy he thrived on when he wished he didn't.

A slice of London he felt more comfortable in than the slice, the life, his brothers had offered him like a piece of angel cake on priceless bone china.

Which would distress them to know.

As he passed a set of filthy windows on Old Nichols Street next to the residence he sought, he caught sight of his image in the rain-slashed glass.

Cracks and more repair with tattered newsprint. His hair was the color of the Cork Distilleries whiskey he stocked at the Blue Moon, darker than it'd been when he hustled these streets, his body broader, his jaw rigid. But his eyes were *less* wary, less aggrieved. And for some bizarre reason, he felt remorse over leaving that terrified boy behind. Leaving this life of misery and poverty behind.

He despised himself for fitting in so well in fucking Mayfair.

Simon shoved aside musings he'd thought, *every* time, he'd resolved, until he returned, halting before a portico of nondescript construction. A decaying set of cement stairs took him to a weather-beaten door and a rusted knocker in the shape of what he assumed was a hummingbird. His request for entry was undemanding, the requisite four raps answered immediately. Ragsdale, Josie's barbarous majordomo, gave a swift nod as he opened the door, his hand caressing the butt of the pistol shoved in his waistband.

Simon took the carpeted stairs two at a time, realizing it was a reckless endeavor, coming here in the light of day, seeking solace instead of sex, as any other man entering Josephine's would be seeking. Henry jostled him, having completed the trip with him, a blast of air rather than the feel of an actual body colliding with his.

When Simon tromped into the parlor where he knew he'd find her, a fleeting surge of fury reeled through him. He'd been unable to save her, his childhood friend from the mudlarking days. The desperate, despicable days. Unable to offer the sister of his heart another solution until it was too late.

Josie glanced up from her knitting, a fleeting assessment. A judgment that would be right on the money because she knew him almost as well as he knew himself. Halting her clacking needles, she gestured with one to the sofa across from her. "*Sit.* I can see something beyond our normal business is on your mind. I wasn't expecting you until next week. A new girl needing placement. But we can get to that after you tell me what's wrong."

He blindly followed instruction, sprawling on the brocade sofa, his legs going out, his head back. Josie's ceiling needed repair, a spider crack spanning an entire corner. He would have the Blue Moon's steward add it to the running list of maintenances. Yanking his hand through his hair, he sent streaks of rain sliding down his cheek to collect on his collar. With a shiver, he slipped a farthing from his waistcoat pocket and rotated it between his fingers as Josie halted her knitting to play hostess. Feminine succor, comfort for both of them in the routine. Pouring tea, stacking biscuits on a plate edged with what looked like daisies, murmuring observations he wasn't required to satisfy. Not with her. She knew how to calm him better than even his brothers. Better than whiskey and, sometimes, better than sex. Her perfume, delicate, discreet, circling the space. Closing his eyes, he breathed in one of the few sensations of *home* in any memory he wished to carry.

Josie reclaimed her seat, fished out her yarn bundle and put her needles into play. It looked like she was halfway to creating a scarf, some godawful mix of gold and fuchsia. "You're soaked to the skin. No gloves, no overcoat. Where is that Inverness cape I saw you wearing on St James last month? My, you looked an Oxford man. You've done us proud, darling boy. Former bandit of the night. Not a lick of Old Nichol on you. You've got the life. Unless one glimpses eyes the color of the finest chocolate and sees the hopelessness." She tapped the needle against her bottom lip. "Care to tell me what this impromptu visit is about?"

"I gave her my gloves," he said stupidly, flexing his chilled fingers. The supplest kidskin to be had, Welsh, specially ordered and just in from his tailor the week before. They would have come in handy during his stormy dash into the slums, *dammit*.

"*Her*." Josie's knitting needles reclaimed their task, her lips curling to hide what he assumed was a smile. She ducked her head before Simon could confirm the suspicion, but his mood curdled anyway. "That answers my question. Why should I be shocked? You run back here every time you get frightened by your new life. But you've never run back because of a woman. More resentment with your brothers over their heavy-handed management, that silly tiff when you were almost expelled from Oxford for stealing the Roman antiquity from the library. But never the need to escape a *woman*. Hmm…"

"I'm *not* running from a woman. I needed to walk. Clear my head."

"Clear your head by strolling from Mayfair to Old Nichols? In the blinding rain?" Josie glanced out the window at the congested mass passing her residence, the sound of a man's shout and glass breaking a clear reminder of where they were. Her needles clicked as she shrugged a slim shoulder and resumed her project, accepting of her circumstances, forgiving of his good fortune, as always. "It's been almost twenty years, Mac. Doesn't that life fit yet?"

Simon shot a breath through his teeth, slapped the farthing to the table and cradled his hands around a teacup, wishing like hell the delicate china was filled with gin. *Mac*. Besides Josie, only his mother had ever called him that. A nickname even his brothers didn't know about. "I'm not frightened."

He took a sip, the taste of chamomile and cinnamon dancing along his tongue, calming, as she'd planned. "Unnerved, perhaps. Unsettled. I don't know why this is the case after all this time. I'm lucky, I know it. Schooling only an aristocrat, even one hanging on to society by the nick of his fingernails, would receive. Quality clothing, a loving family. A home. Two, in fact. Mayfair and Julian's estate in Oxfordshire. A *profession*." He sighed and tapped the rim of the cup against his teeth. "I love the Blue Moon like I birthed it. There couldn't be a place I cherish more in this filthy city. Mine, thanks to someone else's good grace."

Josie paused, placing the half-completed scarf on her lap. "You lose yourself dissecting the boundaries between who you were and who you *are*, Mac. It's a tireless route, bouncing between them. When is there time to simply live? Accept, move on?"

Simon spanked the table with his teacup. "Is that what you do, Josie? Simply live?"

She lifted her head, her eyes glittering, as lush and green as spring grass. "I *chose* this. I opted to live in squalor and fight to get others out. I foster every woman I can, giving them a *future*. This business is a ruse, you and I both know, except for the women who truly wish to sell themselves and will never turn back. And for them, I provide the best situation possible." Josie lifted a brow, her expression chiding. "You speak as if this is *my* life's purpose, not yours. We built this together, Mac. Have you forgotten you're my covert benefactor? Or that this undertaking was *your* idea after seeing how well creating a new life from a lie worked for you." She gestured to the world outside her cozy little parlor with the knitting needle, a string of yarn tangling around her wrist. "How many of my girls have you employed so

far? In the Blue Moon and at your brother's resi-
dences, the homes not requiring a person to have a
magical gift? Ten?"

Bracing his hands on his knees, Simon rose to his
feet. "Thirteen." Josie wasn't a drinker, but she had to
have liquor somewhere in this chamber.

If they were going to explore his secrets, he
needed a drink.

"Oh, yes. Mollie McCurley. How is she working
out?" Josie smoothed her hand over the scarf, fretted
at a knot in the yarn. "I worried. A duke's seat is
aiming very high, and her stutter is quite pronounced
if she's nervous. We worked for months to even out
the rough edges of her manner and her speech but
still…"

"She'll be fine. The Duchess of Ashcroft is an
American and as unconventional as they come.
Everyone equal, no kings, no titles, all that rubbish. I
asked that Mollie be attached as a maid to her new
project, a girl with quite a few jagged edges herself."
Simon dropped to his haunches before a scuffed cup-
board and loosened the bottom drawer, a bottle of
Irish whiskey rolling to the front with a pop. *Bingo*.
Yanking it free, he gave the cork a twist and drank
deeply.

Josie sighed. "I have glasses in—"

"No need." Simon took another pull, the liquor
burning a delightful path to his belly.

"I hate to ask, but is one of your specters here
with us?"

Simon dragged his wrist across his mouth and
jammed the cork in the bottle. Alcohol was swimming in his head—but better hazy oblivion than
unchecked Emma. "Henry. Bootmaker."

"Blacksmith," Henry murmured from his spot
against the escritoire.

"Blacksmith," Simon echoed. "A very amiable fellow."

"Thank you," Henry said, "you as well."

Simon wrenched open another drawer, this one littered with hair ribbons, a button, loose change, and at the back, a broken pencil and scrap of wrinkled paper. He pulled the pencil and paper out and slid to the floor, his back resting against the cupboard, his legs outstretched.

To keep his hands occupied and lessening the urge to steal, Julian had taught him to sketch. Only thing was, he wasn't good at drawing while he was an excellent thief.

Surprisingly, however, the trick worked every now and again.

"Your brothers don't know about me, do they? The women you're saving from an absolute horror of a life? You couldn't even tell the one who smiles all the time, the man they call the most gorgeous in England?"

"Finn," Simon murmured and sketched Henry with swift strokes, his disheveled hair, the cowlick riding up in front like a rogue wave in the sea. Collar nearly hitting his chin and ruffled sleeves, attire not seen since the late 1700s. Tilting his head to inspect, he licked his thumb and muddied the charcoal edge just as Julian had shown him to do. "They left the slums and never looked back. Humphrey, too." He gestured with his pencil, a quick jab. "Julian's a vis-count and never belonged here, anyway. And Finn turned into a gentleman the moment he dipped his toe into Mayfair's seductive pond. They don't under-stand my need to retain parts of this sad life, parts of that sad boy. So, no, I don't tell them I've been coming here since I was old enough to sneak away. They don't know about you, about the network we've established." He added Henry's curling mustache, thinking it looked more like a scar in the finished product. "They know Simon Alexander, not Simon MacDermot. I've never been able to share him easily."

"Did you ever tell them your mother was a light-skirt, compelling you to now risk so much to help these girls?"

Simon flinched, the pencil going wide across the page. "*No.*"

"Maybe it's time to tell them. Quit trying to jam these loose pieces of yourself into a puzzle that only makes sense to *others*. It's acceptable if two such distinct realities don't quite fit and too taxing to try and make them fit. You can't live a life like that."

He'd often thought he *should* tell them. Then, his random disappearances and clumsy fabrications, when pressed, would finally make sense. The somber mood he often had trouble liberating himself from. His sporadic requests to place a female domestic in one of their households.

He knew he needed to tell *someone* who he was—and was fiercely annoyed to realize that someone was Emma.

"So, darling Mac, you're here because…"

"I required a moment to breathe. My family is coming to town for the duke's ball next week. The lot of them. Children, too. It will be utter madness. And this girl, the duchess's project, she demands my attention, in part. It's complicated." He put too much pressure on the pencil, and the tip broke off with a snap. "If you need me, I won't be able to get away easily. Send a note to Mackey—"

"Wait, go back to the duchess's project. I hear a catch in your voice. Is this the woman you mentioned? *Her*?" Josie's hands twisted the yarn into submission as she probed his soul with a gaze so fervent he was forced to look away. "The one with your gloves?"

Simon flipped over the wrinkled paper and started a new sketch, this one of Emma. *Let's face it*, he thought, *that's who you wanted to draw the entire time.* "You remember the girl who showed up at Julian's estate in Oxfordshire? Ten or so years ago? The one I couldn't talk to? The one who stole the Soul Catcher?"

Josie gasped, her knitting needle hitting the carpet with a soft thump. "Oh, Simon, you finally found her." Scooting to the edge of her chair, she smiled broadly while his frown grew. "How did you travel back? Was it incredible? What was London like then? Were the clothes very odd? Did she remember you?"

Emma's reaction when she'd first seen him flashed through his mind, a joyous spill widening her indigo eyes until they completely conquered her lovely face. She'd not only recognized him. For one moment, she'd looked as ecstatic as he *felt*.

"I think I'm still in love with her. Just like I was when I was a daft boy of sixteen," Simon whispered and let his head fall back against the cupboard with a clunk. *How bloody senseless was that?* With a loathsome snort, he reached for the bottle, but Josie was quicker, on her feet, snatching it from him before he could make the situation worse by getting drunk in the middle of her parlor.

"We're not solving this problem with gin, Mac. And you've tried solving it with half the women in this city. It's time to find *you*. Maybe this woman can help you do that. She's one of us. A beggar, at heart. Supernaturally gifted, as you are. You have nothing to hide, no one to hide from."

He closed his eyes and allowed the rookery's tenacious essence to seize his senses. The sound of carriage wheels striking pitted cobbles, a hawker selling sweets beneath Josie's window, fried fish and laundry soap drifting into his nostrils, stale smoke and the Thames battling for control on his tongue. "I found it unpleasant, investing my heart. The return wasn't agreeable. And as an Alexander, I've been taught all about agreeable returns. I run a business, a successful one, based on nothing *but* agreeability."

Josie went to her knee beside Simon. Paper crinkled as she removed the sketch from his hand. "Is the girl you've been waiting on to return for ten years the lost cousin of the duke I've read about in the newspapers? I know you're very close to him, almost like a brother, you've said. Is she the duchess's new project you speak of? The woman all of London is desperate for a glimpse of?"

Simon opened one eye, fixing it on his oldest friend. If he loved Josie in that way, if she loved *him* in that way, life would be so much easier. "She's going to bring me down again if I let her. I spent years wondering where she was and why she didn't come back. I still don't know. Foolish, perhaps, but it pains me."

Josie rocked back on her heels, Simon's sketch of Emma fluttering to the faded carpet. "Your answer to finding your lost love is to create a life for her well above your own? Placing her out of reach, should the ruse be accepted? A future with some posh toff? When she could be with *you* if you'd let yourself figure out who you *are*."

"It will be accepted," Simon whispered and levered to his feet. Did Josie think that made him *happy*? He didn't want to imagine what would happen should Emma become an overnight success, which *was* the plan for a duke's cousin. A prosperous future, a future that would never include marrying a viscount's bastard. "There are downsides. She's head-strong, not one to let a few meaningless rules get in her way. Reckless, impulsive." He crossed to the window, rain falling in sheets and sending a river of filth racing along the street to accumulate in the half-choked drains. "She's also intelligent. Shrewd. Capable. Sensible, I suspect, beneath the swagger. She'll deceive them all and laugh while doing it." He tracked a raindrop down the dirty pane with his thumb, his heart stuttering in his chest. "It might even be amusing to watch."

If only he believed that.

"But what about you, Mac?"

Simon pressed his palm to the glass and stared at a life he'd left behind, a citadel of the underworld living among the *ton*.

What about him?

He'd keep coming back to this very spot, even if it defied his family's strategy to secure his happiness.

And he'd go on loving Emmaline Breslin, he supposed, against his goddamn will.

CHAPTER 7

"*H*e did *wot?*"

Emma collapsed on the edge of her bed, a tricky endeavor in the gown she wore. The bustle jutted out from her bottom like a bundle of straw, at the perfect angle to balance a tea tray on. How had fashion come to *this*, she wondered and watched her maid, Mollie, strut around the room like an actress ready to break into song. Emma questioned where on earth they'd found the girl. She knew nothing about employing domestics and running fine households but guessed Mollie belonged in Mayfair even less than she did.

And that was saying something.

Emma fell back on the bed with a sigh, marveling at the comfort of the feather mattress shifting beneath her. The most snug bed she'd ever settled upon, without question. "He left me. In the ballroom. Yesterday, during my lesson that wasn't a lesson but a chance for him to bloody one-up me. When I'm a woman who doesn't like to be one-upped." She socked the counterpane, pretending it was his rock-hard jaw. "At the end of a waltz. Walked away, ran more like it, before I even had the chance to curtsey. And I'd been practicing that curtsey for days!"

"That's an Alexander for you. Probably had a p-p-prior engagement, if you gets my drift." Mollie sniffed and rubbed her forearm beneath her nose, something Emma noted the girl did when she wanted to slow her speech and take hold of her stuttering. "Simon, ah, he's known for 'em. Engagements with females that is. It's the way with the men in that family. Or so the chatter says. The ladies love 'em, they do."

"I don't care what engagements he has," Emma seethed, giving the counterpane another punch. Cad. Bounder. *Rotter*. He could show that birthmark on his arse to every wench in London for all she cared. But he would not turn his back and ignore a curtsey she'd spent hours perfecting.

"Course you do, missy. Can't help w-w-who you like, even if he is a scoundrel who sees spirits. I heard the lower house staff talking about his latest ghoul, Henry. And the duke and his fires, the duchess and her mind attic. Land sakes, this house is peculiar. I listen, quiet like, so folks talk right in front of me. The s-s-stutter makes them think my mind doesn't work well. But you have your own odd talent, so that evens it out if you do favor him. The oddity that is." Mollie flung open the wardrobe doors and grabbed a nightgown, giving it a clumsy unfurl before tossing it over her shoulder and turning to Emma with a pitying expression. "I seen the way you looked at him that one time, when he popped in at breakfast. You're sunk but good. Maybe you could use your fancy disappearing act on *him* the next time"—she snapped her fingers—"poof, into another room with ya'. Take that for leaving me unaided on the dancefloor!"

Emma's cheeks burned to realize the way she felt

about Simon was noticeable. Rising to her elbow, she shifted atop the massive bustle as she struggled to kick off her slippers. Lovely silver ones she was coming to adore. Even if they pinched. But she loved them almost as much as she loved her beautiful gowns, except for the dreadful corset she had to wear to squeeze *into* the gowns.

This life, this grand, grand life, was one she feared she could get used to. "Mollie, may I ask how you ended up in a duke's household of all places?"

Mollie whimpered and crumpled to the crimson velvet settee. "Do I n-n-not please as a lady's maid? I'm learning to say the H in all my words and not belch and keep my opinions to myself cause I'm not paid to share them. Lowly, they are, truly in the mud, what I think. I told Miss Josie a showy place such as this was aiming too high. Mayfair! T-t-too high, indeed! I woulda been h-h-happy with that stinking-rich banker who needed a scullery maid. But, no, Miss Josie had to place me with a duke!"

Emma scooted to the edge of the bed, the slipper dangling from her left foot dropping to the floor. "Goodness, Mollie, that isn't what I meant. You're brilliant. I've never known a better lady's maid."

Mollie's brow cocked high as she sniffled. "Have you known another lady's maid, missy? I'm guessing not. I reckon the cousin of nobility fib is stretching it, though you have my promise, I'll never tell a soul you aren't what they say you are. To the grave, our secrets. Mine and *yours*."

Emma shook her head and laughed softly, kicking her other slipper free. How was she to dupe the entire of London if she couldn't dupe a servant?

Mollie snickered and gave her nondescript black skirt a cheery pluck. "That's the way of it. We both mean to make the best of this splendid opportunity."

Her voice dropped to a ragged murmur. "Leave the bad behind."

"Was it bad?" Emma whispered, grasping with a dull ache how lonely she was. For *home*, even when 1802 hadn't been splendid in any way. When she'd had to watch her back, worry every minute about how she was going to pay the next month's rent, food, candles. Steal when forced, lie all the time. Be nastier than she wanted to be, every single day.

But she missed the apple tarts her neighbor, Mrs. Watkins, made for her once a month. Missed the aroma of wheaten bread coming from Sampson's bakehouse on the corner. Missed the children, gap-toothed, their faces streaked with dirt, their clothing riddled with holes, who'd smiled at her as she strolled the docks. She missed her scruffy pillow and the quilt her mother had made for her when she was seven. She missed her favorite boots, the ones that had holes in the soles that she patched twice a year.

The tricky part: she hadn't expected to be offered a new life—and then only have seconds to decide whether to accept the offer.

But she could, *would*, make the best of it.

Because this life provided more than fresh quarter loaves Mister Sampson sold her on the sly.

She could turn a knob and have warm water shoot from faucets *right in the house.* She had her own tub and a basket of stylish soaps the duchess had given her, colorful cubes that smelled of lavender and peony, enough for a thousand washings. Oranges and *grapes* were available every morning at breakfast. Last night, she'd sneaked down to the duke's pantry and perused the incredible variety of staples on the shelves. Milk that sold for leagues more than the 1802 price of two pence, half-penny a quart. Vegetables. Fish. Meat. Every hearth she passed was crammed with firewood, the windowpanes sporting not even *one* crack. The newspapers scattered about were recent editions, not stained, months-old rubbish. The books in the home's library smelled of ink and leather, the spines cracking when you opened them because most had never been opened before.

The duchess housed a library in her mind, her supernatural gift, and did not need an *actual* library.

Regrettably, for her heart, the most marvelous thing about 1882 was Simon Alexander.

For him, Emma would strive to be as polished as the duchess's priceless silver.

Emma snapped out of her musings to find Mollie slumped on the settee, sobbing, her head propped on her bent knee. Emma slid from the bed and crossed the room, crouching next to the girl. "What's wrong? You can tell me. Have I upset you in some way?"

"My s-s-sister." Rubbing her fist across her pinkening nose, she shook her head furiously, her mass of coal-black hair spilling from her mob cap to hit her shoulders. "I'm sorry. When you asked if it was bad, it *was* bad, Whitechapel, but not so much for me. I got out but left her behind."

As Emma listened, Mollie unleashed a desperate tale of two sisters. Mollie, saved by a benefactor, the other, Katherine, a year older, a young woman who hadn't been able to escape the destiny of the slums.

"When did Katherine get involved with this man you say has ruined her?"

Mollie wept into her starched sleeve in between uttering broken apologies for her behavior. "She h-h-had a right fine job, a learning position at a dressmaker's in Bethnal Green. Mostly domestic uniforms and reproductions of the lavish dresses you see in the shops on Bond Street." She gestured to Emma's gown as if to say, *like yours*. "Katie has a way with copying the posh designs, thus the new position once the dressmaker seen her walking down the lane in one of her creations. Could sketch them right up and cut the patterns, too. G-g-gifted, like you but without the time travel. She'd taken a turn at what they call a plain sewer at the garment mill in Bethnal Green. But the air is filled with fibers, and anyone there more than a month coughs something awful for the rest of their d-d-days. And the dyes, don't make me reveal what those poisonous liquids do to a soul." Mollie swallowed, slanting Emma a fearful look, twisting her hands together.

"And...?" Emma prompted.

Mollie yanked her mob cap free, sending midnight strands of hair streaking across her cheek. "The owner of the factory, Mason Thomas, he's a m-m-mean one. Greedy and tight-fisted. Broad as a barn, strong as a bull. Doesn't provide food except for scraps of bread and water when folks work twelve-hour shifts. Children, too. Ones as young as eight years old slaving away on his garment floor. He got his eye on K-K-Katie. She's a looker, all right. She quit, up and left the second he approached her with his base desires. He has a wife and three children already!"

"But he found her," Emma whispered, a tale she'd heard a hundred times before.

"Ah, that he did." She dragged her cap across her nose and hiccupped. "One evening, leaving her shift at the dressmaker. Cornered her in the lane just behind. It was force, I tell y-y-you. And now, she's holed up in some squalid flat he's got for her, miserable. No options, no life. A baby on the way at some point, sure as the d-d-day is long. She can't leave, she says, not after *it* happened. Even Josie couldn't talk her out of that place." Mollie ironed her hand down her modest but serviceable domestic uniform. Kicked her feet together to display unattractive but glossy, new boots. "When I have all kinds of a future. If I could o-o-only go back to that day, before he attacked her, I would give my life to save her."

"What if we can do that? What if *I* can?" It would be the first time in *this* time, beyond the desperate ventures she'd waged in 1802—going back to help Mrs. Marsden cross the street before the cart ran her over, making sure the doctor was notified when Eileen Churchill went into labor that last awful time —that she'd found a way to use her gift.

Maybe Simon would forgive her if time travel came to have true meaning.

Maybe she would forgive herself.

Emma rose, crossing to the bedside table. Gleaming mahogany with glossy pewter hardware, an elegant piece unlike any she'd ever owned. The blue velvet pouch was in the top drawer behind the copy of *David Copperfield* Simon had given her. When she opened the bag, the swish stone rolled into her hand, a glittering ball of fire. A powerful sensation pulsed through her as she clutched the gem to her chest.

To protect, to transform.

To *amend*.

She turned to Mollie, who eyed the flickering stone with all the admiration it deserved. "Tell me the exact day, the exact *time*, Mason Thomas found your Katie in the alley. We'll be back before breakfast, no one the wiser."

She hoped with not a little trepidation that she could keep this promise.

CHAPTER 8

Simon just knew it was going to be a ghastly evening.

He'd had a nagging itch between his shoulder blades since leaving Josie's the previous night, unwelcome advice and intolerable realizations stinging worse than the driving rain in which he'd sprinted back to the Blue Moon.

Love. What the bloody hell did he know about love?

He understood death, the line between the living and the deceased gossamer-thin in his world. People stepping in from the past to plague him, then stepping out again as suddenly. Appropriately, the only woman he'd been compelled to consider his own floated like a feather between eras, in his grasp, then gone again. Uncertain, when his other relationships were certain without desire for them to be.

Bracing his hand on the balustrade of the balcony high above the gaming floor, Simon surveyed his domain. Let the crack of dice, the din of conversation, the aroma of brandy, cigars and macassar oil soothe his nerves. The shout of victors, the whimper of those losing their wealth and their souls, rising to echo off the paneled walls of his study.

This day…bad to worse.

Baron von Delton had won a substantial sum at the *vingt et un* table, which happened on occasion but made Simon feel like diving into a bottle of gin and never crawling out. The puerile poet who'd been coming in every night for two weeks finally depleted his reserves, then got into a drunken altercation with the third son of an earl that was sure to hit the scandal sheets. Karina, Simon's oft-companion and currently one of the most popular actresses in London, had shown up at the alley entrance, eyes puffy, dress hanging off her shoulders, looking gorgeous and pitiful, a skill she employed to no end. He'd ushered her into a private salon promising to return when he had no intention of doing so, leaving her in the capable hands of the Blue Moon's manager, Benjamin Squires. Who'd looked like he wanted to rip Simon's head off for giving him such an odious duty. Simon imagined Benji, a former rookery thug, would have liked to show his displeasure in a way that would've had him scuffling on the gaming floor with his employer.

And, while reviewing the evening's annoyances, there was Finn.

Overprotective, interfering Finn.

The single person he'd loved above all others.

Simon glanced over his shoulder at his brother, who sat sprawled at the desk in the dimly lit alcove of a space Simon liked to think of as *his*, a fountain pen's nib pressed to his bottom lip, his index finger trailing slowly down the ledger columns as he added figures in his head.

"Don't you have a newborn to attend to?" Simon shoved aside the urge to swipe the etched gold cufflinks Finn had left sitting on the edge of the desk and instead tugged his hand through his hair. The strands were overlong. Bedraggled, Karina had said. Although she'd whispered it like it was a *good* thing in that dry tone she used to great effect in darkened bedchambers.

"Just making sure you don't bankrupt us with this von Delton debacle," Finn murmured, his gaze tracking the figures before him. The pen had left a spot of ink on his lip that Simon guessed half of London would love to lick off. "I only gifted you forty-nine percent, my pet. I hold the remaining fifty-one if you recall. The final decision, and responsibility, for this establishment is mine."

Simon bounced his fist off the railing and rose to his full height. "That's a crock of— "

Finn threw his head back and laughed, his cerulean eyes dancing. Simon hated it most days, but he could see why the *ton* thought his brother the most gorgeous man in England. He *was* horribly pretty. A pretty jackass. "You're so easy, lad. *So* easy." He flicked the ledger closed, tossed the pen atop it and stacked his hands behind his head with a stretch and a smile that ceaselessly won people over from the first tilt of his lips. "We'll make a killing tonight, no worries. Fairly, I might add, unlike most gaming establishments in the city. Thankfully, we're not required to send ourselves to hell in order to run one." Finn yawned and gave another heroic shrug of his broad shoulders. "When the men arrive worse for drink and not too bright to begin with, it's an economical gambit from the get-go. Heck, we offer a service no other hell can by having a professional read their minds. To save the despairing few who would throw themselves into the Thames over their foolishness, I share my supernatural gift. I don't want their downfall on my conscience for a fistful of blunt."

Simon wiped his thumb over his lip. "Saint Alexander, champion of the exploited, you have a spot of ink on your…"

Finn popped his boots on the desk, dashing his hand over his mouth. "Ah, these pens with endless streams of ink. I can't get over it. Technology proving its worth, right before my very eyes. How your girl lived through her era, what with tallow candles and oil lanterns and water arriving at the house in buckets, I can't fathom."

"She isn't *my* girl. And it wasn't that bad," Simon murmured, thinking of the candlelight washing over Emma in the dreary depths of the public house, his first glimpse of her in years. The way his heart had clutched and released in a feral flutter.

He'd known at that moment that nothing had changed.

"Not your girl," Henry scoffed from the dark corner where he'd decided to settle himself.

"I hope you enjoyed traveling back, possibly being unable to return. Because that's the *last* time." Finn's voice splintered, a familiar argument about to rise between them. The League wanted to know everything about Emma and her gift—but Julian and Finn didn't want that to include letting Simon test it out and travel again with her.

Ever again.

Simon pushed off the balustrade, realizing the fight he'd wanted may be coming from his brother and not Benji, which wouldn't be the first time. "Do you realize you're making these threats to a twenty-seven-year-old *man*? I'm not a grubby urchin, begging for your advice."

Finn's polished-to-a-high-sheen boots hit the

floor with a thud as he rose to a stand. "Eighty or eight, that was the last time-travel you'll be doing if I have anything to say about it."

The brothers stepped forward at the same time, two paces apart, fists clenched. Finn had Simon by a solid inch in height. But Simon was younger. And meaner. Finn didn't like to fight, and honestly, wasn't very good at it.

The study's door hinge squealed, and Simon looked over Finn's shoulder to see his eldest brother, Julian, stepping into the room. The viscount took one look at their harsh expressions, the fighting stances, and sighed behind his fist. "Not again."

A beast of a man barreled into the room behind Julian, sending the viscount forward two steps he hadn't counted on taking.

The only ungifted member of the League, Humphrey was Julian's best friend from childhood and as close to Simon as his brothers. Humphrey's gaze bounced between the two men, squaring off in the middle of the room. "Christ, am I going to be fixing split lips again? I suppose I have to take my brother-in-law's side, even if he's just a daft, beautiful bloke."

"Take his side, fine by me," Simon snarled and gave Finn a shove, his temper heating. "You married his sister. I didn't. All's fair in war and family, right?"

Finn reached to rub his chest, his smile growing. Rolling his shoulders, he whispered a vile obscenity, then knocked Simon off his feet before he could take a breath. The clip to Simon's jaw that followed was trifling and rampant with brotherly love.

Before Simon could return the favor, Finn rolled to his back, his hand going to his temple and pressing hard. "She's here. In the cloakroom again. *Injured.*" Closing his eyes, he released a muted growl that had the men surrounding him, Julian dropping to his knees at his side.

"*Who?*" Julian whispered.

Finn flicked his hand toward Simon with a grimace. "His woman."

Simon scrambled to his feet, pushed past Humphrey and stumbled down the staircase, the raucous activity in the main salon lost to him as he muscled his way through the crowd, the sights and sounds of a vibrant gaming chamber a blur, his skin gone clammy and cool.

Injured. *Injured*.

She'd traveled in time. Against their agreement. Against the *rules*.

He smacked the cloakroom door open with the heel of his hand, bouncing it back against the wall. Mollie was huddled beneath the rack of coats, coiled protectively over Emma, who lay motionless on the floor, her cheeks pale as snow in the meager gaslight, the Soul Catcher captured in her outstretched hand. The stone pulsed like a heart, a prism of amber light unlike anything he'd ever seen emerging from it, splattering the room.

Julian stepped behind him, crowding into the small space. "My God, it's on *fire*. Have you ever…"

"No," Simon whispered and went to where she lay atop the scuffed planks, his pulse a bumpy drumbeat in his head.

"We traveled back, through r-r-rainbow colors, a flash of sound like thunder, but not. It went through my body like a punch. Bethnal Green. My sister," Mollie panted, her hair hanging in a limp tangle down her back, her chest riding swift breaths beneath a torn bodice. Scurrying aside to let Simon move in, she gestured crazily, on the edge of hysteria. "We saved her… Katherine. Before Mason Thomas g-g-got his hands on her. I don't know how it changed things... Her life path... I only know it did. I'll go now and find out. I have to g-g-go *now*."

Settling on his knee next to Emma, Simon brushed aside a strand of hair fired with amber clinging to Emma's cheek. Her breathing was steady, her color improving. She was going to wake soon, and when she was strong enough, he was going to have it out with her. Her recklessness was going to *stop*. "Julian, can you arrange a carriage for Mollie to Bethnal Green?" Josie had told him about Mollie's sister and her abortive effort to save her from the clutches of a garment factory owner who routinely ruined women with ease and little conscience.

Using a riskier method, Emma's rescue attempt had been successful.

He trailed his thumb across the sleek curve of her jaw, his fingers trembling. Her gown was torn at the shoulder, her cheek scratched and bleeding.

Success...but at what cost?

Simon grasped Mollie's wrist when she struggled to stand. "What happened?"

"We was in f-f-fine shape. Got Katherine out of harm's way and tucked in a safe spot. Was headed back straightaway. Before breakfast, before a-a-anyone knew. Just like Miss Emma planned."

Simon inhaled sharply, rage pouring through him. "*And?*"

"The time tracer c-c-caught up with us. Stepped out of the mist like a phantom. He touched her, and she went down like old Freddie Two-step, a pugilist who's not adept-like in the ring for what it's his profession. It's only c-c-cause we were already sliding back here that we got away, to my thinking. That uncanny r-r-rock flickering like a wick gone bad. We whooshed from the past to this very spot like we'd marched through a doorway, simple as that when it's not so simple. We weren't supposed to come b-b-back here, but Miss Emma said your name when the tracer touched her." Mollie yanked her wrist from Simon's hold and wobbled on shaky legs. "So here we be."

Julian stepped into the fray, gently grasping Mollie's shoulder and drawing her to her feet. "Time tracer?" As the League's leader, Julian managed a thousand-page volume listing everything he and his group of mystics knew about the supernatural world. This information would be something he'd desperately want to record in his chronology.

Mollie palmed her brow and swayed, beginning to feel, Simon guessed, the exhaustion he had after his adventure in 1802. "Miss Emma said he follows the ones who gambol through the ages. A watchdog of sorts. Always trying to bring them back."

Someone was chasing her through time.

Simon gazed at her, his mind racing, wondering what else she'd failed to tell him.

As if she felt his regard, Emma blinked and sighed, her lips moving in wordless entreaty.

Simon leaned in to hear her whispered words.

Her eyes opened and focused on him, her gaze such a glorious shade in the muted light that his heart stuttered. "I can't breathe," she said, the Soul Catcher throwing crimson facets across her face and his chest.

He unfurled her fingers, took the gem from her and pocketed it before she woke fully. It dimmed the moment it left her touch. "Relax, you're back. You're going to be fine."

She licked her lips and tried again. "Can't breathe. *Corset.*"

Simon glanced toward Julian. "Take Mollie, will

you? Help her locate her sister. Then, I'll get Emma
back to the duke's. And Henry"—he looked to the
haunt loitering in the doorway just behind his
brother—"a moment, please." Henry gave a proper
salute, then faded like a wisp of smoke into the night.

Julian opened his mouth to speak, advice Simon
didn't want but perhaps needed, then shook his head.
"Twenty-seven-year-old men don't need direction,
now, do they? Wasn't that what you were telling Finn
upstairs?"

Tears pricked the backs of Simon's eyes, and he
was damn glad the lighting wouldn't allow his
brother to see them. "Thanks, Jules." *For everything*, he
wanted to add but wouldn't dare.

A rare occurrence, Julian's lips kicked as he ushered Mollie into the hallway, closing the door behind
them.

Simon looked back to find Emma had shifted to a
half-sit, her breath coming in shallow fits and starts,
her hair a glorious tangle of auburn and gold swimming past her shoulders. She frowned, her cheeks
flushing. *Bloody corsets*, Simon thought and reached
for the knife in his boot. "Turn around," he ordered
and flicked the blade free.

Emma glanced from the knife glittering in the
gaslight to his face. She swallowed once and presented her slim, delectable back.

Against his will, Simon's cock stirred beneath his
trouser close, arousal coloring his ire a shade darker.
"Hold still," he gritted between his teeth and reached
for her.

She dipped her head and swept her hair to the
side, offering a gently rounded form for his consideration. He had the urge, irrational but evident nonetheless, to press his lips to the nape of her neck, to
mark her skin with his teeth. As she gasped, strug-

gling for breath, he pierced her gown at the waist and split the fabric up the back, an ocean of emerald silk falling open beneath his blade. Of course, her corset was a violent splash caught somewhere between gold and russet, tantalizing against her pale skin. The laces were easy to destroy, pleasure he shouldn't be experiencing flooding him as they fell away, strings dangling.

Her back was finely-boned—and freckled. A light dusting along every bend and dip of her spine.

Perfect for a man waiting to be led to the right spots.

He fought the urge to toss her over his shoulder, hide her away in his bedchamber at the top of the stairs and never come up for air. Make her beg for mercy as he prayed for deliverance. As he'd always dreamed.

With a gasping inhalation, the first full breath she'd had in hours, he'd bet, she moved to press the ruined corset and gown against her bosom, gazing over her shoulder with a feral twist of her lips. "You don't have to look so happy about the obliteration," she whispered in a ragged voice that told him that she, likely against her will, was affected by both his touch *and* his savagery.

Her response revealed much about her in the hazy darkness, things he didn't want to know. *Or use.*

Hoping his erection would die a quick death, Simon rocked back on his heels, closing his knife and jamming it in his boot. "Is that any way to talk to the man who just removed you from your torture device?"

Emma yanked a coat from the pile that had fallen to the floor and jammed her arms, one at a time to keep from exposing more of her body to his hungry gaze, through the sleeves. They hung well past her hands, dangling nearly to her waist. "I wager that's not the first time. Corset removal."

"With a knife?" He raised a brow when she looked back at him, daring her, challenging himself. "It's not."

"You despicable cur!" she spit and shoved to her feet. When she got there, she closed her eyes and braced her hand on the wall for balance. She looked pitiful, the overcoat leagues too large, draped over her shoulders, gathered in a sorrowful heap around her ankles. Her gown a disaster, her cheek and chin smeared with blood. Her skin having paled to the color of chalk, except for the rosy slashes sweeping her cheekbones.

He held himself from going to her, protecting, nurturing, but just barely. A caretaker for haunts since the hour of his birth, he wasn't volunteering to care for *her*, too. "Time tracer," he murmured and deliberately rose to his full height, an intimidating stance. The poker chip was in his hand before he could stop himself from tunneling in his pocket to retrieve it. "Care to tell me about that?"

Emma blinked, her mouth falling into a round, little O he wanted to shut with a kiss that would curl her toes. Bemusement looked marvelous on her.

Simon rotated the chip between his fingers, watching her try to puzzle her way out of her dilemma. "Don't lie now; it's too late. I know enough, and you're going to tell me the rest."

Emma gave the coat sleeves a brutal roll, exposing delicate wrists and a light sprinkling of hair that glistened in the light. "I don't owe you my story."

Simon lobbed the chip in the corner and stepped in, snaking an arm around her waist and dragging her against him. She fit like she'd been made for him. Which, at one time, he'd thought she had. "You damn well *do*. I risked my life to save *yours*. That, my darling Emma, is payment owed. And as you can see from my booming business in the salon behind us, I know well how to collect."

She tipped her head, catching his gaze. "Collect, then. Go ahead, Alexander. Do your worst. Take your payment. I dare you."

His hand roamed her back, curling possessively around the nape of her neck. Her skin was flushed, slightly moist, her scent, lavender this day, circling, entrapping. She smelled like the duchess's soaps, every last one of them. A new scent every day, driving him mad with desire. And anticipation. "You'd love that, wouldn't you? Make me lose what I'm about." The words came out harsher than he'd intended, more truthful, closer to the bone. *Damn her.*

Her lashes lowered, quivering, her tongue coming out to wet her bottom lip. "With all your women, how could a gutter rat from the Hamlets possibly make you lose what you're about?"

Simon's resolve splintered.

She was too tempting. His fascination too real.

Her eyes blazing, goading when he wasn't a man to be goaded. Her warm breath struck his cheek as he stood there debating, the scent of mint rolling off her tongue to tangle around his. A darkened cloakroom and the sounds of a gaming hell sliding into the background.

One kiss…

How much could one kiss change?

And wasn't a kiss what he'd always wanted from her?

He didn't think, question, strategize. He simply acted. Hand rising to cradle her jaw, fingers plunging into her hair, tilting her head and *taking*. Simon caught her against him, his lips capturing hers, dragging her almost off her feet.

The contact bursting with everything he'd denied every other woman.

He kissed Emma like it was the only time, the last time, his one *chance*. Like she'd returned instead of leaving and wrecking his heart.

He kissed her like it was forever.

CHAPTER 9

*D*evastating.

The thought circled Emma's mind that she'd been waiting for this kiss her entire life. A horrifying thought. Simon wasn't hers, would *never* be hers.

So she should let him go.

But when he loosened his hold, letting her slide down his broad chest, retreating, she went up on her toes, hand snaking around to circle the back of his neck, mouth opening beneath his. She touched her tongue to his bottom lip because he'd done the same to her, and he groaned low in his throat, pulling her so tightly against him, two bodies became one.

She met his every thrust until they established a mindless rhythm, animalistic and raw, a rhythm that tilted her world on its axis.

A battle for control, a battle for breath.

A battle for sanity.

A kiss unlike any she'd imagined existed.

And with this man, she'd imagined many.

"So this is you," he whispered against her lips, his voice rough, fevered. "Ferocious, uninhibited." He walked her back, stumbling over coats until she was pressed against the wall. Taking a halting inhalation, he braced his forearms on either side of her, caging her in. Pinning her between his hard, hot body and cool plaster. His gaze met hers, his eyes the color of deep twilight, a murky, beautiful spill. His lashes lowered as his focus did the same, following a trail from her neck to her toes and back that felt like he'd set her on fire. Her gown gaped, her breasts unbound behind the fragile structure of a ruined corset that was close to slipping from her body. Trailing a finger down the middle of her chest, he halted at her belly. Then trailed the finger back to her collarbone, a sluggish crawl setting goosebumps racing across her skin. Her nipples pebbled, aching, begging for attention they'd never received and were unlikely to be given.

The punch of pleasure from his languid caress weakened her knees, her determination, her ire. Her ragged sigh was not lost on either of them. He was changing her, changing *them*, right before her eyes. As if he spun their future like a coin between his talented fingers.

"Are you going to kiss me again?" she asked, appalled but too eager for his touch to care.

A worrying fold crept between his brows as she studied her.

Her hand rose without invitation, her thumb smoothing the line with a tender touch. In response, Simon turned his head, caught her palm between his teeth, his tongue following to appease. The bite was pain. The lick pleasure.

She groaned through open lips as her heartbeat erupted, aggravated and aroused beyond measure.

If she waged war, it was easier than she'd imagined winning the subsequent encounter.

She followed instinct, hand sliding from his cheek

to his chest, ribs to his belly, heading lower, to the hard length pressed against her thigh. He whispered an oath and captured her wrist before she reached her destination, wrenching her arm high above her head. "You incorrigible minx," he murmured and collapsed into her, seizing her lips and every thought in her head and tossing them into the wind.

Frenzied, his hands were all over her. In her hair, cradling her cheeks, gliding down her ribs, grasping her waist and drawing her in until they were joined hip to hip, thigh to thigh, his incredibly hard shaft a powerful presence between them. She followed his savage lead, nipping his bottom lip while struggling to remove her arm from his hold. Though she wasn't sure she wanted him to release her.

And he didn't. Not for one second.

This unknown facet, that she'd given a man control and *liked* it, sent her pulse in a dizzying spin. Sent heat—pure, primal *heat*—flooding to her core.

It was madness, the blaze they created. The Soul Catcher smoldered like an ember from its spot deep in his coat pocket, a more forceful glow than she'd alone caused it to emit. Even in her innocence, she imagined he hadn't created this combustion often.

But the image of him with another woman wouldn't let her go.

That he'd experienced *this*, in part, with some random actress or opera singer or widowed hag— and the memory of what she'd seen in the countess's bedchamber when she'd tried to return to him—sent a bolt of fury through her.

He's not yours, Emma. And he never will be.

Shoving him back a step, Emma heaved a gasp into the leaden air and yanked her arm from his grasp. This time, his dark gaze full of fire and fury, he let her go. However, with his chest heaving, he didn't step away.

And he didn't try to hide how her kiss had affected him.

Scowling, he dragged his thumb across his bottom lip, his lids fluttering. "I don't know why you're vexed. I gave you every opportunity to slap my face and walk away." His gaze fixed on her for a long moment, then drifted off. "When you ask a man if he's going to kiss you again, expect the answer to be yes."

Everything changed in that moment.

Fury turning to love, ire to uncertainty. She would never look upon Simon again without knowing exactly how he tasted. How he gently stroked his tongue against hers, increasing the intensity only after she let him know she was ready. How his biceps flexed as he held himself back from crushing her to the wall, when she knew he *wanted* to crush her. His hot breath in her ear, his teeth sinking into her skin. His rigid length pressed to her thigh. His hips intimating a dance she wanted more than any waltz on earth—a dance that would lead to doom.

So intimate, every piece of it. Yet, he'd never thought to wait for her.

But such was a man's desire.

Insatiable, or so she'd heard.

She waited until his gaze met hers, his jaw ticking from suppressing emotion and speech. He crushed his feelings something awful inside until he looked like he was ready to crack. "I came back, Simon. Five years after I left. My ma"—she expelled a sigh, started again—"my *mother* was ill. And the tracer trackin' me, every step. He's like one of your haunts. His existence unending, ageless. His duty, or so he says, to keep travelers in their own time. To curb the disorders made by going back and changing. Traveling forward and seeing." She frowned, her hand going to her bodice when her gown and the corset beneath it started to buckle. "Like today, saving Mollie's sister. Things I can do, use my gift, you see. Ways I can help, something good from this mess of a life I've found myself mired in. God, that mongrel would have hated it. That I helped someone. I've done it before, modest interference. Traveling back and keeping someone from a grievous injury, say. It's not the first time I came to someone's rescue, is all I'm telling you."

Simon burrowed his hand in his coat pocket, coming out with the swish stone. *Her* swish stone. *Her* man. Its ferocious radiance had eased to a faint flicker. Nothing like the blaze when she held it. Or when they'd kissed. He rolled the gem between his palms in what she could see was his way of calming himself. She felt the urge to protect—the stone *and* the man. Insanity, all of it. When neither was hers to safeguard. "When he touches you…" He swallowed, his jaw flexing.

"One brush of his pinkie, and it's like I took a punch to the jaw. Lights out. He casts a spell. Sounds like something from a penny novel, but it's the only way I can describe it."

"Never *again*," Simon said in a rough snarl, bouncing the stone between his hands. "The League is protecting you now."

Emma felt resentment stir. If he thought… "He *will* find me again. Your precious League or no. He always does. He travels time as well as I do, which is, not perfectly. But he travels. And he'll try to bring me back. This is my fight. It always has been. I think he even wants me to help him. Becoming a jailer, like he is. I'll die first." She laughed cruelly and yanked ruined silk to her neck. *What the hell. Tell him.* "I might have let it be your fight. Before. I came *back*, Simon."

He halted, the stone falling still in his hands. Tilting his head in bewilderment, he asked, "You mean you made it? To Oxfordshire? You found me?"

The scene she'd stepped into in that garish bed-chamber rushed into Emma's mind in full, bleeding color. She growled and stomped past him, across the room and out the door she flung open.

"Wait," he shouted, his long-legged stride quickly catching him up to her. "I'm missing something here. Which, when dealing with women, isn't unusual. You're furious. You've been furious since I dragged you to 1882, and I don't know why. When I'm the one"—he thumped the hand holding the swish stone against his chest, crimson sparks spattering the wall —"who should be. You never told me, we never spoke, but you said that you were coming back with your eyes. I didn't have anyone else, Emma, to talk to, except people long gone and a pack of overprotective brothers. No one who understood what it was like coming from where we'd come from, being con-nected to such a cheerless life and still *yearning* for it. Because I could see you had, and you did. I *needed* that."

I needed you, he could have said but didn't dare.

She hauled the neckline of her gown to her chin and halted at the end of the hallway, wrinkled silk fisted in her hand. Lifting her arm, she rapped on the scarred walnut door leading to the alley. Three times, quick and hard, like he had the first time. Two knocks came back. Emma slanted Simon a heated look and repeated with one.

Mackey opened the door, his grin rising when he saw who stood on the other side. "I thought those blows sounded right feeble. But you got the cadence best as a judge, darlin'. A crafty one, you are. I can see why you've been loafing 'round."

"We meet again," Emma said, throwing out a curtsey she hoped Simon could see was elegant enough to please a queen. Unfortunately, she was a fast learner of waltzes, curtseys *and* cyphers allowing women in and out of back entrances of gaming hells. The duchess had her bending and scraping until she'd declared the effort perfect, and Emma's knees ached.

But, by God, she was going to fool them *all*.

"Meet again, we do." Mackey tipped his bowler hat and bowed, not bad form for a ruffian, if Emma were asked to assess. Which, of course, she'd never be asked to do. "Same chit twice in one week. A record for our boy. I fear you got him by the short—"

"*Mackey*," Simon snapped, "round up the carriage if you please."

Emma snorted softly and descended four stairs to the grimy cobblestones. "Quite haughty for one from St Giles, isn't he, Mackey? Polishes up nicely, though, I must admit."

One of Mackey's shaggy eyebrows rose until it slipped beneath the shadow of his hat brim. "Tragic place. Where the Great Plague started, first poor victims buried in the churchyard of St Giles-in-the-Fields." Tapping his muddy boot on the cobbles, he gave his employer a painstaking examination, as if this information provided a connection he hadn't anticipated having. "Me auntie comes from over that way. Grape Street, right horror of a lodging, but she'll leave when she kicks and not a moment before. Stalwart, like most of the females in my family. Blast, like *most* females." Seeing the conversation was going no further, Mackey tipped his hat and hustled away, gesturing for the carriage they kept parked at the corner.

When the silence began to chafe, Simon took the stairs with a hop and landed beside her, blowing out an exasperated breath. "Are you going to tell me what has your knickers in a twist?"

"I want the swish stone back," she answered without glancing at him. If she did, with that kiss swirling in her belly, filling her chest with what felt like flaming cotton, it was going to end with her pressing him against the gritty brick and begging to have another go. She covered it well, but her knees quivered, her hands trembled. Her lips stung. Her thighs burned.

And between her thighs...

She'd never felt more like a vulnerable female, a desirable woman. Regrettably, she wasn't sure she liked it.

"Give it back? No ma'am. I'm not applauding bad behavior."

Blood bubbling from the emotional mix—resentment, longing, helplessness—Simon created in her, Emma presented her back, turning to watch the Blue Moon's carriage, that after circling the block, rolled down the alley on its journey to retrieve her.

"We make a deal, here, now, in this splash of misty moonlight, Miss Breslin. If you comply, I'll consider giving it back at the ball. Not one bloody trick between now and then, not even traveling from the breakfast room to the duke's garden unless you *walk*. The next time you think of placing yourself in danger, don't do it under my watch." From the corner of her eye, she saw him pat his pocket, the Soul Catcher's glow evident beneath the soft linen of his coat.

There had been others parts of him, ones she was desperate to explore, hidden but not well, beneath fabric this evening. Hard as a stone. She kept herself from looking past his waistband to see if this was still true.

"The ball is in ten days. So I won't see you until then?"

His pause was interminable, his boots scraping stone as he shifted from one foot to the other. "After that kiss, a little distance might be for the best," he finally said, his words as tentative as the fog. "The sensible avenue to take."

Sensible? She didn't want sensible. She never had. Not with him.

Instead, she wagged her head, her gown drooping, the corset's sharp edge digging into her breast. Her nipples were still rigid as pebbles, she'd love to tell the toad. "Nothing to it. Forget it ever happened."

"*Done*," he whispered, pretty as you please.

The carriage halted before them, Mackey out like a shot, yanking down the stairs and gesturing grandly for her to make her way inside. "My lady. Yer chariot awaits."

"Christ," Simon muttered.

When she was settled on the velvet squabs, the gigantic overcoat in a puddle around her, she glanced out the window to find Simon standing in the same spot, his face drawn in lines of battle. After scratching his chin with his shoulder, a cautious signal, he dug deep in his checked waistcoat and came out with a handkerchief. *SA* embroidered on the corner in somber gray thread. "You may want to wipe the blood from your cheek before you face the duchess. It's going to be enough to explain the damaged clothing. But you made this bed, so it's only appropriate you lie in it." He shoved the strip of cloth into her outstretched hand, their ungloved fingertips brushing, sending a bolt of heat through her body.

And, she prayed to all that was mighty, through

his.

Giving up, she sighed and flopped back against the seat, pressing the handkerchief against her shuddering belly. Touching him was going to be a danger hereafter. Another problem that blasted kiss had introduced. When she was prepared to make it worse. The minute they got out of sight, she was going to lift the wadded linen to her nose and breath the deepest breath she'd drawn all day. Inviting his scent into her soul.

He stuck his head in the window before they rolled away, determined to get the last word. He was tall enough, *plenty* tall enough, to lean right in and over her. Incredible, when the Alexander brothers didn't share a drop of blood, that they were near the loftiest men in London. "I want to know everything about this time tracer, a minor detail it would have been fantastic if you'd shared before. Julian will need to record your considerations in the chronology, discuss it with the League. I don't believe it's something we ran across in our research to find you. If we're going to protect you from him, we have to know *how*. And *why*."

She was tangled up in emotions she craved and loathed. No one, *no one*, had ever stepped in to protect her. She'd had no father, and her mother had been ill every day Emma had known her. Her granny too old, then gone before she knew it. The feeling of being safeguarded was magnificent and...frightening. As tangible a weight as the coat draped across her shoulders. Though she wasn't prepared to accept it. "I saw you with the countess when I came back. My 'knicker twist,' as it were. Or *hers*, should she have been wearing any."

He rocked out of the carriage, then back in, moonlight a hazy wash over his ruthlessly handsome face. The mist had curled his tawny hair about his ears and jaw, and she wanted nothing more than to knot her fingers in the overlong strands and draw his lips to hers.

"Countess," he whispered, baffled. Shaking his head, his hand came up to grip the window frame, his gaze searching her face. His fingers were long and slim, the nails ragged as if he chewed on them. A spot of ink marked the rough pad of his thumb.

Intimate details she unwillingly cataloged, hating the both of them for the need to.

"I didn't have first-rate control then. I practiced, but it wasn't, it still *isn't* perfect. I even ended up in Scotland once."

His fingers clenched until his knuckles whitened. "Brilliant."

"No, it truly wasn't. Cold as a witch's teat there. Anyway, when I returned, I tried to land smack at the viscount's, Julian's, estate in the country, where I met you before. I thought of you and it, that place, but somehow, I bungled the job and ended up in—" She bit her lip and released a pained exhalation through her teeth. "This vulgar pink bedchamber. You and a countess and her tiara. And not much else. Except for that bloody birthmark on your bum!"

"*Oh...*" he breathed, a comical expression of horror on his face. "That's not good."

Emma snorted beneath her breath, unable to think of another thing to say.

"It didn't mean anything. They never do." His lashes lowered, partially concealing his discomfort. "And she wasn't a countess."

Incensed because he'd made no effort to deny what she'd known was the truth, Emma pried his fingers from the window frame and banged on the carriage's roof. Mackey whistled, and the conveyance jerked into motion, throwing her against the squabs. She wasn't going to look through the rear window, *dammit*, but in the end, she did.

Simon stood in the Blue Moon's shadowed entrance, his expression vacant, his eyes haunted. The Soul Catcher shimmered a radiant blue from the depths of his coat pocket.

Then, without so much as a twitch of his pinkie, he turned and walked inside, closing the door behind him.

Emma collapsed, her breath leaving her in a piercing sigh. It seemed she and Simon were always walking away from each other.

Ravenous countesses, unwanted supernatural gifts, London's dense fog and eighty years standing between them.

⁓

He'd had too much to drink.

But the looming distance between his female troubles and his ability to do anything about them were welcome.

Simon's brothers, who'd barreled into a deserted Blue Moon after closing, were not.

"Humphrey, take the gin from him, will you?" Julian advised from his spot behind the desk in the gaming hell's study, a sketchpad balanced on his knee, his charcoal making light strokes across the page. "I worry this is what goes on when I'm in Oxfordshire. He'll be on the floor soon, with Finn not far behind."

Humphrey reached over him, the bottle leaving Simon's hand before he could recapture it.

"Nothing but grief since she stepped into my life," Simon whispered against the rim of his glass, determined to enjoy the last sip if that's all the controlling viscount was going to allow. Emma's fiery kiss was burning a hole in his brain, and he needed alcohol to eradicate the reflection. "Josie doesn't know what the hell she's talking about."

Finn rolled his head to look at Julian. He was half-slumped in a massive leather chair angled before the hearth, one leg hooked over the arm, the other stretched before him. He sat so close to the fire, Simon imagined his boot was getting toasted. "Who's Josie?"

"The madam in St Giles he visits," Julian said without looking up. "Great Russell Street, isn't it? A philanthropic venture, if you can believe it. Child-hood friend. A few years back, they formed a rescue alliance for impoverished women, taking them out of that life and placing them in service. Covert, but I ad-mit, quite impressive. I employ two of them cur-rently, a scullery maid and a governess, believe it or not. The Duke of Ashcroft has at least one or two himself. Finn, I'm sure you have someone he's foisted on you."

Simon pinched the bridge of his nose in annoy-ance. "Old *Nichols* Street. Russell is two over."

Humphrey slapped the bottle on the sideboard, slanted a swift look at Julian, then poured a generous drink. "That pisspot of a neighborhood? What the ever-loving saints is he doing down there? After all the bother we went to getting him *out*."

"Can't help myself," Simon murmured, pulling himself up on the sofa. He braced his arm on the bro-cade cushion to steady himself, swaying. "How long have you known about Josie?"

Julian's hand stilled, his smile, Simon wasn't sur-prised to note, lethal. "Since the first time you went. What were you, Mac? Fourteen?"

"Thirteen," Simon echoed in a leaden tone, chafing, as he always did, under the protective burden of his eldest brother. He should've known his nickname, his charitable venture, his entire *life*, would come as no surprise to Julian Alexander.

Nothing got by Viscount Beauchamp when it came to his family. Nothing.

"Thirteen." Julian used his thumb to soften a stroke in his sketch. "I must have missed a year then."

"I can't forget where I came from, Jules, like you, Humphrey and Finn have been able to. My past haunts me worse than Henry"—he nodded to the ghost who sat in friendly contemplation on the other end of the sofa—"ever could."

Julian scratched his jaw, leaving a charcoal streak on his cheek. "Who said anything about forgetting? Your problem is *acceptance*. Connecting that life to this one. That's the only thing we're better at, Simon. Or maybe it's because we're older. I was about your age when I finally forgave myself for my past mistakes and embraced a future with Piper."

"Who is Mac?" Finn slid sideways in the chair, his lids lowering. "No, don't bother. I'll read your mind and find out."

"I'd love to have the sofa to myself, if you don't mind," Simon told Henry, stretching out when the haunt moved to sit next to Finn. The bountiful amount of gin he'd imbibed was tilting his world almost as much as Emma's enthusiastic kiss.

He'd never had a difficult time breaking away from an embrace. Evading a passionate situation he'd discovered he'd rather not be in once the kissing started. Theirs hadn't been a situation he wanted to extricate himself from. *At all.* Instead, for one frenzied second, he'd considered pressing her down on that godawful pile of coats and climbing atop her.

Something one did with a lightskirt, not the woman you suspected you were falling in love with.

Or, rather, had never fallen *out* of love with.

A woman who, from her artless but picture-perfect kiss, you presumed was a virgin.

Simon had steered clear of inexperienced women and had no clue how to handle one.

Julian angled the sketchpad, frowned, added another stroke. "I've come to believe love is a pursuit for wholeness. Not to sound overly sentimental, but the other half you're so damned incomplete without. Piper helped me to not only find myself and control my gift but to accept what I couldn't change. Accept who I *was*. But I had to locate the courage to take what she offered. Strong women don't make it easy, Si. And they don't give up. But if you want love and intimacy and friendship, the entire package, you're going to have to work for it. Not be terrified by the promise of *more*."

"This isn't love." Simon stretched long on the sofa, hiking his booted feet atop the armrest, staring at the ceiling in place of meeting Julian's probing gaze, the lie he'd uttered reverberating in his chest. "It's obligation. Since you know my secrets, lord and master, consider it another rescue mission, this one simply retrieving someone from the past instead of down St Giles way."

Humphrey snorted and popped his glass to the sideboard with a bang. "God almighty, youth is wasted on pups." Simon heard a clank as he poured, bouncing the neck of the bottle off the rim of the glass. "You dunce. It's been love since that chit first burst into our bizarre world and sent a duchess tumbling from her mare and into the dirt. With a duke riding up seconds after to save her, white knight extraordinaire. Put their love affair into motion that very day. The duchess should be thanking Emmaline Breslin for the assist, which may be why Delaney has such a blinding inclination to make your girl over. Turn her into a bashful cousin come to Town set to turn the *ton* on its ear."

Simon stacked his arms beneath his head, his fingers itching to slip something from one of the men in the room into his pocket. "*My* idea to style her as a duke's cousin. Inspired by Julian, of course, and his sound work on Finn and me."

"Brilliant, your plan. I can see the advantage. Now that she's here, your wandering girl, after you *brought* her to our time at great risk to yourself, you've decided you don't want her?" Humphrey released a deafening exhalation and began to crack his knuckles. "I feel like coming over there and knocking you upside the head."

Simon slanted a watery, one-eyed gaze Humphrey's way, the room spinning sluggishly around him. He was likely going to embarrass himself by hurling in the rubbish bin sitting beneath his desk, and likely soon. "What are you so furious about? Emma's maturing into a society miss before our eyes. Flipped a curtsey at Mackey tonight that would have made Victoria cry. Her speech is improving, mostly. She waltzes as well as a debutante. All she needs now are a few inane topics to prattle on about, watercolors and fashion and the like, and we'll be golden."

"What about your time thief and that daffy maid of hers racing into the past, then coming back banged up and bloodied?" Humphrey halted his knuckle-popping long enough to pour another drink, crystal clanking. "Golden? Since when? Adept at getting the traveling chit to keep her rabid opinions to herself, are you? According to Delaney, she's got about an *ounce* of submissiveness in her, maybe less. Another fiery woman we're inviting into the League, heaven help us."

Finn yawned and slid lower in his chair. "Fiery ones are the only ones we *like*."

"What if she's an unqualified success?" Julian asked quietly, the suggestion exploding like a fire-cracker thrown into the middle of a church service.

Simon rolled to a shaky sit, a headache beginning to thud behind his left temple. "Meaning?"

"Emma's introduction to society, if Ashcroft's ball goes as planned, will lead to invitations. More balls, teas, musicales. The opera. Walks through Hyde Park. Epsom Derby, anyone? Perhaps a proposal. Isn't a strange notion for a beautiful woman, cousin to a duke, to receive one. And matrimony is where most roads in society lead. If anyone can keep her in 1882 long enough to marry her, that is." Julian tapped his pencil on his thigh and tried to act coy, like he wasn't presenting the topic to make Simon think. The old guess-you-haven't-thought-of-this-but-your-big-brother-has ploy.

"Being a success in society is bloody dreadful," Finn murmured, the only one of them, due to his as-tounding good looks, who could be considered a moderate success in the *ton*.

The nagging itch started between Simon's shoulder blades. Setting his jaw, he glanced around for something to steal and seeing nothing—because everything in the room was already his—dug a half crown from his pocket and twirled it unsteadily be-tween his fingers.

Emma. Married. And not to him.

"No comment?" Julian murmured.

"*None*," Simon returned, the coin getting away from him and bouncing off his boot.

"Pointless being possessive of a lass you don't want," Humphrey added for good measure. "Maybe a bonny thing if she marries someone else. You'd never know one day to the next if she's planning to stay in the same year as you, which could make for a rewarding union. Most marriages, the wife never being around is a blessed event."

"Tell them about the problem, Si. The tracer."

This from Finn. Lobbing his own firecracker into the church, Simon thought. "Thanks for the mind read," he muttered, going to his knee to root around for the half crown.

Finn stacked his linked hands on his belly and gave another resounding yawn. "Anytime."

Julian glanced up from his sketch. "Tracer?"

Locating the coin beneath a mahogany drum table, Simon rose to his feet and started an unsteady trek around the study. Just what he needed—Julian asking questions he wasn't sure he wanted to answer. "This didn't come up in my research, and we have nothing about it in the chronology, but there are people, time travelers themselves, who *track* those who travel. From the little Emma's told me, they sound like Bobbies."

"The tracer brings them back to their own time before any troubles occur," Humphrey said from his spot resting against the sideboard.

"Complicating the situation, he casts spells, as Emma describes it, rendering her..." Simon halted in the alcove overlooking his beloved club and rapped his knuckles on the polished walnut balustrade. He didn't need to show this perceptive group his face when rage and apprehension washed over it. Then they'd know everything. "She said he touches her, and she faints. Instantly. Which is when he returns her to her time. Completely helpless."

Julian drew his pencil across his bottom lip in thought. Simon could see the wheels in his mind turning. His brother loved nothing more than discovering elements of the supernatural world the League had no prior knowledge of. "It's likely he could use this power on others. A clear threat until we know the extent of what he can do. We'll add this to the chronology and document as we learn more."

Simon flipped the half crown between his fingers and lost it again, this time over the balustrade. He winced when he heard it bounce off the gaming salon's marble floor with a dull clink. "I want the tracer kept away from Emma, from this family. I'll speak to Ashcroft about increasing the footmen guarding her, the patrols on his townhouse, on yours, Finn's. A few of the duke's former soldiers are still in his employ. If pressed, we need men able to take care of business and take care of it promptly. Back to a time when we have to worry, I'm sorry to say."

"We've never been able to let down our guard, Si, not once in twenty years. Anyway, I think I have a plan," Julian said in a judicious tone that had Simon wishing for another coin to toss, unease a chilling dance along his spine. "The guards, of course, I agree with. We protect our own. But..." He gestured with the pencil to Simon's pocket, where the Soul Catcher continued to glow, a brilliant, iridescent blue. A neat trick it had never done before Emma's arrival. It was as if the stone recognized her presence in their time, as Simon did. A pulse strong as his heartbeat. "Your girl doesn't have the stone, which helps control her travel. Therefore, the tracer will have to come to her."

"*No.*" Simon took a halting step forward. "We're not using her as bait in some damned mystical game, Jules. I won't have it."

Julian continued as if Simon hadn't tendered an

argument. "Her gift is blindingly unique, Si. And extremely valuable to us. Even if she never travels again, stays in Mayfair the rest of her days, we can record every facet of a supernatural talent we know nothing about." He held up a hand at Simon's exacting expression. "What did you find in the chronology during your years-long examination into locating a portal and reaching her? Not much. We had to use our contacts in other countries to begin to dip our toes in that pond and find a way to her. And, now, this information she's told you about there being others who track? It's astounding. Inconceivable."

Simon crossed to Julian, braced his hands on the desk and leaned in. An intimidating stance, one his eldest brother might not appreciate. It'd been a marvel when he'd grown big and broad enough to challenge his family, not be immediately shoved into the dirt. The duke had trained them in hand-to-hand maneuvers, but until a man had the size to defend, skill mattered little.

Simon might go down, but he wouldn't go easily.

"Here comes the temper." Finn stretched his legs out and gave a sleepy sigh. "I love this part. Certainly, better entertainment than that atrocious play by the Prince of Wales I saw last month at the Globe. He's a horrible writer."

"A tantrum every now and then is good for the soul," Henry advised from his spot in the dark corner where he'd retreated.

"Shut it, you two," Simon snapped, digging his fingertips into the desk's smooth grain. "You supported my researching time travel, finding Emma so that we could record every goddamned detail in that book of yours, Jules. Am I right?"

Julian placed his sketchpad on the desk and

scooted his chair forward with a squeal that splintered the charged silence. His stormy eyes pierced Simon through his fine woolen coat. Threatening—telling a little brother to stand down. The touch of gray at Julian's temples giving him an air of wisdom he'd had since long before the gray arrived. "The plan has always been to investigate Emma's gift. Have her join the League once you found her." Julian flicked his pencil like a baton, gesturing to the men assembled in the room. "As my wife, Finn's wife, Humphrey's, have joined. Provide protection and the opportunity to live without censure. To live as one *is*, not as one is expected to *be*. I've devoted my life to creating the League, to safeguarding those with supernatural abilities. And to investigating the occult, yes. I understand, all too well, caring for someone who is at risk, Si. As Piper was. You were a key piece of her rescue, just a boy, but already one of us. What is it now…?" Julian tapped his finger to the bridge of his nose. Reserved, dignified Jules, whom Simon loved to his core.

He could only think, of course, this is how you'd play it.

"Eighteen years, almost nineteen," Simon whispered, well aware of what his brother was doing but tangling himself in the web anyway. Rolling the dice when he hadn't even known a game was in play.

"A long time, that, and now you think to question my loyalty, my concern for you and those who *matter* to you?"

Simon shook his head and rocked back on his heels, chastised. His fingertips itched with the need to twist a coin between them. But he was in the middle of a game—and his obsession with keeping his hands busy was a colossal tell.

Julian sighed, dug a loose button from the top drawer, and flipped it to Simon, who caught it with a one-handed snatch. "If you care about the girl, *I* care about the girl. I propose that we prepare for this tracer to seek her out, perhaps even send signals to him, never knowing, of course, if he receives them. We have those in the League who can communicate without speaking. Telepathic. That footman who arrived from Spain last year and is working for Finn is quite good. If someone can procure an item from this tracer's person, something as inconsequential as a toothpick, and I'm able to read it, God knows what we'll find out."

"Let's go with Spain," Finn said, surprisingly not asleep. "He and I have contests to see who can read a mind faster. I've got him there, but of course."

Humphrey sprawled on the sofa, his colossal frame taking up half the space. "Going after this bastard before he comes after *her*, young pup, if you're not getting the strategy."

"The duke's ball." Simon rotated the button between his fingers. "We could try and draw him out there. Of course, we'll all be in attendance."

Julian smiled, and with his index finger, nudged his sketchpad back into drawing range. "We'll secure protection that will shame Buckingham Palace's. Ashcroft can make it a fortress without a single soul attending having any idea."

Finn grazed his fingers across his brow in a lazy salute. "Count me in."

Julian held out his hand. His wife, Piper, was American, and long ago, he'd taken to the very un-English act to seal a deal. "Well, young pup, what say you? We go after the tracer as a family?"

Simon looked into Julian's steely gray eyes and held out his hand, Emma's passionate kiss circling his heart, uncertain thoughts of the future corrupting his mind.

CHAPTER 10

*S*he was going to apologize.

To Simon. For the trip to the past she'd taken with Mollie.

Emma gave the ivory fan she held a punishing rap against her thigh, recalling how much she hated apologizing. Although it appeared they'd saved Mollie's sister from ruin. Except for meeting up with the tracer and coming back bloodied and unconscious, the adventure had worked. A successful endeavor.

Like a canny wager at Simon's gaming hell.

She would remind him of that *after* the apology.

Emma stalked the fringe of the duke's ballroom in search of the veranda doors she'd seen Simon slip through minutes earlier, this quest leading her in the opposite direction of the retiring parlor she'd said she needed to visit to repair a hem that wasn't damaged. The baron whose dance she'd rejected had offered to fetch her an ice sherbet, lingering in the event she had another open slot on her dance card. His determination stunned her when perhaps, it shouldn't. Society had accepted the falsehood about her being a duke's cousin, accepted her wobbly accent, her sudden appearance in their ranks, her hesitancy to provide details about her background, simply because the Duke and Duchess of Ashcroft demanded it.

Because they'd created a false history for her. Shy, retiring, Emmaline Breslin. Which she was not and never would be.

Even now, the *ton's* gazes clung to her, interested, *too* interested, the men appreciative, the women speculative. She felt exposed and uncertain, sure she was a misstep away from disaster despite looking like she belonged. Her gown was a glorious pewter confection, a color Madame Hebert claimed no one else would dare wear. And she was right.

Ignoring the impulse to fidget, tug her suede gloves high on her arms or twirl her dance card, Emma nodded and smiled, hoping she looked demure, not determined, and continued on her way. She was following instinct, the moment of serenity at seeing Simon Alexander stroll down the ballroom staircase guiding her like a tug to her hand. With every man dressed in black, Simon's navy coat set him apart like a chrysanthemum in a field of weeds, his height making it impossible to ignore him as he'd moved through the crowd. Accepted, even as the by-blow of a viscount, because the duke and duchess required he be.

Same as her.

She wondered what years of living a lie had done to the rookery scoundrel Simon had claimed to be. Had it tangled him up until he didn't recognize himself? This experience was changing her in ways she wasn't sure she liked. Altering the person reflected in the cheval mirror in her lavish bedchamber.

Now, a cultured voice rolled from her lips, her extravagant gown—she smoothed her hand down her bodice—costing more than all the clothing she'd owned in her past life.

The chandelier's radiance, a gaslight glory that still astounded, winked off her silver slippers as she lifted her skirt and stepped through the doorway and onto the veranda. The footman guarding her followed, but not too closely. Drawing a hydrangea-and-lilac scented breath into her lungs that corseting made near impossible, she searched each corner until she found him. On the far side of the terrace, shoulder propped against a column, a charitable wash of moonlight from the most transparent sky London had offered in days tumbling over him. However, a sharp chill and a deadly aroma from the Thames tainted the evening air, enough to keep society behind closed doors. Taking another inhalation she indignantly realized was layered with nerves, she wiggled a finger inside the duchess's choker circling her neck and crossed the distance separating her from her gorgeous nemesis.

She wasn't going to let that ridiculous kiss they'd shared stop her.

Even if the feel of his tongue guiding hers into play, his long body pressing her into the wall at every key spot she could imagine wanting it to, had kept her up at night, staring at a pristine ceiling without even one crack and wondering how she could get him to do it again.

He turned as her step echoed off marble, propping against the column. Taking a lazy sip from the flute he held, he eyed her over the rim. His gaze was relaxed, like a pleasure boat drifting along the Serpentine, taking its fair time, and then some. The orchestra started playing, music rippling over them like a breeze. After a long moment where time felt suspended, a bubble about to burst, Simon gestured with his flute to her guard, who turned, leaving her to Simon's protection.

Again, her hand went to the duchess's choker, another bout of nerves she was going to have him pay for making her feel.

His focus followed the movement, tracking her like a hunter would his prey. "Alexandra, Princess of Wales, has a scar on her neck she hides with jewelry. Hence the abundance of bejeweled collars in the assemblage this evening. We shall thank her for the trend."

Wordless, Emma squeezed the necklace, a small fortune in gems grazing her palm.

With a smile, Simon took the challenge her rounded neckline offered, his gaze sliding low. And holding. More scandalous than any gown she'd ever worn but perfectly fashionable, according to Madame Hebert, her skin nonetheless burned from the notice. "I'm sorry. That's what I came out here to say," she blurted when it appeared he wasn't going to offer a single, encouraging word of welcome.

He froze, the flute halfway to his lips. "Care to repeat that?"

Halting before him, she huffed a breath through her nose, remembered Piper had advised her not to do that in public, then knocked her fan against her waist instead. Four firm taps. "I've found something good I can do with this gift. But I reckon"—she swallowed, opened and shut the fan two times before continuing—"I *suppose* it's not fair, when you brought me here at great risk to yourself, to then turn around and place myself in danger. Using the League's property. A bit of a reckless gambit, that." Her voice dropped, a thready effort to hide her chagrin. "And ungrateful."

"The swish stone," Simon murmured, his gorgeous lips curled to hold back a grin, that if released, was going to have her bashing him over the head with her fan. He patted the pocket of his coat with his flute, and when she looked closely, squinting, she could make out a bulge that must be the Soul Catcher. His captivating, bronzed eyes met hers. "You need spectacles."

She blinked, frowning. Touched the arch of her nose as if a pair were perched there. "I do not."

He shrugged, bringing the curved crystal to his lips, a muffled hum his only reply as he drank deeply.

"You think you're right *all* the time. It's infuriating."

His lips twitched, releasing a sheepish, wonderfully appealing grin. He leaned in to give the dance card attached to her wrist with a mauve ribbon a flick, sending it spinning.

She grew more vexed by the second as she counted off the things about him she found attractive —the dusting of freckles on his cheeks, the glints of gold in his hair, the fiercely stubborn jaw, the long eyelashes that were invitingly flaxen at the tips.

Heavens, he's handsome, she thought wretchedly.

Perturbed, she glanced to the railing at her side, noted something winking in the moonlight atop it. Looking closer, hiding her squint because she did, perhaps, need spectacles. An etched cufflink, a pearl earbob, a silver match case. Lined up along the marble railing like soldiers. Her laugh came quickly, nothing like the delicate interjection the duchess had instructed her to use to remain a ghost in the room, never attracting attention. "Did you steal these?"

He gave his flute a heedless toss into the bushes lining the veranda and trailed his finger along the stone wall as if the rough texture pleased him, then, finally, picked up the cufflink. Rotated the trinket between his nimble fingers without once looking down. "It's possible," he answered, his smirk diabolical. She could see the rookery rapscallion, clear as the mud that had daily coated her boots in her old life. How had the *ton* missed that? Why, sly thievery was written all over his face. "A reasonable bet if you decided to wager."

Emma smiled and reached for the earbob. From society toff to street urchin in the blink of an eye. *This* was the charming, unpredictable man she could love, she reasoned, remembering how he'd dealt with Jonesy, tossing him about like a sack of flour with a reprimand that sounded like the Queen's English. "You're cracked, Simon Alexander, simply mad."

"They see what they want, now, don't they? A bandit among them, but they have no clue." He dusted his hand down his lapels with a shrug. "It's the nifty clothing, the blue-blooded background Julian prepared like a sumptuous meal for their partaking. They consume without thinking."

She stepped back, perching her bottom on the balustrade, positive this was a breach in etiquette. "They do, indeed," she said, alarmed his thoughts so closely matched her own. It would be the perfect time to ask how to navigate this disingenuous life… but she didn't have the courage to delve into weightier topics with that sizzling kiss sitting like one of his stolen objects between them.

The cufflink glinted in the moonlight with each pass through his fingers. He wasn't wearing gloves, and she couldn't help but remember the pair shoved beneath her pillow.

"Your venture to Bethnal Green to save Mollie's sister was fruitful, Emma, darling. She never encountered Mason Thomas. You got to her first. But the threat was an enduring one, so we secured Katherine a position with a dressmaker on Bond Street. We've also posted a footman, who can creatively kill a man in a dozen ways, outside the shop and her residence." He tossed the cufflink in the air and caught it in his fist. "But after my visit, I don't think this Thomas fellow is going to darken her door again. *Any* woman's door if she doesn't beg him to."

Emma's breath hitched at his daring—and his use of the word *darling*. "You went to see him?"

He shook his head. *Not going there*.

"They're whispering about you saving women in St Giles." Emma popped off the railing, moving closer to him. Close enough for his scent, soap and bay leaves, to skim her nose. What she smelled when she buried her face in his buttery kidskin gloves. "I could help you. Step in before the worst has occurred. Help you relocate the women once they're in a safer situation. I know what that kind of desperation is like."

The cufflink slipped from his fingers to the marble slabs they stood upon. "You're not getting involved," he said, bending to pick up the jewelry. "I have enough to worry about without that."

"Like this Josie woman is involved?"

He looked up from his crouched position, and her breath caught. He was stunning, laid out there in silvery, stray moonbeams. Dark and light, shadows and hollows, mahogany eyes burning through her, his face carved in sage lines in the glow. Like a hero from one of her scandalous novels. Judicious, incensed, exquisite. She couldn't have dreamed up someone so perfect if she'd tried. "How do you know this?"

She backed up a step at his ferocious expression, unease at his secrets being exposed. The dart of jealousy pierced deeply, sending rash words from her lips. "I didn't say I wouldn't travel inside the duke's house, only not *outside* it. From one room to the other, I hear things. I pop in and out of closets quite handily. Sometimes only losing minutes. Maybe an hour."

He pinched the bridge of his nose, sighed wearily and shoved to his feet. "Josie's a friend. From long ago. From another life. That's all you need to know."

Emma dug the toe of her slipper in a crack in the marble. "Your partner in this rescuing operation. What a good friend to have." If he'd done with this Josie what he'd done years ago with the countess, and the hundreds of women in between, according to the gossips, Emma was going to have a hard time being gracious, should they ever have the chance to meet.

Simon slipped the cufflink in his waistcoat pocket and, brushing aside his tailcoat, braced his hand on his hip. "Like all the friends you've made tonight. Viscount Gordon, Baron Thornton, the Earl of Hollingmark. Am I missing anyone? Christ, I've never seen Hollingmark laugh before, while you had him practically rolling on the chalked ballroom floor, the aged sod. But at least he released his hold on you long enough to take those breaths." His lips tilting low, she watched in delight as Simon's jaw tensed. "By tomorrow morning, you'll be the toast of London. I've heard talk of a new moniker. Crimson something or the other, because of your hair. They're idiots, the lot of them, but the *ton* knows a rare piece when they see it. They're canny that way."

Rare piece. And a society name, all her own. Emma shifted in her delightful silver slippers, pleasure shimmering through her. "You're jealous," she whispered, joy rounding her cheeks until they stung. "This is grand, to use one of your kind's fancy words. Simply grand."

Simon scowled, arm dropping, hand curling into a fist. "You're daft. I don't get jealous."

Emma tapped the Soul Catcher lodged in his pocket, watching with escalating glee as it pulsed and glowed a clear, luminous blue. "Then why worry about how frizzy, old Hollingmark is squeezing me? It's a waltz. Touching is allowed, isn't it? I wonder why it's such a shock when it's not that shocking an affair, really. Nothing to get your knickers in a twist over, isn't that right? Just like me with Josie. And the dozens of others you've been friendly with. No need to worry when they mean so little." Bouncing on her toes, she trailed her index finger up his chest to circle the hollow at the base of his throat. Then she took a breathless pause, halting to straighten his impeccably knotted tie.

A tortured sigh slipped past his lips, his Adam's apple bobbing as he swallowed.

Emma tucked her finger inside his crisp shirt collar in a deliberate ploy and tugged at it. "It's not like I'm going to let some musty earl of what-whose-it kiss me."

Simon's eyes flashed, but he kept his arms by his side. "Because the Dark Queen of the West End is so frugal with her kisses."

"I used to be," Emma whispered, daring him, daring herself. "But I've decided I should now take my pleasure where I please."

A muscle in his jaw ticked in time with her heart-beat, but he made no move to accept her challenge. "Your grammar is quite improved. Emma Breslin is a fast learner. Better than I was. It was months before they managed to polish off even the first rough edge."

"I want the change more than you, a young boy, could have. I long for the change, even as I worry what it's doing to me to take it."

She watched astonishment roll over this face. "Emma…"

She exhaled gently and pleated her silk skirt between her fingers, her focus dropping to her slippers. "The duchess has me read to her from the newspapers every morning after breakfast. Then they fix my grammar. Piper likes to go straight to the gossip columns. A wicked one, that girl. Like no viscountess I've ever imagined." She lifted her gaze, trapping his before it could skip away. "The scandal rags are full of stories about the unwed Alexander. Reserved, but with incredible skill. With his hands. Volatile when pressed. A string of broken hearts scattered behind him. Who's going to snare you, they venture to guess?"

"Ludicrous drivel." His flash of emotion sent a shudder through her belly, her thighs, weakening her knees and making her long to touch him. "No one, that's who. I'm not marrying. Ever. Finn, Julian *and* Sebastian, the Duke of Ashcroft, each have a child who has inherited a supernatural gift from their parents. Do you imagine I would want that agony?" With a muttered oath, he grasped her shoulders and hauled her against him. "Well, I *don't*. I have enough people to protect without children I adore being added to the jumble."

The puncture of affection beneath her breastbone was razor-sharp, taking her breath. Settling her hand alongside his jaw, she tipped his head down. Brought his lips to hers. "Simon," she murmured against his mouth, having no idea what she was pleading for. Perhaps simply an end to his anguish. Her tongue flicked out, a languid sweep over his bottom lip. She felt his surrender as his body sagged, leaning over and into her, his arms sliding around her, tightening their hold amid the crush of their bodies.

Simon glanced over his shoulder into a far, dark corner. "Leave us, Henry," he snarled, then dragged her against him, his lips capturing hers.

She melted into the kiss, her thoughts dissolving into London's viscous brume. His hand rose, cradling her face, slanting her head and perfecting a fit she'd thought already flawless. His touch resonated like the clamor of a bell through her soul, ripples of desire dancing along her skin.

Then, it changed, the kiss going from tentative to seeking, calamitous. Shattering her self-control and her heart. Her breasts flattened against his chest, her nipples peaking, tender points of awareness in a body catching fire as he continued to claim her. Her hand tracked up his chest, over his shoulder and into the thick hair at the nape of his neck. Tugging the strands, she sighed into his mouth, a sign of acquiescence.

Groaning, he spun them around, pressing her against the column. "Tell me to stop, Emma," he whispered against her mouth, then plunged back in before she could speak. His arm circled her waist, his lips molding hers as he deepened the kiss. Taking more, more, *more*. Turning her inside out, until she felt reborn, a raw mass of sensation.

Shaken, she curled her hand around his hip to keep from stumbling. Time, her gift and her curse, suspended, holding steady as it never had before. Without a plan, she tumbled into the marvel of an unhinged Simon Alexander.

An unhinged Emma Breslin. Drunk on yearning and recognition.

When she'd never felt more herself in her life.

Kissing his way down her jaw, he halted at the curve of neck and shoulder, releasing a hot breath that skated deliciously across her skin. The hand at her waist lowered, tunneling beneath her bustle and curving over her bottom. Then, with a strangled, hungry moan and a shift she felt to her core, Simon brought her up and against his hard length. His lips returned to seize hers, his tongue inviting her in playful, toe-curling enticement. Her fingers were tangled in his hair, her hand kneading his hip through layers of clothing, fighting the urge to slide center and down, reach his trouser close, free his cock to her pursuing touch.

"Simon," she whispered, voice tortured, sentiment laid bare. Nothing to hide, nothing she *could* hide.

He wrenched back enough for her to see his face. His eyes. Wild, a deep, murky brown surrounded by that startling ring of violet. Opposing forces, those colors, one tranquil, one savage.

With a sigh she knew meant he was *thinking*, Simon's hold on her loosened, his connection unraveling second by second.

She dropped her hand to his chest and shoved him back, completing the separation. "You're not afraid of the heat, the passion, but any emotion coming with it scares the life from you. So I understand what you mean about the women being nothing. Because you never *felt* anything. And, now, I think you do."

His lips flattened, a muscle in his jaw tensing. Not pleased, but not arguing, either.

A knot of emotion backed up in Emma's throat at his lack of effort to *keep* her. In any way, shape or form. She stepped back. "This is useless. I'll—"

"This performance sheds light on why you're skipping through time like a rabbit, Miss Breslin. For some curious reason, because of it, I'll enjoy returning you even more."

Emma turned with a gasp, recognizing the threat and the voice.

Simon grasped her arm and shoved her behind him. "Bloody *hell*, Emma. You didn't tell me the tracer is Hargrave."

"I didn't know." *Hargrave*. The journalist who'd been sticking his nose in Simon's business was her tracer. The bastard who'd been chasing her for years through time. Simon and his brothers thought the reporter's interest was the Blue Moon when it appeared it was much more than merely infiltrating a gaming hell.

He must have known about the League, about their supernatural society, about everything.

Hargrave stepped out of the shadows and into the moonlight, his knee-length cape swirling around him. Tall and gaunt, an untrimmed beard covering his face, ebony slashes beneath his golden eyes, he looked determined. And exhausted. She'd often thought, if not for his ability to render her senseless with a touch, she could've fought him and won. "Alexander, we meet again," he said and nodded to Simon. "Now, why do I think you're going to disagree about handing her over? She's already caused one disturbance in this time, altered a young woman's reality. Did you think I wouldn't know about that?"

Simon's voice dropped so low she had to struggle to hear it. "When I say run, take my hand and run. Don't think, *run*." Then, he turned his attention back to their nemesis without missing a beat. "You've laid a keen wager, Hargrave. Because I *am* going to disagree about handing her over. We've been waiting for you. Hoping you'd step into the light, where we could have a fine look at you."

"Ah, your League, is it?" Hargrave took a stumbling step forward, a crooked smile tilting his lips. A gust caught his cape and sent it shooting like a dusky vapor behind him. "I have a job to do, Alexander. Or, what was it in the rookery days, before a viscount stepped in to liberate you from your deprived existence? MacDermot? See, I grew up in Spitalfields, not ten streets away from your grubby hole. In the 1740s, though. Strangely enough, I heard about you before I ever arrived in your time, whisperings in the occult world while I traveled through it. About a boy with enchanted hands, a devil who could filch a jewel off Victoria's crown while it sat perched atop her head. A boy the deceased sheltered. A boy who sheltered the deceased. You're legendary in our bizarre sector for having a foot, much as time travelers do, planted in dual realities."

Simon rolled his shoulders and laughed, a sound frosty enough to send a chill down her spine. "The circumstances of my birth and removal from St Giles matter not. You're welcome to my secrets, but you're not welcome to the girl."

Hargrave shook his head sadly, gave a half-hearted shrug, then rushed them in a move no one expected. Although Simon was bigger, leagues stronger, and from what she'd seen, well-trained in hand-to-hand combat, Hargrave had a gift for casting spells. Knocking people off their feet with a simple touch.

When his knuckle grazed Simon's chest, Simon went to his knees with a pained curse that rang through the night.

Emma walked backward across the veranda as Hargrave advanced on her. He crooked his finger, his teeth a sallow glint in the darkness. "Come, dear heart. Your dire predicament in 1802 isn't my responsibility. Returning you to it *is*. I only follow what must be. I can't be bothered with what *is*."

Hargrave tracked the look she directed at Simon as he struggled to rise, the tracer's expression souring. "I see what's in your eyes, darling, even if your thieving lover can't. You want me to render him senseless for the rest of his days? Then fight me on this. Challenge your destiny, and we'll see where that lands us. Lands *him*."

Desire and regret an unbridled pulse beneath her skin, Emma surrendered without a battle.

She'd survived leaving Simon before. To protect him, she could survive leaving now.

Love rained down upon her like the watery London mist, ghostly and unreachable but bolstering her resolve.

Bowing her head, she closed her eyes and waited for time to catch her.

CHAPTER 11

*H*is gorgeous time traveler was going to be the death of him.

Dazed, Simon braced his fist on the terrace's cool marble, his head pounding, the Soul Catcher throbbing like a wound from his waistcoat pocket. Yanking the gem loose, he folded his fingers around it, the flood of conflicting forces—strength and calm —expected, as he well knew the stone's power. A dense fog had rolled in off the river, delivering a vaporous, stinging drizzle to his cheeks as he lifted his head and gazed into the distance.

Across the veranda, only Emma's indigo eyes were visible in the cloaked mist. When she closed them, extinguishing hope, and bowed her head, accepting a return to a time that would be the death of her, crimson crowded Simon's vision. She'd never had anyone to protect her—and she wasn't sure how to fight. How to *trust*. He recognized that defeating inclination more than she'd have believed possible after seeing him with his brothers. He'd fought against trusting anyone until Finn broke through the wall he'd built around himself.

Allegiance, when one had been mistreated, wasn't easily given or gained.

As Hargrave reached for Emma, Simon snarled and stumbled to his feet, his mind dizzy with terror.

"You're our protector, but for once, let us help *you*," Henry said from behind him, frigid air flowing past as the haunt elbowed him aside and crossed the distance to Emma in a thrice.

Simon watched in astonishment as Henry snatched Hargrave by the collar of his cloak and tossed him over the balustrade as if he weighed less than a babe. Then he turned, gave Emma a shove in Simon's direction and issued this advice, "Go to another time, a week in the future and hide out for a bit. I can't do more to interfere, and he won't stop, this man, in his search for you. But maybe you can throw him off his conniving route while you devise a strategy. You and them brothers of yours can surely come up with something."

It was an odd time to have a piece of the puzzle of his life fall into place.

His haunts had been guarding him all along. And he had been harboring them.

Jolting himself from his stupor, Simon grabbed Emma's wrist and dragged her against his side. His hands trembled, fed by emotions he wanted to reject, feelings he wanted to deny. "You thought to give in, give *up*?" he whispered, fury a fever in his blood.

Emma's gaze kindled, her lips falling open. With an oath he was unsurprised she knew, she yanked her arm from his grasp.

"*Go*," Henry shouted as Hargrave extricated himself from a hydrangea bush and staggered to his feet, head in his hands as if he wasn't sure how he'd ended up in the duke's shrubs. "There'll be time for quarreling later, as it seems it's all you two do."

Emma held out her hand, one that quivered almost as much as his. "Give me the swish stone."

The drizzle had spiraled into a downpour. Rain clung to Emma's eyelashes, misted her creamy skin like dew on a petal, molding silk to the gentle curves of her body. A drop highlighted the freckled birthmark on her cheek he wanted to press his lips to. She wasn't beautiful, not enough to compensate for his blind attraction. His undeniable desire to memorize every facet until, if he had Julian's skill, he could sketch the art of her on a canvas.

No, she wasn't beautiful.

But she was stunning, courageous, unforgettable...

And he wanted her with a mindless intensity that shook him to his core.

I wasn't expecting this, he concluded, but you're mine, nonetheless. Now I only have to figure out what to do about it.

Decision made, Simon shoved the Soul Catcher into her hand. Took her arm as Hargrave bounded up the veranda steps, advancing on them.

"Take us from here, then," he said, hoping like hell she didn't hear the way his voice caught on the word *us*.

～

Emma awoke, wrapped in him.

Her head pillowed on his shoulder, tucked into an intimate nook on his long body. His breathing steady, measured exhaustion. They lay in hushed familiarity in a natty chamber in the Blue Moon that Simon had described well enough for her to transport them there. A week into the future, maybe two, she'd guess, not so far as to cause undue angst within his family.

When they'd landed, she'd struggled to lead him to the bed before he'd collapsed, fully clothed, boots and all.

Time travel, to those unaccustomed, was a ghastly physical strain.

She'd settled next to him because she'd feared leaving him in such a weakened state.

Then fallen asleep herself, only to wake in his arms.

Blinking in the drowsy sunlight streaming in the window, she lay quietly, pulling the tranquil tenderness of the moment over her body like a counterpane. The muscular ridges of his belly beneath her hand. His heartbeat, steady and solid, vibrating against her cheek. His firm thighs trapped beneath the leg she'd thrown across them. Tangled silk sheets and the faint scent of lavender drifting from them. The tick of a clock. The rumble of an establishment coming to life belowstairs. The flickering glow of the Soul Catcher on the bedside table.

Before she could stop herself, she'd raised to her elbow and gazed down at him. *His face is a bloody wonder,* she reflected with a weary exhalation. Not to mention the lean, hard body laid out there for her exhaustive perusal. Her blood began to thump, her breath streaking from her lips as she imagined turning his head and kissing him. Letting him roll over her like a wave, hauling her under in forgiveness and hunger.

He was the only man her restless body had ever burned for, pacing its cage, ready to pounce. Lifting her hand, she dusted her fingers over the hair lying limply on his brow, the strands matted from their encounter with Hargrave. His face was relaxed in sleep, youthful, the harshness mislaid. The gentleness in such contrast to his enduring reserve.

The wall he'd built about himself, holding everyone except his family beyond it.

She desperately wanted to be allowed inside that boundary. Too desperately. Dropping her chin to his shoulder, she dragged in his scent. Into her soul, where it smoldered, seeking victory or downfall. Because of the want, the horrible yearning, and Simon's rejection, she slid from the bed on shaky limbs, sunlight a slash across her bare feet, her silver slippers lost somewhere during their journey. Her beautiful gown had a tear in the sleeve, and her delicate kidskin gloves were long gone. Ripping the dance card that had somehow survived the crossing from her wrist, she watched it flutter to the floor.

"A gorgeous woman in my bed, and she thinks to flee," Simon whispered. "Typical dilemma for a bloke, I suppose. Although this sprite looks like she ran a ragged race across London to get to me. A reputation for disappearing from balls because she can't be bothered with them."

Emma released a weak laugh, shook her head woefully and turned to face him. His eyes were open, but just barely, disorientation and fatigue coloring them near black. For a moment, they could do naught but stare, passion a visceral presence, as tangible as the pulse in her fingertips, hands that wanted to *explore*. Wrapping her arm around the bedpost, she gave it a hard hug. Better that than the man sending her a sleepy grin from the warmth of his big bed. "A woman absconding. How about that for a word the duchess taught me? Not the usual game for Simon of the magical hands, from what I've read." She tucked a loose strand of hair behind her ear, wondering in what day between the one they'd left and the one they'd landed she'd lost her hairclips. "The one time I accidently popped into your bedchamber, what I saw…"

"My mother was spirited like you. Full of opinions she didn't mind sharing. The fishmonger used to wilt when she showed up, a flower losing petals. She got the best deal in the rookery on cod, she did. And negotiated for a fair price for anyone in line with her." Simon gave the stubble lining his jaw a buffing rub and folded his arm beneath his head, his muscles flexing attractively. He cast his gaze to the ceiling with a smile that didn't meet his eyes. "She did the best she could. I realize that now. I was mischievous, gifted with a talent for thievery and talking to dead people. Gifts I didn't hide in any way until Julian, for my protection, made me hide them. I brought more burden to her labored life than any youngster should." He sighed into the vast space, his lids fluttering. "She chose to leave this earth, leave me, and for a long time, I was furious about that. But now, I…" He shrugged a broad shoulder, diminishing his pain. "She did the best she could."

"And maybe, just maybe, Simon, so did you."

His arm tensed beneath his head, his fingers curling into a tight fist.

Emma's heart wrenched. As if she needed a naked display of vulnerability to love him more. Perching her hip on the bed, she settled out of reach in the event he thought to touch her. "You were whispering in your sleep. I couldn't hear, exactly, but you seemed shaken."

His head turned, his tormented gaze catching hers. "Night terrors. Poverty, desperation, dread. Those sum up what visits my twilight. Likely the same things that visit yours."

Emma scooted until she rested against the bedpost, stretching her legs and giving her toes an inadvisable wiggle. His gaze shot to her feet, then did a leisurely slither up her body. "You look like you've been pulled through a keyhole," he finally murmured. But when his eyes met hers, his fiery expression said he liked what he saw. "The duchess will perish when she sees the state of your gown. You're going through dresses quicker than the modiste can create them."

"Time travel is hard on the body, the mind. Especially for those new to it." She fluttered her hand down her disaster of a bodice. "And it appears to be hard on my clothing."

He threw a sharp glance at the window. "Where did we land? My family is going to be frantic. Julian and Finn will scour London until they find us."

"A week later, maybe two. I'd know if I was off by more."

Simon propped an elbow on the mattress and settled on his side, head in hand, his other coming to a nonchalant rest beside her right foot. "What looks the same? In my time?"

She tried very diligently not to imagine Simon's index finger, currently tracing a gold thread in the counterpane, sliding the paltry distance that separated them and writing words on her skin instead of silk. Cheeks flushing, she shifted her gaze high, focusing on the elaborate ceiling medallion surrounding the pendant light. This one, a leaf design with bumps, like a strand of pearls, bounding the edge. She'd never seen such a luxurious architectural feature before arriving in 1882. "What looks the same? Clouds, those fat, fluffy ones you think you could grab hold of and be carried away. Stars jammed like raisins in a pudding. Rain hitting my cheeks. The cheery laughter of children." Her gaze tumbled back to him, her belly twisting at the penetrating look on his face. He listened to her as no one in her life had.

"The duke's brood runs wild through his house. It makes me happy and sad. Reminds me of my little cranny down on Milk Yard. Lots of children there, scrappy darlings." She lifted her hand to her mouth, chewing on her thumbnail as she sometimes did when she was flustered. A revolting habit, according to Piper, who hypocritically chewed on her nails herself. "Despite all this luxury, I miss that hovel, which I know defies intelligence and good sense."

He pressed his hand to the counterpane, fingers spreading wide. "It's not crazy. I miss St Giles to the point that I find myself back there once a month, sometimes more. Helping Josie with her mission, which gives me a reason to go. My *only* reason. Even with dreadful memories, horrendous ones, sitting like a famished mongrel on every corner, I long for those dirty alleys. The haunts following along for the ride. My brothers…" He twisted his fingers into a fist, taking a wad of a counterpane that had cost more than all of the furnishings in her Milk Yard dwelling with him. "They don't understand my need to keep a piece of that boy, keep a piece of that *place*." His gaze, which had wandered off like one of his corner mongrels, refocused on her. "But you do."

She took a shallow breath, understanding his comment. This conversation meant more to him than it appeared on the surface. "I reckon I do."

He gestured to the ceiling, knowing how fascinated she was by gas lighting. "Something called electricity has arrived in England."

She wrinkled her nose. "Electricity?"

His smile was deliberate, and sweet. As glorious as champagne bubbles erupting on her tongue, the first she'd ever tasted at the ball this evening. "There's a station on Holborn Viaduct powered by coal. Which, in turn, powers a carbon-filament bulb, what they're calling a light bulb. Sixteen lamps along Holborn Circus to St Martin's Le Grand glowing every night." His lips tilted, his coffee eyes sparking. Then, unbelievably, he blushed. "I could show you."

Simon was a nurturer, she realized, astounded. His haunts came to him for safeguarding, which she believed he was only beginning to comprehend. He guarded them, and they guarded him in return. Too, he cared greatly for his family, made an effort to rescue women from a sordid life in the slums, had traveled through time to save a girl he'd never actually spoken to—only felt a connection, as she had.

He had a temper. He thought he knew what was best for her. He was conceited. Arrogant. Entirely too male. Argumentative.

Handsome, charming, courageous.

A thief, and possibly, with good cause, a liar.

Verdict? He wasn't perfect.

But he was perfect for her—and she wanted him.

Making her decision, Emma shifted until her ankle bumped his wrists, her gaze never leaving his. A blatant invitation if he chose to take it. "The rumors go that you have talented hands."

His chest hitched, his lids fluttering to cover the heat flaring in his eyes. Then, with a sigh of defeat, making his own decision, he trailed his crooked knuckle up the sole of her foot and over the arch of each toe. "You shouldn't be here. Should have left the second we arrived, and you steered me to this bed. But we both know that, don't we? So no use, really, belaboring the point."

Emma anchored her hand against the mattress, her body lighting from within. An absolute blaze. Goosebumps raced down her arms as a fierce beat started tripping between her thighs. Head swimming, alive with sensation, arousal torching any effort she might make to leave. "Is this your bedchamber? Did I get the right one?"

"You got the right one," he said as he sketched each bone in her ankle.

"Are we…alone? No haunts?"

Teasing the newfound, sensitive arch of her foot, he blew a taunting breath across it. "We're alone."

"This is where Mackey says you bring—"

"*No*, Emma." He halted his seduction, his hand stilling. "This is my private chamber. It used to be Finn's years ago before he got married. Not a place I bring anyone. *Ever*." He chucked his hair from his eyes with a self-deprecating snort and toss of his head. "Look around you. This room is filled with pieces of me I don't share with the world. My flaws line the walls."

While he skimmed his thumb over the ball of her foot in a purposeful rhythm, she did as he'd suggested and examined the space. Books with cracked leather spines in a spill on the floor; a scuffed desk shoved in a dark corner, surface littered with all manner of writing utensils and sheets held in place beneath a paperweight shaped like a ship. Shelves lining the walls, teeming with scraps of life he'd stolen from another's and brought to his. Cufflinks, earbobs, coins, cigarette cases, hair clips.

"Quite the collection," she murmured, with his touch, her mind only half on his treasures.

"It's a problem. At least, I realize that." Then he destroyed her by pressing his lips to the hollow below her ankle. "I sell the items after a time, give the funds to Josie for her efforts."

Closing her eyes, she hummed, caught between the desire to demand he stop and the desire to *beg* him to continue.

As if he'd heard the latter plea, his teeth caught

her skin in a gentle nip, his tongue laving the spot just after. Her body erupted, heat rolling through her.

Her gasp was uncontrolled and shattered the silence.

"Stop me now," he commanded in a rusty voice. "Because my resistance is leaking away like tea from a cracked cup. When you and I should be figuring out what to do about this mess with your time tracker, not rolling around in my bed. But I'm helpless when it comes to you."

The mattress shifted, and when she opened her eyes, he was there, on his knees, before her. Through the open curtains, a dreamy band of sunlight washed over him, highlighting the raw vulnerability on his face, an emotion she knew he'd rather hide should he know she'd seen it.

Lifting his arm, he trailed his fingers along her jaw and into her hair. A searching yet resolute touch. "But you're not going to stop me, are you?"

She mouthed the word—*no*—caught his neck and brought his lips to hers, sealing their destiny.

CHAPTER 12

*S*imon had sampled his fair share of women.

Often, in what felt like a gamble against himself, against life. A dare. To see how much and how *little* he could feel at the same time. See how fucking lonely sharing his body with another person could be without love added to the mix.

But this...

Enchantment, obsession, *greed*.

Emma. Her soft, sweet lips opening beneath his. Her fingertips marking his cheek, guiding him to her when he needed no guide. Her hair a lemon-scented enticement, a velvet shroud flowing about them, the silky ends dancing across his collarbone, his shoulders. A few paltry layers—silk, buckskin, cotton, linen—standing between them.

Between glory and doom.

Between what he desired more than all was holy and what he feared straight to his core.

In a place, in a way, he'd never let himself be seen.

"Show me," she whispered against the side of his mouth, drawing him into a deeper kiss, "show me."

With that simple appeal, he was lost.

Bending, he looped his arm around her waist and

brought her, kneeling, against him, his cock hard, throbbing beneath his trouser close, a fact he could no longer hide from her.

Surrendering, he shifted his hips until his rigid length met her warm essence, a tattered groan rolling out of his mouth and into hers. Letting her know, perhaps, what she was getting into. Life on the streets didn't afford impoverished women ignorance of the ways of the world, not as it did for society misses, but he imagined, from the shy way she'd touched him, that Emma didn't have *actual* experience.

A fact that made him so goddamn ecstatic it scared him.

Her hands went to his coat, tugging until, with one arm yank, then another, he was free of it. His waistcoat buttons were her next project, her murmur of complaint causing him to loosen his hold and assist with the disrobing. Their tongues tangled, clashing, a chaotic kiss, the contact as feral as his thoughts.

He wanted them naked, and he wanted them naked *now*.

"Hurry," she implored against a sensitive spot beneath his ear, taking his skin between her teeth as he'd done to her ankle and biting. Harder than he had, the minx.

Ripping two buttons off his shirt in his haste to rid himself of the garment, he pressed a chortle into the crown of her head. "Emma, darling, I've never divested myself of my clothing with such rapidity. Even with talented hands, the practice takes time."

She took hold of his shirt cuffs, snatching one arm free, then the other. Her gaze slithered up his body. Lingering for a long, arousing moment on the smattering of hair on his chest. The hunger reflected in her eyes when they met his took him by surprise.

"I want you," she said, her voice layered with amazement. Resolve. Desire. "I want you."

His remembrance of the episode was fragmented after that artless declaration.

Recollections colored by piercing moans, moist skin, fevered kisses, questing hands. Impassioned commands, frenzied avowals. His boots hitting the floor, her gown ripping down the back. Breaking the kiss, he rolled to his feet and removed his trousers and drawers, not once considering slowing the pace. Not when Emma was biting and licking, touching him *everywhere*. His stomach, his thighs, his cock. His earlobe between her teeth, his nipple beneath her searching fingertips. Disclosing luscious desires he was thinking but feared *saying*.

Her passion echoed off his bedchamber walls, surrounding him in a cage of yearning.

She followed without a hint of shame, slipping from the bed, whipping her disaster of a gown over her head and tossing it to the floor. Then presenting her slim, lightly freckled back—assistance with her corset. He worked the hook and eye closures with skill he knew he should conceal but didn't once strive to do. Chemise, drawers, petticoat, the duchess's priceless choker, all gone in a matter of seconds…

Until they stood before each other clothed in nothing but uncertainty.

Or, as Simon watched Emma take him in with a sweeping glance and a wicked grin, maybe that was just him.

A shimmer of unease rolled through him. The kind that made him wish frantically for a coin to spin between his fingers. One of the stolen cufflinks sitting on a shelf across the way.

He was too far gone, too mad for her.

Desperate in a way he'd never been, never imagined.

Lifting her hand, she traced a crescent scar on his shoulder. "Where did you get this? Looks like someone took a blade to you."

He shrugged beneath her fingers. "Fighting with the duke's men. Training since I was a boy." His gaze shifted to her adorable toes in apparent avoidance. "So we can protect those we love from men like Hargrave."

"Oh, no, don't think to go running away from me. Don't drag him into *this*." Clicking her tongue against her teeth, she stepped in until his arms could only surround her. Her body was hot, trembling when he powerlessly pulled her against him. "Don't think to back out now, Simon. Not when I've waited years for you." Then she buried her hands in his hair, walked him back until the mattress hit his thighs, tumbling them to the bed.

Laughing, he let her control the skirmish for a minute or two before wrestling himself atop her, tunneling his arms beneath her and capturing her lips, ending her domination. She reared up as they grappled, not taking the shift lightly, her hips mimicking moves he hadn't yet started. After a moment, they settled into a matching rhythm, bodies fitting like they'd been created for each other.

Of course, she'd be a natural, making love like a warrior.

Which frightened him.

However, he wanted her more than he feared his ruin.

"We'll go slowly," he vowed and, disputing his statement, kissed his way to her pert breasts, clamping his mouth hungrily around her nipple, tongue lashing the pointed nub until she moaned and clutched his shoulder, digging her nails into his skin. When she began to pant, the little growls affecting him mightily, he moved to the other, the peak pebbling beneath his lips, that, and the sounds she was uttering, hardening his already stiff cock until it hurt.

She heaved a breath, a sigh, her body bowing into his touch, her legs locking around his. "*More*."

He rocked his hips against hers, let her pick up his tempo. The tiny pulses of pleasure hit his spine and spread to his buttocks, to his shins, until his skin was aflame. One of the duke's incinerations, charred destruction. When he felt the first tremor rock her, he steered his hand south, over her hip, between her thighs, to her moist, silky-smooth folds. "Let yourself feel; feel it all."

Working his finger gently inside her, he almost went over the edge himself when she shuddered, her eager exclamation hitting his neck. Capturing her moan, he kissed her while thrusting his tongue and finger in tandem, pressing her deeper into the mattress. Her hips matched the melody only they could hear, breasts mashed against his chest, legs tangled, until she was wild, her hands on his back, nails clawing. Leaving scratches he honestly couldn't wait to view in his mirror the next morning. Love marks he would gladly hide from his valet.

"I want," she whispered against his lips.

"Then take," he returned and slid a second finger deep.

Her hips surged, meeting his stroke. "It feels like floating."

He closed his eyes to the sight of her, rosy cheeks and plump lips, cerulean eyes dazed from his rough handling.

To him, it felt like *love*.

Her hand muscled its way between their bodies.

Insistent, untrained. Lighting him up like a match to a wick.

She'd tried to touch his cock once before, and he'd stopped her. But, this time, he had no intention of stopping *anything*.

"Like this." He pulled back enough to give her room to explore. Wrapping her fingers around his shaft, he gripped, squeezed, moved her curled fist up and down, showing her what he liked. Measured movement, a pause at the crown before starting again.

"So hard," she breathed.

A bemused gust shot from his lips, followed by a ragged groan when she created her own variation, her hand sliding low and cupping him. Emma smiled at the sound, triumphant as only a woman in sexual control could be. "You're enjoying this."

Simon nodded, overcome, his breath coming out in a pant. "*Yes.*"

"Then I won't stop," she said and seized not only his body but also his heart.

Smiling, laughing, they stroked and kissed, shifting, sighing, whispering entreaties and secret cravings, ones he'd never shared, their scents mingling to fill the bedchamber, creating a unique fragrance he knew would be forever imprinted on his mind. The counterpane twisted around their writhing bodies as they sought pleasure. It was a race, a war, a loving combat. Knocking his arm aside, she moved his cock into position and gave a wiggle of her hips that embedded him just the slightest bit inside her.

An unsophisticated, wondrous entry.

Rising, he braced on his forearms over her, exhaling in a puff against her shoulder. "Emma…"

Rubbing her moist folds against his rigid length

until he saw stars, she shook her head stubbornly, her lips pressed tight. "I want this, Simon. I want *you*."

He reached, cradling her jaw, tilting her head until his gaze snagged hers. "Emmaline Breslin, I've wanted you, although I didn't truly know what that *meant*, since the first moment I set eyes on you. Even when I couldn't speak to you, when you were trapped halfway between your world and mine, I *wanted* you. More than want. Ravenous *need*. Don't ever think, no matter what happens, that you aren't mine."

Then he tumbled across nearly a century and into her.

~

Simon handled her like crystal when Emma wanted to be handled like stone.

She wanted his passionate fury, not an act he strove to lessen in magnitude to protect her body or his heart. So when he began to thrust gently, and she realized she didn't have all of him, she whispered lewd desires in his ear, curled her hand around his hip and brought him closer. She tangled her leg around his and surged against him to lock him in. The prick of pain was distant, manageable, and over quickly.

She wanted her innocence and his reticence *gone*.

"Dirty cricket, Breslin," he murmured before dipping his head and seizing her lips, his hand streaking to her waist to hold her steady for his assault.

It was a struggle for control after that. Animalistic and greedy.

And *real*.

His weight atop her, his ragged moans rolling over her like a roaring sea. Simon as she'd never imagined him, never imagined anyone. His nails scoring her skin, his scent filling her senses. His teeth clipping her neck, her shoulder. She felt each part of him like winter raindrops, stinging to her soul. His calloused fingertips, his stubbled jaw. The sound of wind whipping against the shuttered windowpanes, their bodies slapping as they followed an intimate melody. Dropping his head, he shifted his hips, touching a new part of her and sending quivers through her body.

"There, yes." She curved into her delight.

Together, they were a wonder.

Tangling her hand in his hair, Emma fisted the other in the counterpane, holding on to the present. Feeling a moment's panic at her escalating ecstasy, she opened her eyes, recording his beauty in full measure. Tawny hair, damp from exertion, sticking to his brow, the sleek nape of his neck. His broad shoulders blocking the dewy light pouring in the window. Gaze lowered as he watched their bodies connect, lips set, jaw hard, breath racing from his lungs. His hips angling until just the tip of his shaft was enclosed within her, then a hard thrust back.

Again and again and again.

When he caught her staring, his eyes dark and fathomless, she felt the world begin to tilt.

Too much sensation, too much emotion. Curling her toes, taking the air from her lungs, making her *yearn*.

The bedchamber whirled, time circling like a wrathful storm.

His hand went to her cheek, drawing her eyes to his. "Stay with me, Emma," he whispered roughly, his movement atop her calming. "We can stop. I don't want you to leave me. *Don't leave.*"

With a furious grunt, Emma rolled him to his back and, their joining unbroken, began to move, legs astride his hips, his cock buried deep inside her, as she'd imagined in her fantasies.

His gaze met hers, his lips falling open. "You're trying to kill me, woman."

She dragged his hand to her waist, linking fingers, begging for guidance. "Only in the best way."

Then time, because she willed it to do so, stood still.

It could have been 1802 or 1882. 1750. 1935. Alone, in an ever-darkening bedchamber, she and Simon were ageless. An eternal symphony of passion and love. Seconds to minutes to hours as they possessed each other in ways neither had thought to possess, never hoped to. A kiss gone damp and careless in its zeal. Tender becoming eager, effortless becoming strenuous. The experience answered questions, acquainting her with Simon in a way far beyond language, beyond touch. Beyond oxygen, beyond light.

Kismet, destiny, fate, and in that fervent hush, she heard the reverberation of his soul.

The spasm, a fierce, desperate clench in her thighs, swept her away, her cry of delight echoing through the chamber, his sharp inhalation following. Simon didn't relent, didn't give her time to catch her breath, instead skated his hand over her belly, to her core, his thumb finding her nub and caressing, sending her into a dizzying universe of pleasure and sensation.

She collapsed atop his chest, her ear pressed to his pounding heart, her mind howling. Laughing softly, he took her lips, kissing her fervently while he moved inside her, prolonged strokes heating to fiery ones that rocked the headboard against the wall with spirited thumps. She groaned into his skin, her body a quivering muddle. When he shouted his release, his arms trembling, moist skin fusing them, she could only think there could be nothing like this anywhere else, in any time, with any man. What she'd known from the rookery, what she'd seen in murky alleyways and the corners of grimy public houses, had not been *this*.

This was love and illumination and forgiveness.

"I may not survive." Simon ironed his hand down her back to her buttocks, where he tucked her in tighter against him. "Holy hell, I feel dizzy all of a sudden."

She tilted her head until his face came into view. His eyes were closed, gold-tipped lashes brushing his flushed skin, a bead of sweat rolling down his jaw toward his collarbone. Lips bruised, cheeks bright, he looked overwhelmed and beaten.

While she felt *powerful* to have brought him to such a place.

"Quit gloating," he mumbled in a roughened voice. "You rolled me to my back and kept me inside you. Quite the trick, humbling a man known for them. One I'll never in this lifetime forget."

Emma hummed and traced her pinkie down the dark patch of hair trailing the center of his chest. It tickled her fingertips and invited a kiss she couldn't hold back. So, even with the leagues of women who'd shared his bed, she'd been able to do something he *liked* without knowing what she was doing, only blindly following instinct. She wondered when she would get a good look at his taut bottom, and the birthmark she remembered was on his left cheek. If that wicked countess had gotten to see it, Emma certainly felt *she* should be able to. "Beginner's luck," she finally replied, a blush of recognition sweeping not only her face but her entire body when she realized she ardently hoped they'd do this again.

Soon.

He grunted a non-answer, his weak kiss dusting the top of her head. "I could argue about natural talent, but I won't. Those with incredible skill usually don't want to hear about it."

She drew a circle around his nipple and watched it harden. "I have other ideas." Then, blowing lightly across his skin, she held back a grin as he groaned. "If you'd like to hear them."

Simon rolled her to her side until they faced each other. "Do you have any notion what year it is? For a moment there, I thought we were headed into the past. I heard an engine, a noise in the sky, a sound I've never heard before." He brushed aside her hair, pressed his lips to a wildly vulnerable area beneath her ear. "If we're going to fuck our way through time, I'd like to know which time it is."

"I'll tell you about them someday. Flying machines. Airplanes." She returned his caress, smoothing a kiss over the pulse beating in his neck. Feeling mischievous, she let her hand wander, heading to a part of him that was reawakening, hard and ready, against her thigh. "Does it truly matter where we are if we're together?"

He arched into her touch, his voice fraying. "Depending upon the specificity of your suggestions, I don't suppose it does. Although I'd like to hear about these flying machines someday."

Emma tilted his head, seeking his kiss. "I can be very specific. Girls from Tower Hamlets are known for being *meticulous*." A new word, that one, straight from the duchess's mouth to hers.

"Meticulous. That's my girl," he whispered and pulled her atop him.

And with his persuasive talent, he made time disappear.

CHAPTER 13

Not my girl, London's girl, Simon thought caustically, throwing an irate glance down the Duke of Ashcroft's central hallway as he stalked along it three days later. There'd been a mound of calling cards scattered across the console table securing the main entrance. So large a pile that some had fallen like discarded flower petals to the marble floor. He'd flipped through six or seven, his temper flaring—earl, baron, second son of a duke, solicitor—before shoving them in his waistcoat pocket. A theft he'd be damned if he'd feel guilty over.

Not when these men were salivating over something that was *his*.

With a grimace, he sneezed into his fist. And the flowers. Crowded across every vacant surface until the gallery resembled a bleeding nursery. Like the one on Albemarle Street that Finn frequented when he'd made a masculine, husbandly error in judgment.

Simon rotated the dented gold button, also pilfered from the console table, between the fingers of the hand not holding Emma's gift, eyeing the bounty spilling from a dozen vases. *Roses.* Yellow, red, white.

Who, but a man who *didn't* know Emmaline Breslin in the slightest, would send roses?

Emma was not a rose girl, he could tell the lot of them. Asinine society lads. Simon's hand clenched around the violin case, housing a splendid instrument the Duke of Ashcroft had personally helped him select. He hoped he'd gotten it right, picked something that would please her. Simon wasn't sure it would, a musical instrument she'd mentioned once in passing, but with a dreamy expression he'd been unable to ignore.

Anyway, it seemed a better bet than fucking *roses*.

A vision of Emma on her back, her lips parted, these husky mewling sounds slipping free, thundered through his mind. Took hold of his cock and said, *remember that marvelous moment?* Took hold in a way that had him halting to adjust his suddenly tight trousers.

He'd experimented with her during those short hours as he'd never experimented before. Watched, demanded, *begged*. He'd never been able, he supposed, or willing, to be so free. To whisper veiled desires into someone's ear and have them react. Smile and laugh—then *do*. The deed, one necessary to a man's survival, had never felt *right* with anyone else even as he'd heartily agreed to doing it because he was, after all, a man.

But this time...

He caught his faraway reflection in a beveled mirror he passed and halted in place.

Obsessed. He was obsessed.

With a woman who'd left him, much like his mother had. A hurt he wasn't sure he could recover from twice.

Emma's scent lingering in his mind, the feel of her skin indelibly imprinted, like the wavering lines on his fingertips, ones a soothsayer in the League had recently told him signified the finding of his true love and a long life.

"What to do about your girl?" Henry asked from his place before the mirror, which he peered into, searching for a reflection that wasn't there. "In my time floating around, life to life, I've seen many a man fumble *this* part, let me tell you. But you're the only bloke I could actually give me humble advice to, which is liberatin', I have to say. I feel quite bold with my words this morn."

"Lucky me," Simon said and continued down the hallway, wondering why it was that the haunts were like shadows evaporating into the mist when you needed them, always around when you didn't.

"Leave on good terms with the little filly, now, did ya'?"

Simon glanced into the first parlor he passed, finding it empty as a bawdy house on Sunday morning, wondering where Emma and the duchess could be. Delaney had invited him for tea, matchmaking, or possibly, considering the calling cards and flowers filling the townhouse, *not*. "Is it my fault Julian tracked us down at the Blue Moon and took her back to the duke's posthaste? Looking worse for the wear, the both of us. The right decision, the proper move, getting her out of my gaming hell, my bedchamber in said establishment, I should discretely add. But then, you keep all my secrets, don't you? We arrived two weeks after the ball, in the same year, thank God, but my family was frantic. They'd been combing London, looking for us the entire time."

"But you waited three days once they retrieved her. Until this upmarket invite from the countess forced you against the wall, so ta' speak. It don't look agreeable, seeming as if you didn't want to talk to the

THE HELLION IS TAMED

chit after entertaining her in that gambling den of yours for two long nights. Hiding, like."

"Duchess," Simon murmured, giving the elegant emerald and gold sitting room Delaney never used a swift scan as he passed it. Popping the violin case against his thigh, he blew an agitated breath through his teeth. "I have a fantastically successful enterprise to manage. Contracts to negotiate, a slew of workers to oversee, shipments to coordinate delivery of, account ledgers, multiple, that make my eyes bleed to look at them. The second son of a marquess intent on losing every shilling he has, and my brother, Finn, being so kind-hearted as to ask me to step in and talk the idiot out of it. Plus, Josie has a new rescue for me to locate a position for. This one is educated enough to pass off as a governess. Baron Digby needs one for his twins, now that his wife ran off with his valet."

"Oh, the baroness was a wicked one. Naughty. The news of her even traveled to our side." Henry clicked his tongue in ghostly judgment. "Right so, them children need a tutor. You're doing fine deeds left and right, young Simon. Proud of you, I am. You protect and are protected."

Henry's words warmed him, though he struggled to hide his response. "A nifty situation ripe for the plucking, that's all it is." He spun the button between his fingers, the cool metal curve beneath his fingertips calming. "Taking advantage of an opportunity, which God knows, I'm good at. Quickest solution so I can get back to running my business."

"Business to run." Henry wiggled his pinkie in his ear, his whistle sharp with skepticism. "Woman to run *from*, ya' mean. Although if you don't want to run"—the haunt flicked his arm in the direction of the back lawn—"she's out there. Flitting about in the gardens. All full of grace and charm. Looks like the kindest picture of a lady. One of our own, rising from the ashes." He chuckled, the tattered lace on a Regency-era sleeve Simon had only seen in paintings dancing with the movement. "Don't believe it, though. She spent the morning teaching the staff to play hazard. Loves the kitchens more than any other spot when no quality chit spends time amongst *those* folk. Servants liking her says quite a bit. A fine caster you've got on your hands, Simon, my boy. Quite fine, indeed. Rolls the dice like she were born to 'em and nice, too. Nicked every soul who dared to play with her, but in the end, she returned the winnings. Earned over a pound, all told."

Simon strode to the wall of windows lining the gallery, caught a flash of canary yellow mixed among the lush sea that was the duke's expansive lawn. The Soul Catcher hummed to life in his coat pocket, recognizing Emma before he did. He leaned to the left, squinted. There, she and Delaney seated on a marble bench in the side garden, a sterling tea service settled on a table before them. Simon narrowed his eyes, his body tensing. Rounding out the group to a lovely trio was the Earl of Hollingmark, rather impressive when Simon wished he looked more like a toad. A man who'd made it known to all who would listen that he was open to marriage again, no immeasurable dowry required. His late countess had been a rare beauty. And a wealthy one. It seemed he was in the market for another gorgeous gem, much like the gem housed in Simon's pocket.

Simon's heart kicked in his chest, memories of his lost night with Emma circling his mind and snapping like a pack of wolves. The flood of possessiveness was disturbing for a man unaccustomed to ownership. *Temper,* he reminded himself. He'd been known, on multiple occasions, to make tactical errors under volatile duress.

He shoved the button in his trouser pocket and rounded on his haunt. "I can't go out there with *this* in my hands." Thrusting the violin at Henry, he gestured to the sweeping staircase that led to the upper floors. "Deliver it to whichever chamber is hers, as I'm sure you know which one that is. Someday, my friend, we need to discuss your voyeuristic tendencies."

Henry's bushy sterling eyebrow rose, his lips pursing. Taking the violin with the tenderness one would reserve for a babe, he tipped his chin toward the hallway they'd traveled down. "All them flowers had notes. Poetry, even. If I leave this without tribute, she'll think the duke sent it, being a musician himself." Henry's thumb snaked along a grove in the case, a rough caress. "How will that advance your agenda?"

"This isn't a strategic military campaign; I don't have an agenda." Simon muscled through the terrace doors, the side garden down a short stack of stairs and to his right. A gust of wind flavored with the Thames, azaleas, roses…choices and fate…hit him square in the jaw. His gaze immediately found Emma, looking like cream topping a fairy cake in a gown the color of sunlight and possibilities. Goosebumps swept his arms, raised the hair on the nape of his neck until he shivered from the effect. His cock, willing, hungry since the moment Julian had dragged her away, rising at the sight of her. He denied the impulse to let his perusal take her in from head to toe.

In their hours together, he'd been unable to get enough of her. But in the most simple of ways. The brush of her knee against his, his ankle caressing her calf. Tracing the pale blue veins beneath her skin, the charming freckle on her cheek. Whispers in the darkness, hands clasped.

Laughter, joy, contentment.

Insignificantly significant connections he'd never made or needed before.

However, the point he couldn't get past, something that, when he recalled it, made him stumble as he entered the duke's lush garden, was that he'd almost told her he loved her. Felt the need in the quiet hush, after they'd made love a second time, to admit this, open the rusty chest that was Simon MacDermot. *Mac.* To admit he was considering forgiving her for leaving him if she'd forgive him for not waiting for *her.*

He'd been grateful she'd been asleep when the sentimental urge hit.

Mooning over her for years as a boy, only to find he was doing the same as a man, was marginally distressing.

He sneezed into his fist, *goddamn roses*, the sound interrupting the trio at an opportune moment.

Delaney swiveled on the marble bench, something murky in his expression lightening hers. She loved nothing more than romantic drama, he thought with a scowl.

"Simon, join us." The duchess patted the empty spot next to her. He noted no empty spot next to Emma, moving into the center of the garden with a halting step. Hollingmark had claimed more than half of the bench she sat on, his arse crushing the trim of her butter-yellow gown.

Three hulking footmen stood on the outer edge of the lawn, patrolling in the event Hargrave got it in his mind to approach Emma so soon after his last attempt. They nodded when Simon glanced at them, their dour expressions

never shifting from kill-at-any-moment perseverance.

"Yes, join us," Emma said, throwing him a terse
look, her eyes flame-blue, letting him know she was
still angry that he let his brothers separate them—
and then making it worse by not coming after her
immediately. Or the very next day, at least.

Simon ripped his bowler from his head and
whipped it against his thigh. Then, perching on the
edge of the duchess's bench, he waved away her offer
of tea, and instead, made a game of twisting his hat
brim into submission while trying hard not to stare
at Emma's gown, the most gorgeous he'd seen on her
yet. The bustle was ridiculous but stylish, rounding
out her slender figure. A floral motif, chrysanthe-
mums if he wasn't mistaken, woven into the silk in a
pale green thread that glimmered in the sunlight. Her
auburn hair contained in a chignon that exposed the
gentle slope of her neck to his hungry gaze.

"This looks cozy," he murmured finally, unable to
help himself, his tone saying what his words didn't.

Delaney choked on her tea, her cup rattling the
saucer as she banged it atop her thigh.

"*Don't*," Emma mouthed across the short distance.
Don't, you, dare.

"This ain't a good start," Henry advised from his
spot next to a hydrangea that looked to be swal-
lowing him in lavender blooms.

The earl gazed curiously around the group, canny
enough to realize he didn't comprehend the whole
story. "I was just asking Miss Breslin if she's ever at-
tended Epsom. The running of the Derby's next
week, at the Downs. The Duke of Westminster's
horse, Shotover, took Newmarket. Could be the one
to win, first filly in over a hundred years to take two
in the Crown if she does."

Simon gave his hat brim a snap, eyeing the earl's cufflinks. Oval, etched with some sort of scrolling design around the boundary that he found fetching. Capped with a ruby, tiny but quality, he could see, in the center. Catching the earl's eye, he said, "Didn't you visit the Blue Moon after Newmarket this year? Finn had to break up a petty spat with that Wellington chap over a horse he'd told you was well suited to juice in the grass, rainy conditions that day and all. Considering your unfortunate wagers on the beast, that didn't turn out to be the case." Simon clicked his tongue against his teeth, thinking he could get a mint for even one of the cufflinks. "No, no, I have it wrong. It was his mistress you were quarreling over. The opera singer from Wales. Perhaps you thought to make her *your*—"

"Simon," Delaney whispered between clenched teeth, "*behave*."

The earl bounded to his feet, his teacup tumbling from his knee to the grass. "Alexander, if it were a different time, I'd call you out for this nonsense."

Emma said nothing, stirring her tea with a chilled expression he couldn't decipher.

In for a penny, Simon thought with a sigh. Tossing his hat on the bench, he braced his hands on his knees and rose with a lazy stretch, knowing full well he was going to tower over the earl once he got there. "Pretend it's another time, Hollingmark. I'm the youngest in a family of brothers who delight in pummeling me into the dirt. Her duke"—he jacked his thumb in Delaney's direction—"has done it quite a few times himself. Former soldier, so no easy mark. Me, either, now that I've had so much practice. Try your best, and we'll see where we end up." He stretched his shoulders with a pop. "Make a day of it."

Emma hopped up, squeezing herself between the

men with as much grace as possible and without actually going so far as to touch either of them. She'd learned well; Simon could almost believe she'd been born to this life. When he knew it wasn't the first time she'd broken up a brawl, though this news would have surprised the hell out of the earl. "I would love to attend the Derby with you, Lord Hollingmark. Thank you for asking," she said, a bit breathlessly. Fury, though it probably sounded like reticence to those who didn't know her. "I look forward in great anticipation to the event."

The earl flashed a broad smile, his steely gaze shooting to Simon. "Well, I'm obviously delighted when you said you had to think it over first. Emmaline Breslin leaves the party if she's not enjoying it, as this town has come to find. Disappears almost. We shall, as Mister Alexander suggested, make a day of it, my dear. I'll do my best to keep you entertained."

"You botched this one, but good," Henry muttered. "And not even the prime gift of a violin to make up for it. I already deposited that, without poetry, to her suite."

The earl grasped Emma's gloved hand and brushed his lips across the kidskin tips. "I must take my leave, Miss Breslin. A noon meeting with my solicitors. I'll be in touch. Next Wednesday morning. Mark your calendar." His gaze again shifted Simon's way, the sneer twisting his lips a blatant challenge. "I'm thrilled by your acceptance, by the by."

Simon faked another sneeze, stumbled, his arm brushing the earl's. The cufflink slipped into his hand as easily as knocking an acorn from a branch. "Sorry, old chap, all the blooms, don't you know."

Delaney rolled her eyes, linking her arm through the earl's and leading him from the garden before Simon had the opportunity to score the other cufflink. "I'll be back in a moment, Emma darling. The footmen are there on the lawn, and Mollie is in the conservatory, should you need her."

"Yes, yes, we're well and truly chaperoned," Simon said as they walked away, the earl's swagger so pronounced Simon wanted to color his creamy linen shirt with the green of freshly cut grass by dragging his body across it. Delaney was an American and found society's rules and regulations as confounding and foolish as he, a lifelong Brit, did. But they were forced to play the game. Or be ousted from the communal ledge they stood upon.

"You arrogant ass," Emma snapped once the duchess and the earl were out of earshot.

"You senseless chit," he returned, irate for no good reason. And he knew it. Bounced the cufflink from one hand to the other, making sure she saw it. "Enjoy the Derby. Such a magnificent *event*."

"I will. You better believe I will." She huffed a breath and spun on her heel. "Henry, be gone!" Then she marched across the lawn, toward the conservatory, conceivably in search of her missing maid. A maid *he'd* saved from the slums and brought to her, she should know.

Frustrated, he watched her pert bottom swing from side to side as she stalked away, debating if he should hike in the opposite direction to his waiting carriage. To another adventure. Lady Lydia Davidson, a widow with what some said was the most talented mouth in England had sent him a note last week, a rather bold invitation to tea, a tea that would be *fun*. So he wasn't desperate. Or lonely. He sighed and rotated the cufflink between his fingers. Well, not any lonelier than he'd been his entire damned life.

The feel of Emma's pert bottom in his hands,

lifting her onto his cock as he leaned against the headboard of his massive bed, her legs wrapping around his waist as she settled atop him, sending him deep, flooded his body with a tremor of repentance that had him going after her like a fox on the hunt.

When he entered the conservatory, it was empty except for the woman he stalked and a king's ransom of orange trees. Just Emma and the stinging scent of citrus, his girl standing in the shadows, facing him, eyes a sharp indigo glimmer. Her hands going into fists and rolling out of them at her sides. Her ginger-snap hair had tumbled from its confinement and lay in a puddle across one shoulder and rounded breast.

He stared, unable to approach as his body screamed for him to do. As the Soul Catcher screamed for him to do, a lightning pulsation in his pocket. He'd wondered at his immediate and visceral attraction. Had always wondered. A supernatural meeting, the inability to talk. A girl from another time, a curious, lonely boy, searching and starved for self-worth. Yet, he could see the allure now, with a man's wisdom. Her strength, her certainty, called to him as solidly as thievery did. She'd known who she was, accepted herself when he'd been tossed in a rising tide of antipathy over things he couldn't alter.

She'd stepped into his world, recognizing him in a way few had. Recognized his eccentricities, his mystical gift, the ghostly circle of people included—should anyone choose to share a life with him.

And wanted him anyway.

He'd learned to mistrust on the streets of St Giles, *mightily*. Watched his mother step in front of a carriage because she didn't want to live—or didn't want to live with *him*. He'd made every person who cared about him work twice as hard to prove themselves when he'd been desperate to let them in. Julian, Finn,

Piper, Humphrey, Victoria. And to what end? When he was simply a thief. Hot-tempered, rash, obstinate in a most uninviting manner.

Why would a woman such as this—formidable, clever and so breathtakingly beautiful—want him?

A quiver started in the pit of his stomach and rose, settling in his chest. Then, a whisper of sound, her husky sigh, acquiescence or perhaps surrender, shot from her as she took a faltering step forward, his name leaving her lips to settle over him like freshly fallen snow.

A tender sanction, a soothing plea.

Neither he could ignore.

They met in the middle of the deserted space, the kiss nearly knocking him off his feet, the earl's cuff-link hitting the stone slab. His fingers in her hair, yanking pins free to scatter like petals. Her hands cradling his jaw and bringing him down until the fit was seamless. The kiss was past due, payment for misdeeds and misunderstandings. Jealousy. Possession. A vicious edge, crimson bleeding into his vision. His skin aflame.

He backed her up with a rough step, into a wobbly bench, and then the wall. And there he held her, imprisoned between medieval stone and his body. Took her hands and pinned them by her side so he could look, *think* without her touching him.

She wasn't the only one who'd waited years for this.

Emma gasped and wrenched high on her toes but not free, her passion turned to rebellion. He could feel it in the stiffening of her spine, her angled hip beneath the curve of his knuckles. Bumping against the firm ridge of his cock, a blatant presence beneath buckskin he couldn't hide, she rubbed against him like a cat, purring, that little mewling sound that had unmanned him before. And she knew, from the wicked sparkle in her eyes, exactly what she was doing.

Entrapment of another kind. *Her* kind. A feminine, fearsome snare he wished desperately to be entangled in.

When he let her go, instead of shoving him away as she should, she slid her hand between them, setting her palm over his rigid length. Curled her fingers, conforming her grip to his shape. Stroking until he felt his heart kick, once, twice, in his chest.

"I'm afraid of what I feel for you," she whispered and squeezed his cock, almost bringing him to his knees. "But I want to *know* more than I want to be afraid. Those things I saw in dark, drunken corners and alleyways, the hunger, the desperation. I understood the act and what bodies looked like doing it, but I didn't understand anything until you touched me. It's humbling to imagine that what my mind and body have been telling me about you all this time is true. I know myself…and it seems I know you. I know *us*."

She pressed her lips to his, her tongue tracing his bottom lip and nibbling until he released a ragged groan, without plan pressing her harder against the wall. "And I will, no matter what happens to us, have you. Have *this*. I've earned it, you see. I didn't travel those eighty years for nothing."

It seemed this was a promise she intended to keep. To herself, if no one else.

"How much time?" he asked, his voice whisper-thin against her jaw, her neck, tilting her head until he was swimming in the blue of her eyes. "Before Delaney comes to retrieve you?"

Her mouth fell open in invitation, one step toward fulfillment of her promise. "She'll have to check on the children, which turns into spilled milk, requests for more cookies or the reading of a fairytale. Someone hiding, someone crying. A half-hour, maybe a little more. But we mustn't tear my clothing. No time to disrobe. But I've seen it done such. A swift...joining." Her smile grew, her hot gaze sweeping his body.

She liked his physique, he could tell. From the aroused beat of the pulse in her neck to the way she sighed out a prolonged breath he guaranteed she hadn't known she'd held. Her studious attention made him swell, his posture, his cock *and* his heart.

She made him feel greater than he was, stronger, smarter.

Made him feel the future was bursting with hope if he could forget the past.

It was more than love to be elevated like this. And though his heart stayed in the shadows, his body leaped forward.

Taking Emma's hand, Simon dragged her down the center aisle toward a utility room he remembered stood at the back of the conservatory. Jostling her inside, he turned back, and with a hoarse grunt, shoved a marble plant stand before the door. Not enough of an impediment should one of the duke's burly footmen come calling, but it was certainly enough to keep a curious duchess out.

He didn't let her speak, stepping in and seizing her lips before she could say something else to ruin him. Utter avowals he wasn't prepared to answer, offer declarations he couldn't yet return. Her hands fisted in his shirt and brought him closer, her tongue an assault inside his mouth, seeking to intensify a connection already too intense. A bruising onslaught, his arms full of her, his mind rupturing with sensation. He closed his eyes to it, to her, let the sound of the wind scuttering through a split in the wood, and her muffled moans drive him a little mad, right there in the duke's vacant utility room.

It seemed an ideal place to change course, for better or worse.

The bench behind them was an appropriate height. Perfect, tagging him right at the hip. And sturdy enough, he determined, when he kicked it. Lifting Emma to it, Simon hitched her skirt high, spread her thighs and moved inside her warm, welcoming circle.

She was his obsession, his ambition, his avarice.

And in that untamed moment, he both loved and hated her. Required and feared her like the blood racing through his veins, the oxygen spilling into his lungs.

Despite the fear, he plunged in with everything he had.

CHAPTER 14

*S*ometimes a kiss becomes more.

From the pale glow of a fresh flame to the white-blue of a raging fire in one second. An inferno. Blistering heat.

Emma was both present and not as he tormented her.

Fingers tweaking her nipples through layers she wished he'd ripped away, even though she'd asked that he not. Thumb covering the swollen bead at her core through her combination, flicking, circling. Knowing, in his vast experience, how to unlock not only pleasure but recklessness. Madness. Excitement escalating past what one could hope to manage and rationally *think*.

His teeth on her neck, her jaw, his words a delicious pirouette in her ear.

She raced blindly to keep up. Tangling her fingers in his hair, rubbing his scalp with her nails as he groaned into her mouth. Wrapping her leg around his buttocks and pulling him tighter against her. Digging her hand into the corded muscle of his hip, urging him to establish a rhythm.

Inside her. What was he *doing* down there?

She arched against his hand. "*Now.*"

"I'm trying, darling. Patience. What is this bloody undergarment you're wearing," he whispered against her lips.

"Ah," she said, unable to string together enough words to tell him that her modiste had suggested the newfangled piece combining drawers and a chemise —after Emma had complained about the many layers required of a lady's proper wardrobe.

With an oath, he released her lips, dropped to his haunches and whipped a knife from his boot. The blade glinted in the razor-thin band of sunlight puncturing the cracked slats. "Hide what I'm about to destroy in the kitchen's rubbish bin in the morning before the staff empties it. You can get back today, the calamity being beneath your skirts, without anyone being the wiser." Then she felt the whisper-edge of metal, an initial tear in her undergarment, his fingers widening the opening as the knife clattered to the stone floor.

A blast of chilled air hit her thighs before his mouth restored her warmth.

Her head dropped back, her hands going into his hair for balance, afraid she'd topple off the high bench. This, *this,* she'd never seen nor imagined. Not out of a bedchamber, not with him kneeling before her.

Simon's mouth settled over her, his tongue doing vile, wondrous things. His hands were bracing her thighs apart, then moving to loop her legs over his shoulders as he edged in. Deeper. His tongue stroking, fingers thrusting, lips sucking. Moist heat, silken skin, the stubble on his jaw abrasive and glori-ous. The muscles of his back flexing beneath her heels, an experience she'd never in her life expected. As if it were a dream, she began to lose herself. The sounds coming from her throat were raw, uncontrolled. The movement of her hips as she chased pleasure unmatched, feral.

She would've been embarrassed had she time to think.

As it was, she let sensation ride as she rode him. Undulating, a jolting, shuddering journey to completion. His erotic demonstration was broken only by his words. Filthy and joyous. About her beauty, her scent, her taste…and the glorious feel of her body closing about him.

Tight, wet, *perfect*.

She could have come from those lyrics alone.

His arm snaked behind her back, steadying her, intensifying the exchange as she began to rupture into a thousand brilliant pieces. Flashes of light behind her eyelids, electric pulses along her skin. She cried out, palms slamming back to level on the bench as she arched into her pleasure. His muscles tensed beneath the legs draped down his back, his declarations of ecstasy almost as riotous as hers.

Relentless, he pursued her with his lips and tongue until she pushed him away in gratifying agony.

Removing her legs from his shoulders, he rose, staring down at her with an ardent expression she was too dazed to decipher. His eyes glittered, black as pitch in the hazy light. The surge of possession streaking through her was harsher, more wrathful, than love. A tempest. Like her granny would've said, a glitch of the nastiest kind. To *want* such as this could only spell doom.

She didn't want this brutal yearning, a ferocious

desire to reach the isolated parts of a man unwilling to share.

As Simon had stated, she'd be the ruin of him. Not his salvation.

He wiped her indecision away with a kiss. The taste of something foreign—*her*—on his tongue, a feminine scent she was unacquainted with clinging to his skin. With a wrenching motion, he unbuttoned his trousers, took himself in hand, and because he'd readied her so very, *very* well, sank into her in one deep, penetrating thrust. Circling his arms around her, calling hers to wind around his neck in response, her legs going high on his hips, ankles locking over his buttocks, he drove his thighs into the bench with a pounding rhythm as he sent them to heaven.

There was anguish in his touch, in his kiss. Impossibility. Longing.

And far beneath, hesitation that pained her to recognize.

When the bench shuddered and started to collapse beneath them, he laughed ruthlessly, ducking his head into her neck, circling his hands beneath her bottom and bringing her to his chest. The rounded bead he'd taken between his teeth, his lips, her center of pleasure, flared to life with the shift, her core rubbed against his pelvis in some magical way that lit her up like one of the duke's infamous fires. Simon didn't pause, sliding her along his shaft in gradual, leisurely strokes while she gasped and angled for purchase, under his control completely, delight misting over her like London's dense fog.

Silence, except for two scattered heartbeats, savage moans, the faint creak of a loose shutter banging the wall.

And in the distance, the call of children.

"*Now*," she murmured into his starched shirt collar, her tongue tracing the flaring pulse above the crisp fold, tasting salt and something uniquely Simon. "Before we're interrupted." Impatient, she sank her teeth into his neck, marking him. "Or I can take us back a few minutes—"

"No damned time travel," he rasped and stumbled back, pressing her against the door, the beveled ridge bumping her spine. "I'm close. So close. And I know, from the tremors racing through your body, that you're close, too. So let us be in this moment, please, without being in the supernatural."

With a sense of urgency, he tilted his hips, his gaze centered on her as he recorded her reactions. She watched his keen mind house what was going to make her come. And come quickly. Hard thrust, slow glide, lingering until his tip met her entrance, then a robust return. Her startled catch of breath, her hoarse cry—*yes, there*—when he angled to the left, he followed like rose petals she'd scattered across a path she wanted him to take.

Suddenly, she had a violent urge for them to come together. Another experience she'd never imagined.

Emma had erotic weapons at her disposal; she'd recorded quite a few things *he* enjoyed as well.

Her touch was bruising, as he liked, nails scratching, fingertips pressed hard against his skin. A frantic kiss, her teeth taking his bottom lip and sucking, until his arms shuddered around her, her stance shifting with his shaking knees. Choking on each other's moans. She swallowed the taste of their joining until it flowed through her like an enchanted essence.

When the fever hit him, he braced his hand on the door by her head and urged his hips against hers until she was pressed between scuffed oak and a long, damply glistening body.

"Yes?" he asked frantically. "I can't...not another minute."

"*Yes.*" She groaned into his neck, closed her eyes to the extreme beauty of their intertwined bodies. Then she let pleasure catch her. Skin lighting as she twisted to capture every frantic vibration, like grabbing snowflakes in the wind. Her world tilted, years and minutes, *ages*, filtering through her like smoke. She held on to him, *only* him, letting time whisper past, race forward, slide back.

With a hoarse cry, he lowered Emma to her feet in an exhausted slide down the door. Gave her a lingering kiss, dusting her cheek and chin, his knuckles brushing her jaw. Then he went to his knee, crouching, hung his head and gasped for breath, his wounded exclamation echoing off the walls. She watched his fingers spread wide on the stone floor and marveled, amazed, at how attracted she was, still. With every beat of her heart, every throb of blood through her veins, she wanted him. Even after the most explosive orgasm of her life.

Now, this moment, wanted him, if he'd have her.

To hell with who should find them, she cared little.

And she knew, no matter how wrinkled and gray he'd become, that this wanting would never change.

With a sigh of defeat, she let the door guide her to the floor, her own collapse, knees coming high, chin resting on them. Her legs had announced, quite abruptly, that they would no longer support her.

How beautifully remote he looked, kneeling before her in the duke's dusty spare room, weak from taking his pleasure, from giving her the most explosive of her life. Skin moist from their exertions, the scent of their joining filling the small space. His back rising and falling with his inhalations, a herculean effort to reclaim himself when she'd given up on reclaiming anything. At least, she'd stolen a piece of him this time, as he'd stolen a piece of her the last. Consummate thieves, both of them.

Only, he was the better thief, there was no disputing.

But the question laid out before them, a precarious gamble, was if Simon Alexander was going to allow this burglary or not. Looking at him, it didn't seem like he wanted to.

As if he'd heard the question, he swiped his hair from his brow and gazed up at her. Dark eyes glittering, his lips, rosy and plump from their assault, flattening as he debated.

"Is it always like that?" she asked in a voice that betrayed every blasted thing she wished, upon seeing his sullen expression, to hide.

It was like watching a gas flame, a particular hobby of hers at the moment, flutter and die. Emotion flaring, then burning out. Until, before her sat a pillar of stone, his protective cloak cinched around him. "Sure, Emma. I fall to my knees, weak as a babe, every time I fuck someone."

Emma picked at a notch in the stone slab she rested upon, erosion from centuries of living, maybe even loving of the kind they'd shared. Simple to see, Simon was pushing her away. Begging her to get exasperated enough to flounce back to the duke's bloody mansion without a discussion they needed to have occurring. *Fool*, she thought, *jackass*.

What a life they could have together if they'd only chose to *have* a life together.

They understood each other, recognized the low-rent parts of the other, the rookery allure that clung like a curiously attractive scent. She knew him, whether he liked this fact or not. And he knew her. They were damaged, mystical souls, quite ideal for the other.

But that didn't mean—

"Have you forgiven me?" she said, partly into the fist she'd brought to her lips. "For not coming back?"

His head came up from his inspection of his trouser close. "Have you forgiven me? For not waiting?"

Emma kicked her leg out with a curse, sending his knife spinning across the stone floor toward him. Her combination now housed a ruinous tear thanks to it—a tear letting in air that was, admittedly, cooling her fevered skin. "I trust you. That's *better* than forgiveness where I come from. And years may separate our births, but you came from where *I* came from. We're kin in this way. Nothing like these posh toffs you surround yourself with. That I'm surrounding myself with to *survive*."

The sound of children's laughter again sounded from the lawn, closer than before. Emma drew a breath scented with the fragrance of cut grass and the river, obliterating their magical mixture tinting the air. She blinked into the bright sunlight piercing the dim space, the life outside peeking in.

She dusted her hand down her bodice. "How do I look if they stumble upon us?"

He paused, assessing, his eyes going hot as he studied her. "You look like you've been abused in the duke's conservatory. I'd take the servant's stairs on the way back if I were you."

Irritation flared, but she kept it contained. This learning to be a lady business assisting on multiple levels, she was coming to find. "Good. I'm glad fer it," she said, letting her old accent flow through her words. If he thought he'd change her until she was unrecognizable, he had another think coming.

Dipping his head, Simon buried a caustic reply in the sleeve of his coat.

"You made me into this, and now you don't like it?" Emma wrenched to her feet with a blaspheme she'd not uttered since leaving the slums.

Scrambling to grab his knife, he snapped it closed and jammed it in his waistcoat pocket, rising to his feet seconds after her. "I'm not trying to make you into anything. I'm trying to save your damned life! Hargrave—"

"Is going to find me and return me to my time. Someday, he *will*. He has no value, no purpose, other than this venture. You should take what time we have together, you foolish man."

"Over my dead body," Simon ground out between clenched teeth, his expression harsher than she'd ever seen it. A legitimate ruffian, someone to fear. This was the forbidding man he'd have been if he'd stayed in St Giles. If the lads in Tower Hamlets had faced him looking like this, they would've scampered into the night.

No fancy education or first-rate clothing could hide this brutality.

Crossing to him, she grabbed his wrist and squeezed as hard as she could to make him understand because it seemed he didn't. "If it comes to that, I leave. If it comes to *any* of your family, anyone in the League, being put in danger to save me, I return to 1802 on my own, do you hear me? I'll be gone like a vapor in the night before I put anyone besides myself at risk."

He whispered a vile curse and whirled, yanking open the door, sending it into the wall with a dull thump.

Taking two steps for his one, she pursued him down the conservatory aisle, feeling his walls rising, brick by brick. How could she make him trust her? She'd only leave if it meant *protecting* him. She'd never leave otherwise. But her words seemed like another abandonment, a vulnerable juncture for the boy inside him.

Even if he didn't realize it.

Halting abruptly, his gaze roamed the space until she realized what he searched for. With a sigh, she pointed to the far corner. "There, beneath the orange tree."

Crouching, he snatched the earl's cufflink from the floor. Then rising, bumping into her because she'd stepped so close, he slapped it into her hand. "You can return it at Epsom. Say you found it in the grass and mooned over it for days. Felt closer to him, having something of his with you. Tucked under your pillow with one of those roses I'm guessing he sent."

"You daft man. *Your* gloves are tucked under my pillow! A blood-stained handkerchief you gave me weeks ago, too, if you must know."

He blinked, processing this information as a man typically does, *slowly*.

She fisted her hand around the cufflink until the rounded edge bit into her skin. "After this, us, *that*"— she hiked her thumb over her shoulder, toward the utility room—"you'd send me off with Hollingmark? I should punch you in the nose. Or like my granny taught me, kick you in the nethers."

He opened his mouth, closed it. Rolled his shoulders. Exhaled. Chewed his bottom lip until she feared he'd have it bleeding. His beautiful bottom lip. "*Emma*." His hands went out in a gesture of surrender, then dropped to his side. "If I were a writer, and

I started composing my thoughts during my last life and continued straight through to my next, I still wouldn't have enough time to put into words all I feel for you."

Her heart dropped, her throat closing around her feelings. This was love, then, wasn't it? Awkward and halting, shy and reluctant, but so lovely. All Simon. "Then *be* with me. It's easy. *Be* with me. It's what we've known we wanted since, well, since forever. I'm not asking for marriage, even, as I couldn't care less about a silly slip of paper. And I have no family to care for me."

With a snarl, he swept his hand over the shelf housing a variety of earthen pots, sending them to the floor with a clatter. Pieces of pottery danced around her feet, pinging off her slippers and her stockinged ankles. "I don't know how to *be* with anyone. You don't understand the corner I've painted myself into with you. How unfit I am to give you what you need. What I had to do to survive before Julian twisted me up inside. *He* doesn't know. Finn, whom I've told my darkest secrets, who knows me better than anyone, doesn't know. Not everything." He glanced over his shoulder, and she caught the ominous flicker in his eyes. The chill hit her, racing toe to cheek like an icy bath. He wasn't going to let her in. That's what his expression said. *Stay out.* "I wake in the night with terrors. St Giles, the slums, right there, beneath me. Bloodied hands, shouts no one was there to hear. Not to mention the haunts, who are *never* going to leave me, Emma, not for one moment leave me. I walk into a room; they walk in behind me. Who but one imprisoned in such a world would want that?"

Affection was a soothing balm. Being afraid to love her was much better than not being *able* to love her. Or *not* loving her, which she didn't think was the case. "You're their savior; that's why they come to you. They need you; they believe in you. You're part of their journey. A safe part, I think. Maybe you're the safe part of mine."

He kicked a shard of pottery into the corner, his gaze anywhere but on her. "I don't want them." His tortured exhale rang through the conservatory, off the rows of polished glass panes. Shoving his messy hair from his eyes, his attention finally circled back to her. The devastation highlighted on the handsome, hard planes of his face frightened her, the sunlight she stood in unable to thaw her chilled heart. "And maybe I don't want you."

"You're going to let me go," she whispered, her mind clouding with the knowledge. She couldn't grasp that this might *truly* be his intention. Even after their spats and battling, that he might let her go. "There are…" She pointed to the house, indicating the console table in the foyer currently displaying her popularity. "Invitations, a dozen of them this morning alone. A ball at a titled gent's somewhere in the country, a musicale a baroness of whatever is only inviting me to because she thinks I'm a scandal in the making. They smell something different about me, this pack of city wolves, yet they can't quite figure it out. Still, having a duke for a cousin trumps all, I'm seeing. I have a choice, Simon, genuine choices aside from you."

He tilted his head to stare through the domed glass ceiling, his hand snaking in his pocket and pulling a farthing free. She'd wondered how long it would take for him to start *that* up. "Then pick. Roll the dice, Dark Queen of the West End. Will it be an earl, a viscount or a marquess? Centuries of near-royal blood for the taking." He slapped his hands together, his heated gaze meeting hers, the coin, for the first time a play she could witness, sliding into the edge of his sleeve. "But whoever you choose, you bloody well better choose to stay in 1882 with them."

His fear was vaster than she'd estimated. Shock was the current emotion racing through her, but rage trickled in like rain through a split in the ceiling. She was willing to unleash the storm on him, *oh*, was she.

Sunlight glinted off the coin as it passed through his fingers. "And just so you know, I'll take care of Hargrave."

"He's *my* problem," she returned, rage bleeding into her words.

Simon retreated two paces, perching his bum on a bench that looked as shaky as the one they'd destroyed in the utility room. If only he didn't look so attractive, a professorial swindler, standing there in a burst of light usually reserved for nourishing citrus trees. Drawing her even as she backed away because he'd pushed her. "He's the League's problem. You're one of us now. You have been since you showed up in Oxfordshire and had Delaney's mount tossing her into the dirt. It isn't *my* problem if you're just catching on to this fact. You came to *us*, remember?"

"I apologized to the duchess straight-off for that unfortunate event. I was only trying to get the Soul Catcher. Desperate. Out of options, time running out. Remember those things, do you, you bounder?"

He laughed then, lowered his head and let the rusty sound roll from his lips. Lips wounded from *her* ministrations. His shirt collar wrinkled from her ferocity. His hair a disaster because she'd tangled her fingers in the strands as he'd thrust inside her.

Made love, though not likely what he'd call it.

It had been love. It *was* love.

"I'd buy tickets to see the Breslin version of an apology. God in heaven, I would."

"Are you trying to hurt me, Simon?" she asked as the wail of the duchess's children approaching the conservatory rolled over them like a wave. "Or are you trying to make me so furious I never wish to speak to you again? Is this reluctance because I *see* you, as you see me? We're alike, the two of us, in an exceptional way that terrifies you."

His coin hit stone, his eyes blazing when they met hers. "I'm trying to *save* you. From me. And, *yes*, you *do* bloody terrify me. My choices when I'm with you terrify me. As it is, I've had you three times without taking sensible precautions. You could be carrying my child this very minute, Emma. Have you thought about that?"

I want your baby. The words rang through her mind like a dull chime, teasing her lips open. Sending her heart into a flurry in her chest.

Spilling emotion she couldn't hide across her face.

In the end, she left Simon before he could read what she'd silently written, as he wished her to do. Shoved the door to the conservatory open, fading sunlight balmy on her cheeks as she turned her face to the sky. She skirted the lawn and the gravel path back to the house, avoiding anyone who could catch a glimpse of her and know what she'd done.

Relinquished her heart, irrevocably, to a man determined to live his life without her.

When she reached the kitchens, she took the servant's staircase as Simon had advised, her ruined combination a reminder of how mad she was to wish she could ruin another. Halting on the winding staircase, her hand braced on the chilled stone, she promised to stop loving a man who couldn't love her back.

This plan survived until she entered her bed-chamber and found the violin. No note, nothing like the godawful sonnets she'd received.

When no note was needed.

Cradling the extraordinary gift to her chest, Emma wept until the sun slipped low in the sky, ending the day *and* her remarkable love affair.

CHAPTER 15

*S*imon usually enjoyed the Derby.

It was what he liked to think of as a commoner's race when he considered himself common to his core. The public was allowed to view for free in restricted areas, drawing a massive crowd of folk from Epsom and the neighboring towns of Tadworth and Langley Vale. Of course, Queen Victoria was in attendance in the upper reaches, where he was allowed to roam freely because of his association with Julian. Well, one level below Her Majesty, to be exact. Bastards of viscounts got knocked down a bit, which he agreed with in democratic fashion. Close enough to note the color of her gown should he care to, a rather atrocious mauve that made her skin look like wax paper.

The environ crackled with loser's cries and winner's roars, peanut shells and discarded wager slips crunching beneath his boot. He'd always loved the scent of gambling. Because there was a scent, a *taste*, he'd noticed the first moment stepping inside the Blue Moon when he was but a lad of ten. Peeking from behind Finn's coattail, eyes round like saucers. His brothers had laughed at his reaction when he'd simply *known*. This life called to him. Exhilarating, and a prudent profession for a man who didn't risk more than he could afford to lose. It wasn't tempting, the reckless squandering, when he spent his nights watching others go down that hell pit.

When he was feeling charitable, saving them from it.

Too, there was always his ability to steal should he need ready funds. Which, thanks to the supreme success of his gaming hell, was never going to be required of him again.

Now, he simply filched for fun.

Fun, he thought irritably, fingering the ruby earbob he'd lifted from Baroness Ampthill when she'd lingered next to him, whispering lewd suggestions about what she'd do if they chanced to meet in her thoroughbred's stable after the races.

He wasn't going to meet the baroness in stable number five, no matter what was rumored about the length of her tongue. He *wasn't*.

Even if—while observing the Earl of Hollingmark place his sticky fingers all over Emma on the balcony moments ago—he wanted to. Desperately. Like a dog in pain, he wanted to hide in the familiar. And sex with someone he cared nothing for was familiar to the extreme.

If only there were a way to make her pay as he was paying—for loving her. Erase the crimson tint filming his vision like a brutal swipe of his hand would the chalk marks on the Derby betting boards. Ridiculous desires when the obsession in question had stated, well, not that she *loved* him, but that she *wanted* him. Wanted them to be together.

For now.

However, she hadn't uttered the three words that truly mattered. The words that would lead him to her and keep him chained there happily for the rest of his life.

I will stay.

He'd had enough people leave him—and he couldn't stomach another.

He had one job. To keep Emma safe and bring her into the League. Not marry her, as he was tempted to do in the far reaches of his mind, down there in the ditch with the items he didn't discuss with anyone. Not Finn, not even Josie.

Leaning against the varnished slab serving as a bar top, Simon stared at the perplexing puzzle of female misfortune across the way, the sounds of the race removing any chance for him to hear what Emma and the earl were discussing. He guessed she could feel his scrutiny because she twitched, tugging at her glove, her eyes *almost* meeting his. Then she shifted her interest to her escort when Delaney forced the issue, the duchess throwing a fiery glance at Simon that said, *don't do this again.*

Turning away, he left Emma to the duke's men, who were shadowing her every move. Former soldiers dressed as footmen, their multi-hued livery lighting up the tavern, hulking blokes daydreaming about ways to exterminate a man in between slugs of ale. They might be bothered to learn that the woman they guarded could waltz out of 1882 before they got so much as a fat pinkie on her. Not like the typical supernatural suspects they protected. Or maybe she'd zip to the future, where she'd taken Simon while they'd made love, the sound of engines roaring through the sky louder than her frayed moans.

It had been her choice not to return them to the present in those fevered seconds, and he'd been fine to be in any time as long as she was with him.

Or perhaps she'd been helpless to, much like he'd been.

He'd made his own rash choices, drowning in that vulnerability. Stayed inside Emma, his passion spent. A gross dilemma for a man who never played fast and loose during sexual adventures. Never chanced a babe, not once. But he'd chanced one with Emma. Three times, in fact. Rolled the dice, and how. A man surrounded by bookmaking, his world comprised of it, frightened to his toes over a wager he'd laid.

A crisp riddle, that. Ironic and profound.

He knew, deep down, in that soul-searching place that made him steal items that didn't belong to him, that he wanted a baby with her as much as she—he'd witnessed the longing in her eyes, right there for the taking, a mad dare for a thief—wanted one with him.

It was his practice. To run.

He'd run from his name and his past. Was running from his future, stuck watching another man fondle the woman he wished to be the mother of his children. Very gentlemanly, the fondling, very proper. Nonetheless, heating Simon's blood as he wondered what the hell he was going to do about it.

"Did you see Westminster's filly overtake Dingham's stud as she rounded Tattenham Corner?" Finn, breathless and half-lit, shoved Simon into the bar as he lurched into the vacant spot beside his brother. "That horse is unbelievable. Un-believe-able. History-making, this win, history. Blunt dripping out of men's pockets like water from a sieve. The Blue Moon shall benefit from the excitement this evening, I can feel it." Glancing over his shoulder, in the direction of Simon's gaze, Finn snickered, brotherly mocking riding air reeking of moist earth, whiskey and horses. "Quit staring, boyo. Unless you have a ring ready to give your beloved time traveler.

Of course, a violin's better than any ring, if you ask me."

Simon sighed and raised his hand to signal the barman. *The Duke of Ashcroft couldn't keep a bloody secret.* If he had to deal with Finn's advice, he wanted a potent dram with which to wash the counsel down. "She doesn't know who sent it."

Finn hiccupped behind his betting sheet, his smile running so loose and free the ladies next to him fluttered their fans and stepped closer, knowing full well the middle Alexander was in frantic and cheerful love with his wife. However, they couldn't help themselves as Finn's good looks *were* staggering. "Bloody hell, Si, take it from a man who botched this process himself. Royally. Our girl Emma's a smart one; she knows who sent it."

"I'm not marrying someone just to advance the League; bring the only traveler we have on record into the fold." Simon pointed to a bottle of Scotch, held up two fingers, then tossed coins on the bar in payment. "Change my life just to fill pages of Julian's chronology. Thank you, but no."

"Ah, brother of mine," Finn whispered against the rim of the glass Simon handed him. "How about, do it for love?"

Why not tell him? When he'd told Finn just about everything else. Or as much as he could. He gave the earbob a spin, the ruby winking in the light. "I'm not waking one morning to an empty bed, only to find my wife has scurried off to 1920 because I said something cross over dinner."

The smile Finn unleashed was wobbly and endearing to the point that even Simon had trouble looking away. The female contingent clustered next to him tittered, the ostrich feathers in their bonnets fluttering. "Have you asked her to stay—and not a threat because of the danger if she returns? Women don't care about danger nearly as much as their men do. Maybe, like you need to hear she won't run, she needs to hear that you want her to *stay*. That you love—"

Simon knocked his shoulder against Finn's, sending his brother stumbling into the crowd of female chicks and ending the pronouncement before it could become a legitimate part of the world. Like a flower pushing through a crack in a cobblestone, existing despite the menace.

"Why you nutty, young pup," Finn grunted and launched himself at Simon, where they grappled and tumbled to the floor. The baroness's earbob tumbled from his hand and bounced across the floor. Another scandal, Simon gathered, fearing Julian's reaction but enjoying the rush of adrenaline, even if he'd never be allowed entrance to Epsom again.

Honestly, he was delighted with the idea of pummeling his brother to bits—until he heard it. Heard *her* over raucous conversation and clinking crystal.

Finn was the mindreader in the family, but Emma's words—*forgive me*—hit his ear as clearly as if she'd kissed a breathless promise into it.

The plea punctured his soul, dread pouring in.

Shoving his brother off his chest, Simon scrambled to his knees. "Emma's in trouble," he snarled, then was off, muscling through the horde crowding the barroom, skidding over ale-slick planks, Finn, he knew, right on his heels.

His family was utterly dependable like that.

The balcony was bedlam, wind whipping his hair into his eyes, the sound of horse hooves striking earth a ricochet through the misty morning, straight through his chest to his heart. Jostling his way to the railing, Simon peered over the side, his pulse skipping when Emma's guards, having given chase, looked up from the level below with bewildered expressions. He was over the balcony railing before the notion materialized that this was his plan of attack and possibly, not a good one. Landing in a crouch in a thankfully deserted spot near the staircase, without breaking a leg, he took the stairs two at a time, hitting the courtyard situated inside the stable closures at a dead run.

There were people everywhere, an explosion of color before his eyes. Murmurs, shouts, the smell of roasting meat and horseflesh. Sweat. Perfume, flowers, leather, dirt.

He'd done a wretched job protecting her, staying away because of jealousy, because of blinding trepidation. The next time he touched her, and there would be a *next* time, he was never letting her go again.

Never again. And he knew what this meant. *Oh,* he knew.

However, when he didn't have to face what he'd just admitted to himself immediately…where the hell was she?

They caught him there in the dusty semicircle—her guards, Finn, the Duke of Ashcroft. His brother's cheeks were parchment, more than a race down a set of stairs would render them. The duke, too, looked stunned, his gaze soldier-alert.

Simon grabbed Finn's coat sleeve, crushing linen in his grip. "What did you hear?"

Finn swallowed, his hand covering Simon's. "Si…"

Simon stumbled back, brought the heels of his hands to his eyes and pressed until he saw stars. When he tried to feel her, he knew with dead certainty that Emma was no longer in 1882.

The panic edging into his lungs, tilting his world

on its axis, was real. *Deserved*. It had taken him ten years, *ten*, to find a portal to travel into the past. Years of research utilizing Delaney's library of a mind, her supernatural gift. Exploiting Piper's ability to strengthen his own. Conversations with haunts from Emma's time period, visits to those in the mystical underworld who'd had interaction with a woman with blazing blue eyes, there one minute, gone the next. According to his contacts, his portal, a forest in a German village ravaged by a recent fire, was gone. Hargrave's work, if Simon had money to wager.

He had money to wager. Loads. But no Emma.

What did blunt matter when he didn't have the girl?

He inhaled a breath of racetrack filth, collecting himself before uttering the words. "What did she say, Finn? In her mind?" Exhaling brutally, he blinked away the sting of tears in his eyes. "How can I find her again?"

Finn brought the tumbler he still held to his lips and polished off the contents. Then he paused, dipped his fingers in his waistcoat pocket and came out with a green poker chip, which he shoved into Simon's hand. "I read Hargrave's. There were too many voices, too many thoughts, excited and scattered, aroused and uncontrolled, I couldn't read them all. However, strangely enough, *his* rose above the rest like yeast floating to the top of an ale barrel."

Simon grasped his brother's lapel and gave him a fierce jerk. "What did he say?"

"I have a possible way out of this mess." Finn unwrapped Simon's fingers from his coat, turned his tumbler upside-down, letting a drop of brandy stain the straw beneath their feet. "There's a woman."

Finn shook his head, clearing it, doing fast magic with the chip in his hand. "*What?*"

"Ah, we'll reclaim your weakness by attacking his," the Duke of Ashcroft said in his nobly ruthless way, his hand going to his jaw as he strategized. Simon could see the wheels spinning. "A cunning strategy for the softest Alexander. Nothing brings a man to his knees like threatening the woman he loves."

"I'm missing something," Simon murmured, wondering why he was the only one missing something.

"*Soft.*" Finn chucked his tumbler at the wall, barely blinking as crystal exploded against brick. "We're going to neutralize the bloody bastard. Using his woman as leverage, with no harm done to her person, of course. We're not those types. But Hargrave *is*. Fortunately, while he was fantasizing about his lover moments ago, he told me everything. Her name. Location. White Chapel. He visits her in this time, his *adopted* time. A milliner. Lucky stroke, that. We station men outside her flat, her shop, make sure she's watched every second, then Simon travels to Emma. Negotiates with Hargrave, who's waiting for him to show. He longs for this confrontation. I read that in his thoughts, too."

The Duke of Ashcroft brushed his coat aside to caress the butt of the knife jammed in his waistband. "Terms of the negotiation?"

Finn slashed his hand out as if to say, *I have this*. "Emma is untouched, lives in whatever time she chooses to. We allow the same with his piece. His sweet milliner will never know any of it. Secrets safeguarded on all sides."

"He didn't exactly *take* Miss Emma." Henry flickered into view like a heat stain shimmering in the distance. "She left willingly, if you call curses no fine woman should utter willing. That Hollingmark fellow had gone off to get refreshments, and Hargrave stepped in. She did the leaving to protect you, lad. He didn't want to hurt her, he said. Didn't use his trick of making her faint; didn't have to. Only wants her to stay in her world. Get out of yours. *You're* the one he said he'd harm. Splash the truth about your peculiar group of mystics all over the *Times*. Expose every one of you to the light of day." Strolling to the wall, he prodded the remnants of Finn's tumbler with a tsking sound. "Claimed he's a correspondent or some such, so he knows how."

"She went willingly? To save me, to save the League?"

Finn and Ashcroft shared a familial look Simon caught out of the corner of his eye, a look he astonishingly felt no ferocity over. The youngest in the close circle of men at the highest level of the League, they were protecting him, as they always had.

"We shield our own. You know that," the duke murmured and began to crack his knuckles, his expression growing less ducal by the second. Ashcroft loved nothing more than the occasional skirmish to keep his skills tight. "I'll send someone to find Hollingmark and make apologies for my dear cousin to explain her disappearance. Let's go with a blinding megrim from being in the sun all day."

Simon tossed Finn's chip from hand to hand, his mind spinning, possibilities rife. Then, a dead weight settled in his gut. He couldn't *get* to Emma. His portal was gone, destroyed.

And, if she thought he was in danger, she'd never come back to him.

"I see that melancholy glance." Henry grinned, the gap in his front teeth wide enough for Simon to slide Finn's half crown through. "I can take you back, boy. And not like your young miss, getting the day wrong, the month even. I can drop you in the exact sodding second of the exact sodding day you tell me I should drop ya'. Light as a canary feather striking snow. None of this bilious feeling like you get with *her* travel. Sick and sleeping for days. But she's breathing, so her gift is what it is. Cozy time travel is one benefit to dying."

Simon curled his hand around the chip, the beveled edge scraping his palm. Relief and rage bubbled in his chest, sending his heart into a dizzying rhythm. "You mean I can travel through time? As long as I take a haunt with me?"

Henry scratched his nose, his watery gaze dropping. If a ghost could blush, this one did. "In a loose manner of speaking, yes. Roundabout way to describe my bequest to ya'. But seems factual enough."

"Bequest. I'll tell you where you can shove your damned bequest. I've shared a life with those on the outside edge of hell since I prowled the streets of St Giles in short pants. I paid an extraordinary price for being different, talking about my mystical tendencies before I knew to keep my mouth shut, and suffering greatly for it. But that is *my* burden to shoulder. However, *none* of you"—Simon stalked to Henry, stabbed a chest that wasn't solid, his finger passing through the haunt's misty image to brush the sun-warmed brick—"thought to tell me? When I spent years trying to find a way to get to her? When I've been surrounded by haunts my entire bloody life, every one of you jabbering dawn to dusk until I thought I'd go mad? And you never once thought to tell me you could take me to her?"

"Weren't allowed to tell. Weren't allowed to take ye. We have higher direction, you know." Henry shrugged, lining up a neat row of crystal shards with the toe of his boot. "Alas, I'm no rule-follower, but it was the suitable decision as you weren't ready." He grinned at the response his advice garnered from his charge, his image flickering like a flame caught in a gust. "Bah, look at that irked face. Consider the cheery side of this, lad of mine. Two time travelers, so-called, joined in this barmy world. Perfect as one of them paintings of your viscount brother's hanging in the National Gallery, ain't it?"

"What's he saying, Simon?" Finn asked in exasperation. "We can't hear the conversation if you recall. If they've passed to the great beyond, I can't read their minds for shit."

Simon glanced at his brother, then tipped his head to stare at the sky when he saw the hawkish way Finn studied him. God knows what embarrassing emotions were written across his face.

Surrender, Simon, just let her in. Let them all in.

Amid his agony over Emma stepping eighty years into the past, so far away he couldn't *feel* her, sunlight pierced the frothy, smut-stained clouds to strike his skin. To thaw the ice encasing his heart. Perhaps the future wasn't as bleak and grimy as the street where he'd grown up, after all.

"We going to get your girl or wot?" Henry asked from behind him, still kicking at the shards of glass, from the sound of it. Whistling softly between that gap in his teeth. "You're mooning, you are. I can always tell when a man is done for. And you, my boy, are *done* for. Roasted like a Christmastide goose. Cooked. No use fighting it another minute unless it's from sheer stupidity. Which many a man has been known to do."

Simon hauled a shallow breath into his lungs, tasting the acrid dust surrounding the race track and, somewhere miles beneath it, hope. Closed his eyes and decided, right then and there, to follow the guidance of his haunt. It wouldn't be the first time. He'd saved Piper's life with the assistance of a long-gone ghost, and since then, for some reason, he'd tried too hard to live life without help.

Even from his family.

It was time he changed. Accepted. Loved.

He could let go of the past—with Emma beside him.

Embrace a new life built on the somewhat precarious remains of the old. The rest? Let it smolder and fall into the ashes of his existence, be blown away on a ripping gust, never to be considered again.

There wasn't a decision to be made, not really. Henry was right about that.

He was going to get his girl.

CHAPTER 16

*E*mma flicked the tattered curtain aside, the street bordering her dilapidated lodgings not much to look at. Just past midnight, the grubby lane was deserted of all but the few stumbling past after leaving the Cock and Hammer on the far west corner. Not even *one* gaslamp to light their path. Reminding her where she was.

Or, rather, where she *wasn't*. No hydrangeas beneath her window to cover the putrid scent rolling through Tower Hamlets.

Mayfair smelled like it looked: posh.

She'd gotten soft. Used to cocoa arriving on a silver tray every morning. Tea every afternoon, sprigs of mint bundled in an elegant posy on the saucer's lip. Silken sheets and a counterpane so thick a hearthfire wasn't required. Lucious gowns you could live the rest of your days in. Nights spent on a mattress that didn't involve feathers jabbing you in the back. Lights operated with a flick of the finger and warm water shooting from a faucet *inside* the house. A duchess and duke you were, bizarrely, coming to call friends.

And *him*. Most of all, she'd miss Simon.

His wicked smile, his rare laugh. The dimple that winked at her when she was vexed, melting her ire like sun striking ice.

His temper, his fortitude, his vulnerability.

His hot breath crossing her cheek. His long body pressing hers into the mattress. His hands diving into her hair as he inched inside her. Filling her in a way she hadn't known she needed, not only her body but also her soul. She desired each piece of him to a degree that frightened and astonished her. More than she'd expected after falling in love with him, at first sight, all those years ago, when they couldn't even speak.

She'd given him up to protect him. A time-traveling girl from Tower Hamlets, nothing special really, but noble when it came to it. Honorable. As much as the society folk she'd been tossing with in 1882. Worthy of Simon Alexander's love had he given it to her, when he was just an ordinary boy, too.

"He's not coming," Emma said, certain she wasn't as certain as she sounded.

While *please come* rang in her head, defying every rationale she had for coming back.

Indeed, Simon would consider this another abandonment. He would know, from one of his haunts or his mindreading brother, that she'd left his time of her own free will. Walked out of Epsom, the aroma of horseflesh clinging to her clothing, the only thing she took with her. Aside from telling Hargrave how she was going to gut him when she got the chance—anyone who'd seen her stroll past with a man dressed, not well but well enough, would've had no idea her heart was breaking into pieces and scattering at her feet. That she was leaving at the end of a barrel as surely as if Hargrave had the muzzle of his pistol pressed to her temple.

"He's not coming," she repeated, turning to face her nemesis. Sighing, she rubbed her bruised cheek, an injury sustained when Hargrave shoved her into the carriage at Epsom.

Hargrave said nothing from his sprawl in the only chair in the room, his muddy boots perched on the only table. Both rickety pieces not far from being pitched on the rubbish heap, lacking even for the Hamlets. Worthless, like everything she owned.

Somehow, her shoddy dwelling looked worse by candlelight.

As did the man who'd brought her back.

Hargrave's eyes were red-ringed, shadowed with fatigue and focused on her in a poisonous manner that made her knees quiver. But his hand trembled when he lifted a slender cheroot to lips chapped by drink and weather, his fragility showing. He looked like he hadn't slept since arriving in 1802 thirty hours before, which he hadn't. Their standoff endured, neither of them trusting the other enough to so much as close a lid. He'd dragged her straight to her former residence on Milk Yard, still hers because, unbelievably, only one day had passed since Simon had taken her home. *Home.* Tears stung her eyes, but Emma blinked them back before the time tracing bastard could see.

At least, Hargrave hadn't felt the need to incapacitate her. But, then, she hadn't resisted. And any power he used took from him as well. She'd seen how his gift weakened him. Plus, she thought he enjoyed the battle. An unconscious woman presented no challenge to a man like him.

In the end, her *gift* was robbing her of everything. Just as she'd known it would.

This time, she and Hargrave were going to destroy each other. Her destiny was like a pulse of lightning, sparking charges in the air. It was undecided if there would be a winner. Maybe they would *both* lose.

She dragged her finger over a split in the wall that kept the room chilled in summer and frigid in winter, fatigue riding hard—though she was unable to show it. "I don't know why you're waiting for him. He can't get back. You torched his portal, or did you forget that crucial fact?"

"Crucial." With a sullied chuckle, Hargrave sucked lustily on his cheroot, then blew a smoky torrent in her direction. "Listen to the swank talk. My, did they do a number on you. Guttersnipe to society sensation in four short weeks. Let me guess. Dance lessons, speech, etiquette. The Mayfair trifecta. The elegance starts to rub off like tarnish from a tea service, now, doesn't it? Pinkie out when you hold a cup and all that. I'm there myself, torn between two worlds. Torn between three, five. Until my head whirls with it. You're not the only time traveler, though there aren't many. Just enough to keep me on my toes. But you *are* the most rebellious, I'll give you that."

"You're not going to get him. You have me, but that's where it stops. I told you I'd stay." She glanced around her home with an aching pinch of despair. The scuffed furniture, the bent bed frame, the sagging mattress. Her mother's patched quilt, made for her with scraps of fabric collected one long, cold winter. Candles on the upturned crate serving as a bedside table. A grand total of four, all she had funds for. "I'll never leave Tower Hamlets, 1802, again. You have my word."

"Your *word*." Hargrave slanted his head, his flat black gaze never leaving her. His smile grew, and she realized she was doomed. Because he *liked* it. The control, the cruelty. He wasn't chasing her through time on principle alone. "Don't be so sure about my not getting my hands on Simon Alexander. He's had me, in some way, chasing *you* for years. Wasted a load of time on the two of you. When time is my game. Besides, I tend to get what I want, dear heart. If I know what I saw in the man's eyes when he looked at you, he'll find a way. Then…one touch, and he'll tumble like a petal I've plucked from a dying rose. I've bested many a beast more terrifying than him. In many a time."

They have people with abilities greater than yours, she wanted to tell him. Opened her mouth to issue the threat before she stopped herself. Why warn him if the League could catch him by surprise? She hadn't been given much information as a new member, but she'd been given some. Enough. They had weapons at their disposal. The Duke of Ashcroft shot fire from his fingertips. Delaney's intellect was far-reaching and fantastic. Victoria blocked gifts. Finn read minds. Julian touched objects and saw the past. Piper was a healer. And Simon, he had a unique talent aside from holding her heart, a deceased brethren who sheltered him, as he sheltered them.

They would protect him. From the misfortune she'd dragged him into by stepping into his world in search of the Soul Catcher, the beginning and the end of her.

When Simon had never trusted her enough to give up the gem anyway.

The sound was slight but caught her ear. The scrape of a carriage wheel against stone. So slight only one standing by a fractured windowpane would hear it.

Inching aside the curtain with her pinkie, she glanced to the street. Simon stood beside a rented hack, his hand still clutching the doorframe. His furious gaze found hers across the twilight. His smile was hard-edged, succinct, devastating. Gorgeous and windblown, looking like he'd stepped from his tailor's shop and straight into 1802, he motioned to someone inside the conveyance and started across the lane.

Mine. The word rang through her mind, tender illumination lighting her soul.

Dropping her head, she sucked a biting breath through her fist.

He'd come for her.

Seconds later, the door cracked back on its hinges.

His typical entrance.

Then Simon was striding through the archway into her squat abode, his broad body filling the space as no man's ever had. She almost laughed to realize that even amid calamity, she was embarrassed to reveal the way she lived. The poverty, the degradation.

Absurd, when Simon Alexander, nay, *MacDermot*, had come from such humble beginnings himself.

His gaze seized her for a lingering moment, then focused on Hargrave. She kept her face impassive—but her body's response was swift, love filling her as he filled the lone room of her dreary abode the moment he stepped into it. Dark slashes beneath his eyes, his cheeks gaunt and shadowed. Enraged and exhausted, as she was. But here. As he'd promised, without promising, that he would be.

When they'd made love, she'd known it was forever.

Until now, she hadn't been sure *he'd* known it.

Hargrave took a long drag on his cheroot and lowered his boots to the floor with a thud, readying for confrontation. "Wasn't locked, Alexander. The door. But thank you for the impassioned entrance. Almost theatrical. Like this pithy play on Drury Lane I saw once. 1838 or so, I reckon it was. Although everything, with you and this chit"—he rolled his shoulders, braced his hand on his knee and rose resignedly to his feet—"is impassioned, isn't it?"

Emma tried to catch Simon's gaze to keep him steady. It wasn't the time for that temper of his to rip through the space like a frigid winter wind. But she was too late; Simon zeroed in on the bruise on her cheek, his hands curling into fists as he took a fast step forward. "I'm going to fucking kill you, Hargrave."

Hargrave leered, deliberately, evilly, the wisp of smoke from his cheroot coiling like a snake about his head. "Guns don't work well on me. Knives, either. I see the bump of a pistol outlined in your coat pocket. I bet, little gypsy, there's a knife jammed in your boot. Superb attire doesn't separate the man from his origins. Miss Breslin and I were just discussing that very fact. Unlucky for you, the gods that made me made me durable for this line of work. I have more lives than a cat. And if I touch you…" He shrugged and swept his hand out, signaling someone falling to the floor. "You'll bother me no longer. Imagine, arriving like some fictional hero to save your woman when it's simply not possible. The future I see is your face pressed against the rotting planks of this hellhole and *my* boot on your back. Under my control, no time travel involved. You and me? After years of this anarchy, it's personal."

Simon plucked the Soul Catcher from his waistcoat pocket and held it near the flickering flame of a candle burning on the mantle of her regrettably empty hearth. The glow caught the sharp edges of the stone, flinging golden facets across the ceiling and the floor. "This is yours, I believe," he murmured and tossed the gem to her.

Reaching, she caught it with one hand. Gasped as the heat from the stone rolled up her arm. Her fingers, helplessly, curled around the treasure as she brought it to her chest.

Simon glanced back at her, love, if she could believe it, looming in his eyes. Like Hargrave had said he'd seen coloring them. Strangely, Simon didn't try to hide his feelings from anyone but her. Maybe he wasn't trying to hide anymore. "It warmed the closer I got to you. Pulsing a blinding blue, like your gaze in the moonlight. Almost led me right here."

"You're a bloody poet, Alexander." Hargrave jammed his cheroot out on the wall, the stench of burnt wallpaper traveling across the room to sting her nose. "That trinket isn't going to help her. Because she's staying *here*. She can keep the damned stone. A treasure from a lost time. A memento from her lost love. Under her pillow like your gloves and that stained handkerchief. I'm even thinking, such a crafty girl being wasted in this hole, that she could help me bring back others who travel. Be trained to do my job, so I don't have to do it. With a little persuasion, of course. Threats, you'd call them." He flicked his fingers dismissively. "All just semantics."

"I would *never*," Emma said, rage riding her voice.

Simon strolled across the room, planks creaking with each step, until he stood a slender pace away from Hargrave. Close enough to touch. Insult in his bearing, provocation in the challenging smile he released to the world. Her man liked to show his temper, he did. She'd be more fearful if she weren't impressed by his masculine show of bravado. She was weak for him, *weak*. "You don't know much about the League, do you, Hargrave? It's not wise to go into battle without understanding who you're fighting. Confidence above skill is never a successful combination."

"You insolent mongrel." Hargrave thumped the heel of his hand against Simon's shoulder, knocking him back a step. An exchange Simon didn't try to defend himself against, his clenched fists never leaving his sides. Emma choked back her cry, not understanding why he hadn't reacted until she watched the time tracer's face pale to the color of ash. "What the —?" Hargrave opened his fingers in a calculated roll, staring as if he'd never seen them before.

Simon snaked a tarnished half guinea from his trouser pocket and flipped it between his hands in a cheeky act sure to further infuriate Hargrave. When she knew it was merely his way to calm himself. "Why did I touch him, and he's still standing, you ask? Have you ever heard of a blocker, Hargrave?"

"Victoria? You brought someone with you? But...*how*?" Emma breathed and stumbled away from the window, halting when Simon gave her a furious, arresting look. Finn's wife could suspend supernatural gifts. Emma had yet to meet her but knew the League planned to see if she could travel while Victoria was close. When the expected answer was no.

"Who the hell is Victoria?" Hargrave growled, dusting his hand through the hair scattered thinly atop his head, a signet ring on his pinkie catching the candlelight.

"My sister-in-law. She's in the hack outside, as is my brother, Finn. Her husband, who'll kill you if you so much as gaze at her unkindly. If Victoria's within, oh, a hundred yards or so of one of the insanely gifted, their power is reduced to ash, like that cheroot you rudely snuffed out on Miss Breslin's wall." The coin flashed as it snaked between his fingers. "Go ahead, touch me again. Throw a punch and see how vicious I've become, learning to protect what's mine. Gaming hells aren't known for civility. Neither is the supernatural world." He tossed the coin in the air and caught it. Then it disappeared up his sleeve. "I'll tell the haunts to step aside. Man to man, this bout, no mystical gifts involved. But you look a tad worse for the travel, so you'd better consider the situation carefully. I'm well-rested, my friend."

Hargrave spat on the floor and gave his mouth a bruising buff with his forearm. "If you think I'll let you take the girl back *without* a fight, you're crazier than they say."

Simon tipped his head back and laughed. "Crazy, am I? Society, once again, has a man pegged incorrectly. It's talking to empty rooms that aren't empty that confuses them. Initially, I considered insanity myself. Truly."

Emma took a step closer, silently pleading. *Simon, stop this; play the game.*

He must have felt her because his hand shot out, his jaw tightening. *His* warning. "To borrow an American expression from my dear friend, Delaney Tremont, the Duchess of Ashcroft, let's get down to brass tacks, shall we? I came eighty years for proper negotiation. Equal trade. Fair-minded, both sides."

Hargrave peeled his coat off, one graceless arm at a time, and flung the garment to the floor. "I'm not a wagering man, Alexander. I don't trade when I own the property outright. Law of our world, you see. I track, I bring back those who travel. You're sluggish on the uptake, boy, when you should appreciate the significance of our unique situation. Let's see what your girl thinks of being bartered like a—"

"Heloise Murphy," Simon said with a lazy yawn

thrown into his fist. "Sorry to blurt it out like that, but I was getting bored. You have mine; I have yours."

Hargrave's breath seized as if he'd taken a healthy punch to the chest. His startled gaze shot to Emma, and he staggered forward, calculating his strategy.

"Don't think to touch her. Ever again." Simon dragged his shoulder against his chin like he scratched an itch and stepped between her and Hargrave. "My promise, if you hold to yours? That the League's men, watching Miss Murphy this very *minute*, won't act. They're stationed outside her charming abode on New Street, her business on Royal Mint. The route she walks every morning through Whitechapel Market. The Duke of Ashcroft, more warrior than aristocrat as you may have heard, has an endless supply of able-bodied soldiers in need of work. And killing, come to think of it. Talk about a melancholic group, now that there's no war to wage. In any time you place Miss Murphy, we'll continue watching you, should you think to spirit her away. I'm guessing she doesn't even know about you, so your chances of getting her to leave 1882 are limited. My haunts will take me to her in seconds. *Seconds*. After Finn reads her mind, and yours, of course."

Hargrave stooped to yank his coat from its haphazard crumple on Emma's worn planks. "You bastard."

"I prefer to think of this as clever design. We've already established a relationship between Miss Murphy and the duchess. Every modiste wishes to style a member of the *ton,* don't you know? We have others with gifts that I could call upon. But I think the plan in place is enough for now. You see, I don't want to drag an innocent woman into this…but love is your burden to manage. I already have mine."

Emma's heart sank, her throat closing. *Burden.*

Simon thought his love for her, if that's what he was finally admitting, a burden.

"You're not going to win," Hargrave ground out in a guttural whisper. But he backed away until his boot heel smacked the doorjamb.

Simon's gaze went to Emma and held. "I already have."

They watched Hargrave give a final, malicious glance around the cramped dwelling, then he was gone, opening her cage and letting her, for the first time in her life, fly free.

Simon turned to her, his eyes black in the amber light cast from the candle. "Emma, breathe, *please*," he murmured and reached to caress her bruised cheek with his calloused fingertip. Touching her so gently, as if he feared she'd disintegrate like an ember on his skin.

She let out a gusting exhalation she hadn't realized she'd held, her vision spotting, the floor beneath her wobbling. Finally, after hours without sleep or food, giving in.

"Burden," she whispered and fell toward him as darkness overtook her.

CHAPTER 17

The sky blanketing London shone pink and battered blue in the hour before sunrise.

A dull wash spilled across the paint-spattered planks in the St Giles warehouse no one knew he owned. The top floor, Simon's private accommodation. Or, rather, it would be someday. A yawning expanse running the length of the building, with few fittings aside from a shipping crate housing bottles of gin and a towering sleigh bed that he'd found in Julian's attic and had moved before Piper noticed it was missing. He'd refurbished the space one rotting timber at a time by his own hand. It's why the work was taking ages and looked reasonably amateurish.

A skilled laborer, he wasn't.

But he loved the place with a fervor that shocked him.

Sometimes, love didn't follow design.

He was learning to accept this fact.

Drawing a breath scented with ale from the public house next door, he let the bitter fragrance calm him. This place, *his* place, a decrepit building five short blocks from where he'd been born, calmed him. Coming back, coming home, when he could now afford to buy half of Mayfair from sellers up to their armpits in debt, was ironic, he supposed.

The deal was, he'd left part of his soul on these jammed streets, affection in his heart for the neighborhood *and* the people. The hawker selling fish for sixpence on the north corner, the costermonger selling exotic nuts and pineapples just off the ships for five on the south. The Irish contingent selling onions and oranges, the watercress vendors packing baskets of greens and striding down the alley to start their day.

They were *his* people. Like the haunts were his people.

Therefore, he'd decided, against what was going to please Finn and Julian, that he would live here. In St Giles. Be a part of his Mayfair family, of the League. Run the Blue Moon. But he'd walk these often dismal streets coming home every night. This community was *his* to improve. He was already in talks with the local magistrate about sanitation, roadways, healthcare, wages.

He had lots of ideas.

Like the women he and Josie were moving not out but *up*. Creating opportunities, as Julian and Finn had for him. But in their hamlets, haring off to a locale they'd no affection for not part of the deal.

It was mostly money that opened doors and slicked the palms providing the prospects, a fact Simon had long ago made peace with. Easy to forgive when he was a player now, too, able to slick as many palms as were thrust at him. He could walk into any drawing room in London—looking like them, talking like them. He'd danced in their ballrooms, woken in their beds. Sipped their champagne and laughed at their jokes. Gone to school with them, even.

Enough that they thought he was one of them.

When he wasn't.

However, he wasn't above realizing this was his way of paying back his good fortune. Of letting his tortured soul heal.

His family, his good fortune. His profession, his good fortune. Even his supernatural gift, his good fortune. His love—he glanced to the bed and the slumbering figure tucked beneath her mother's tattered quilt—his *extreme* good fortune.

He knew, in what fortune tellers liked to call the *look back*, that he'd never have been able to share his life with anyone except a woman who understood what survival and desperation on the mean streets was like.

His heart being taken by a rookery girl made all the sense in the world.

Simon left his inspection of the waking city to check on Emma. She'd been sleeping for—he slipped his watch from his pocket and checked the time— going on thirty hours. Henry had returned them to the *minute* in 1882. The only issue with the trip being that his brothers now knew he owned a lumbering former paint mill overlooking the worst section of New Oxford Street. Unfortunately, Julian and Finn weren't the kinds to linger before popping by to check out his investment. The security of the neighborhood, the safety of the dwelling...and so on.

However, he loved them. Consequently, their behavior was tolerable.

Love brought all manner of disturbance into one's life.

He wasn't up to fighting it anymore.

Swiveling the chair sitting next to the bed around with the toe of his boot, a spindly, fragile effort he'd also pinched from Julian's attic, he looped his arms along the high back and settled in. The button he'd lifted from Finn's coat for kicks in hand, fingers occupied, mind resolved. She had to wake soon for food and drink and to use the utilities, which were admittedly sparse. But this woman, he knew, would see promise in the space, in his plans, in his *life*.

She'd seen promise from the very beginning, when he'd seen little promise himself.

"Something stolen, I imagine, that you're shuffling between those talented fingers," Emma whispered minutes later from the depths of fine bedding. Everything else in the loft was rough, like her mother's quilt, but the bedding he'd made sure was fit for a queen. The same maker Victoria used. So when he slept here, he slept well. And alone. Never having brought anyone to this space.

"You're not a burden," he said, diving in before his idiotic side, incorporating a man's hesitant reasoning, kept him from divulging the truth. *Burden*. The wrong word, although love *was* burdensome if one felt it strongly enough.

He felt it strongly enough.

The quilt lowered, and her eyes found his. In her bright blue gaze, he read all kinds of things. Affection, exasperation, offense. The last chilling and putting him on guard. "I spoke without thinking. Apologies for what rolled out of my mouth."

She scooted high, coming up and out of the tangle of silken sheets, in a shift but nothing else. Victoria had undressed her, but now, he was benefitting, his blood racing through his veins to see her nipples, dark pink and pebbled beneath thin linen. The gentle curve of her breasts. Collarbone, slender neck. Tongue sliding along her lips to moisten them.

He'd undressed to his trousers and shirt and slept beside her, listening to her soft breaths. Nothing but his heart involved.

Now, his cock was stepping into the mix.

When her gaze met his, he found a complementing hunger, emotion sizzling, stinging him where he sat.

Emma looked to the crate acting as a bedside table. The Soul Catcher glowed in a puddle of amber light. A soothing pulse, like a heartbeat, because it was where it should be.

With her.

"You're trusting me with the swish stone now, is that it?"

He shifted on his rump, thinking the chair felt harder than it had seconds ago. She was still irked. *Women.* "I'm trusting you with everything, Emma."

"More than you trust Josie?"

He cursed and vaulted to his feet, leaving the chair rocking on its frail legs. Ate up the distance to the window, braced his arm on the iron frame and gazed out at the bruised horizon. "You're going to fight me at every step. Damned if I shouldn't know that already."

The coils squeaked as she crawled from the bed. An issue he'd have to repair if they were going to use it like he wanted to. He forced aside a frantic urge to swallow his pride, stride over to her and kiss her senseless. Seduce her while destroying those luxurious sheets, until there were no words to be spoken. "I'm sorry for not giving you the Soul Catcher in the first place. It's yours. The League agrees, if you care about that piece." He traced a jagged gash on the frame with Finn's button. "Is this what I'm supposed to say? Josie is—"

He exhaled and tunneled his hand through his hair, thinking it'd been ages since he'd had it cut. Overlong, which he liked. He wondered which man Emma preferred. Unkempt scoundrel or London toff. "Josie is a friend. And never more than. While you're…"

Her arms circled his waist from behind, sending his pulse spiraling. Then, after a moment, she laid her cheek on his back and squeezed tight. "The thought of you with anyone else, those women, the gossip rags. I can't stand it. I won't stand *for* it. I *won't*. Even if you did give me the loveliest violin I've ever seen."

Simon released a relieved whistle through his teeth. She loved him; she did. Hanging his head, he placed his hand over both of hers, trapping her, should she think to leave him. Ever again. It was going to be fine, somehow, all of this. He and Emma were going to find their way through a complicated world. Protect each other, love each other, and go on.

"Em, there's never…will never be another woman for me. How could there be?" He shrugged a shoulder, brought her hand to his mouth, brushed his lips over her palm, the veins running along the inside of her wrist. "When you're all I want, all I've ever wanted. Ask anyone in my family. Piper, Victoria, Delaney. Julian, Finn, Humphrey. Since that moment in Oxfordshire when you stepped out of a dream and into my life, I've never wanted anyone else." He laughed against her skin, power coursing through him when she trembled. "They worried greatly because not finding you meant my life was over."

"Simon," she whispered, her breath streaking through his cambric shirt to warm his skin, "stop."

"No, never again," he vowed and turned, enclosing her in his arms, lifting a hand to cradle her head as he seized her mouth. Her surrendering sigh parted her lips just enough to let him in.

Where he poured every ounce of love, desire, fondness into the kiss, the most important of his life. Of hers, perhaps. Catching her hard against his body, he brought her into the nook created for her and her alone. Lemon and the faintest hint of lavender drifting free, tempting him with every breath he took.

Bouncing up on her toes, she offered herself with a ragged moan that blazed like one of Ashcroft's fires through his body. Her hand snaked into his hair, tugging the strands until his knees threatened to buckle and send him to the paint-splattered floor.

His cock stiffened, a rigid presence she surely felt against her hip. Grasping her shoulders, he inched her back enough to witness her undoing. Her eyes wild, the color of the sea before a storm. Her hair, absent of order and tumbling past her shoulders. Her lips parted, moist, pink.

Lewdly, it made him wonder what other parts of her were moist and pink.

Then she called him back, her mouth hard and hot. A kiss born of freedom, passion, possession. Telling him what she wanted, what she needed. He was backing her in the direction of the bed when he remembered, his brief glimpse of the blistering sunrise reminding him.

He hadn't asked her yet.

He'd never told her how he felt.

"Come," he murmured against her lips. Taking her hand, he led her across the room, her stumbling step twice his to keep up. "I'll make love to you until you can't compose a suitable sentence, can't think, can't breathe. I'll put us both under, days spent in slumbering recovery. I promise, dear God, I promise. But first, this. What I should have said already."

Stopping briefly to toss his coat over her shoulders, he led her to a staircase in the back corner of the loft. It was crooked but surprisingly sturdy, iron like the window frames, and extending to a roof that had one of the best views in the city.

Even if the view originated in the slums.

The stench of the river and burning coal hit hard when they reached the tarred surface, the wind tearing at their clothing and hair. Nevertheless, his heart lifted. The sight of London waking was gorgeous.

His one wish at that moment: to share the view, to share his *life*, with the woman he loved.

"*Oh*," she sighed and got so near the edge and the insubstantial wall reaching her knee that he shuddered and looped an arm around her waist, pulling her back against his chest.

"Not too close. You want to scare me to death, woman?"

"Simon, this is *magnificent*. I can see Tower Hamlets. See that spire? My little street is right next to it." She stretched her slender arm and pointed into the distance.

He grinned, pleased to the tips of his toes, gazing over her shoulder at his community. "It is, isn't it? But once you get down there, among the people, traveling the alleys and lanes, it's different. Better. Life shows itself, like a roll of the die at the hazard table. A neighborhood reveals itself when you walk the streets. That's why…" He swallowed, nervous, now that he'd come to it. "I'd like to live here." He nodded toward the stairs they'd just climbed. "In this loft, once I get her ready. I've done most of the repairs myself. But for the rest of what I'm planning, I need help. There are craftsmen all over this township who need work. We'll put in a proper kitchen and sitting rooms and parlors or whatever we require on the floor below. Another bedroom or two. We have more space than we need. Although it won't ever look like a Mayfair townhouse. Won't look like anything this town has ever seen. Of course, my office is at the Blue Moon, and I'll work there. But I..." He sighed, letting out the breath and the admission. "I want to live *here*. In St Giles. With you. Unconventional, to utilize an abandoned warehouse like this..."

She tilted her head down with a shy laugh, her stomach quivering beneath his hand.

He made her turn into his arms, even if they were both embarrassed to acknowledge the future blossoming between them. Proposals had to be presented face-to-face. "I want to save this community. Or try. My pack of haunts will help me. You'll help me. I've finally found a way to use my gift. And maybe you have, too. We can travel together safely, reach those in circumstances before the circumstances break them. But we have to live here, not at the Alexander family home or above the Blue Moon, to gain their trust, to make any association work. Besides"—he shrugged and glanced at the sunrise setting fire to the sky, wishing he had a coin in his hand to settle his racing heart—"I want to be here. I pray you do, too."

She settled her hand on his jaw, tilting his gaze to hers. "Is this a proposal, Simon Alexander?"

He felt the blush light his cheeks. She laughed and pulled him into a kiss, lingering until they were breathless. Until the air crackled with passion. Intent. Promises. Desire. *Love.*

Emma did a delighted spin on slippers that had seen the worst of eighty years, the ends of his coat slapping her hip. His nerves stretched taut, waiting for her response.

Her smile grew, plumping her cheeks. "Paint. In the loft. On the floors. Was it once a factory?"

"Previously, yes," he whispered, his heart hammering. "Now, whatever we want it to be. A reinvention, as it were. Of lots of things."

"Such an unconventional garret. A spot that suits you so well. I can tell from the glow in your beautiful brown eyes that you love it. As to us living here together, I want you to know, marriage, that's not necessary because—"

"Oh, *no*." His hand went to her wrist to halt her nervous swaying. "We're getting married, Emma. Don't reject me because you think I don't need it. Need *you*. I long for you to be my wife more than I long for my next breath. I've talked to my solicitor about securing a license if that's the route we go. Or we'll have banns read and do this properly. We'll have an intimate ceremony or one tasteless enough to make society's teeth ache. A duke and duchess in attendance, among others. Your parish is St Anne's, isn't it? Years after you left, but it's still there."

She pressed her lips together, smothering her amusement. His mood lifted to see she was pleased with this cheerless production. He was no romantic, though he wished he were. "There's a fee for banns to be read, you know, darling man."

Laughing, he trailed his thumb down her throat in a prolonged caress that made her purr. "Fifteen shillings and sixpence. I checked. Costly, but you're worth it. Even if I'm not."

Her eyes were shining when she lifted them to his. "If this is because of what happened in the conservatory and the other times, I promise you, no babe resulted from our…interludes. I'm without a child; you're safe."

His heart stuttered, a deafening thump in his chest. "I don't want to be *safe*, Emma. I want to have children with you. *Our* children. I adore you. You and only you. I adore your strength, your wit, your intelligence. Your kindness. I want you because you and I understand each other in a way no one else *can*. I never thought to utter words of love to anyone outside my family. I never thought to have my *own* family, that I would be given the chance." Leaning, he kissed her cheek, her jaw, the delicate arch between neck and shoulder, taking her frayed groan and letting it enliven his soul. "I love you. Do you hear me? So much is held on the shoulders of those eight letters. Letters that don't seem appropriate to their weight. To express them should require volumes, a library of emotion. Not the world, to be left to eight simple letters." Capturing her lips, he kissed her quickly, passionately, then let her go. Took a step back to allow a slice of London's dense but welcome air to settle between them, clear his mind. "But that's the flawlessness of the sentiment; perfection in the simplicity."

"The weight of eight letters," she murmured and gazed out over his city. *Their* city.

"Eight letters you could return if you'd like."

She glanced back, her expression trapped between exasperation and fondness. She looked wonderful in his coat, he decided. "I love you, you daft man. MacDermot *and* Alexander. I love both equally. I always have." A flash of fire lit her gaze. "To quote the duchess: we were waiting on the gentleman."

"You're going to make a go of it, then? With me? And accept my humble apology for making you wait? This time—and before."

"Oh, yes, the countess. And her bloody tiara. I may never get over that." Emma's shoulders lifted in vexation, relaxed with her decision. When she stepped into his arms, Simon had no choice but to wrap them around her and hold on tightly. "I'm going to make the very best go of it. No matter that you botched it the first time. I'll even strive to become acquainted with this Josie person since she's your friend. If I'm going to help you, I have to accept her."

"You're not only going to accept her, you're going to *like* her."

"We'll see," she whispered against his shirtfront. "I'm somewhat possessive of you, I've found."

"Stubborn chit."

"Arrogant cur."

Over her head, he watched the sun soar above the red and gold speckled horizon, the wash of color bringing out the amber in her hair, the pinkish flush darkening her skin. He wanted to preserve this moment, place it on canvas to gaze at throughout life.

After a moment, she gave a wiggle in his arms. "Your bed was very comfortable. Quite."

With a smile, he pressed his chin into the crown of her head and tightened his arms around her. "Do tell."

"There's a loose spring in one spot I'd hate for you to hit." She made a huffing sound and looked up, her eyes as bright as the sapphire in the ring he'd ordered from Julian's jeweler last week. The one he was picking up tomorrow and hoped she'd like. Because with this woman, he was never entirely sure of anything. Part of, he realized, the attraction. "Unless you've shown someone *else* how comfortable it is already." She struggled to back away, teeth bared. "I reckon you have. What am I thinking? The *Times* has written about it, I bet! In that case, I kindly rescind my offer. How's that for fancy talk?"

Simon bowed forward and laughed until he gasped, clutching his belly and coughing, all the while, her ineffectual fists cuffing his side.

"I haven't, Em. Stop it. No one. I've brought no

one here." He glanced up, barely missing a final swing she'd unleashed. "My bloody family didn't even know, until Henry dropped us on the corner outside, that I owned a paint factory in a rather troubled neighborhood they wish I could leave behind."

She poked her finger against her chest, her lips forming a delighted O. "Just me."

He kissed her brow, drawing the lapels of his coat together at her throat. "Just you. Only you."

"Well, then." Taking his hand, she dragged him across the roof, a splash of unspoiled sunlight warming their backs. "What are you waiting for?"

He took the stairs behind her two at a time. "Not a thing, Emma, darling."

He wasn't waiting on one bloody thing with his girl ever again.

EPILOGUE

Three Years Later
Where a Warehouse Has Become a Home
St Giles, London

*E*mma watched from the window as Simon stepped gingerly down from Finn's carriage to the cobbled lane, her heart beating faster as it did each time she saw him.

As it would until the day she died.

Love was fierce and, at times overwhelming, seizing her breath and her soul.

But she would never run from love again.

Frowning, she rubbed her thumb across a streak on the windowpane. Simon was still limping; an injury sustained three weeks ago during travel to 1875 to rescue one of Josie's charges. Emma laughed with a puff that fogged the glass when her husband waved Finn off, scowling as he climbed the front steps, entering the warehouse with a door slam that reverberated through the residence. Their majordomo, Dimitri—hired because a majordomo was required even if one lived on the edge of what society considered civilization—rarely got to the warehouse's main entrance before Simon muscled his way gracelessly through it.

He was irritated of late, perhaps justly. His brothers *had* been overprotective since Emma had returned with Simon to the Blue Moon following their rescue mission, where he'd proceeded to leave a trail of blood from the alley to his study, then decided, as chaos erupted around him, to elegantly pass out on a vacant settee. Even Henry, who was still around after all these years, had been distraught—or so Simon later told her.

Today was his first trip into the city since the accident, returning to his position as a vestryman for the St Giles District Board of Works. Of course, Finn had decided to swing by the Palace of Westminster to escort him home, where Simon had had an afternoon meeting with an MP he was courting who'd accepted the invitation because of Simon's last name but would help him because of his ideas and his passion.

Simon Alexander was making a name for himself, one all his own.

Finn had likely asked after his little brother's health four times before they hit Tavistock Square, making Emma smile as she gave the windowpane a light tap. His family loved him and treated him as a boy even as Simon approached the wizened age of thirty. That might not change, a fact she'd accepted, but he hadn't. The brothers' Alexander also thought it marvelously amusing that Simon had chosen to cycle between such disparate lives. Elected official; gaming hell owner.

Julian was elated, Finn appalled.

Little did they realize, but her husband was determined to change the world.

Starting with his tiny, downtrodden piece of it.

After she and Simon had promised to do so on the

night of their wedding, lying in a naked tangle in the bed upstairs, they'd immediately set out to fulfill that promise.

To each other—and themselves.

Supernatural gifts were of little use if the gift wasn't shared. Their work had given life meaning.

"If you're standing by the window, he'll know you were waiting for him. The nurturing is starting to drive him mad, dear."

Emma turned, having forgotten for a moment that Josie was sitting by the hearth in the corner of the warehouse fashioned as an office. "*Oh*, you're right," she whispered and hurriedly crossed the room to settle behind a gilded bronze writing table Simon had gifted her last Christmas, as the ink-spattered one she'd been using had rocked with each movement on its wholly uneven legs.

They heard Simon before they saw him. Heard *them*, Emma thought, her heart near to bursting as Simon strolled through the arched brick doorway with his hands full of boy.

Arthur looked just like him, a replica right down to the dent in his cheek. Except for her son's startlingly blue eyes, her contribution. Aside from birthing him, of course. Her joy at seeing them together was enormous. Simon was a wonderful father, striving to be the man his birth father hadn't been— and everything that Julian and Finn *were*. He couldn't stand to be away from Arthur for even an afternoon. He'd carry him to his quarters at the Blue Moon every day if she'd allow it.

Simon tossed Arthur over his shoulder, the boy squealing and kicking his legs in delight. "Josie," he said with a salute of his hand. Then straightway, her husband was before her, wrapping his hand around the nape of her neck and drawing her up and into his body, issuing a brief, blistering kiss that left her breathless. "Later," he whispered in her ear.

The heat of his promise sank through layers of fine wool and muslin to warm her in places only he knew how to appease.

Pulling back with a wicked gleam in his chestnut eyes, Simon winked.

"Papa, present," Arthur beseeched in his sing-song voice, yanking on his father's coat and leaving a chocolate smudge on the sleeve. Just two years of age, he expected a present any time an adult entered his vicinity.

Laughing, Simon shifted Arthur in his arms, tunneled his hand in his trouser pocket, coming up with a piece of peppermint and a silver matchbook case. He handed the candy to his son and, with a swift glance at his wife, worked the case beneath the edge of his sleeve with a magician's ease.

Emma sighed and held out her hand, tapping her slipper on the polished planks.

Shifting from one foot to the other, Simon muttered beneath his breath but, in the end, relinquished the case. "Lyons, the MP I met with, won't miss it. Interesting thistle pattern etched on the front that I couldn't resist. Good hinge, too. Doesn't stick like mine."

"I thought we'd agreed about the larceny." She slipped the case in her skirt pocket, embellishments to her gowns Madame Hebert had created for instances like these. "Elected officials don't go around stealing things."

"Hungry," Arthur mumbled around a mouthful of peppermint.

Josie rose to her feet, her arms outstretched. "Let me. I know just what he likes for a snack. Apple slices and buttered bread." She swiveled so only Emma could see her and mouthed *tell him*.

Simon placed his son on the floor and gave his bottom a swat. "I'll be in for a story, Artie, after your snack."

"The tiger one," Artie said, his hand tucked in Josie's as they strolled from the room.

"Indeed, the tiger one," Simon murmured, his gaze fixed lovingly on his son. When they were alone, without a word, he pressed Emma back two steps into the wall, slanting his mouth over hers. "It's been too long since we've made love. I'm frantic for you."

Emma grinned, breaking the kiss. "Simon Alexander, it's been two days."

He nibbled on her jaw, then moved to a sensitive spot below her ear, eliciting a frayed groan from her. "*Frantic*."

"I have something to tell you." Her head dropped back as he rolled her earlobe between his teeth and sucked lightly. "I can't think when you do this."

Her tone must have alarmed him because he froze, his hands falling to his sides. "Hargrave?" he asked in a feral voice.

Emma bracketed his jaw between her palms and kissed him softly, calming him. "Not once since you let him know the League would never let him go if he didn't let *me* go. This is good news. Incredible news. Only the second time I've been so blessed news."

Simon blinked, cheeks flushing. Then, stumbling back, he slumped on the edge of her desk as his breath scattered, rushing from his lips in a gush. "A baby." His throat clicked as he swallowed, his eyes going fever-bright. "A baby."

"A *summer* baby. Only fair, since Artie's our winter treasure." She watched her husband run through the possibilities, some of them dire, and stepped in until he had no choice but to wrap her in his arms and drag her close. "It will be fine. We'll be fine. I barely had a complaint last time. Honestly, I enjoyed it."

"You're the toughest woman I know, Em. But I still worry." Pressing his cheek to her bosom, he drew a choking breath, his voice frayed. "Don't let me ruin this moment. I'm overcome. I love him so much, you so much…" His words crumbled like a sandcastle consumed by a rogue wave. "I want to give you everything. Protect you from every danger."

Emma tilted his head until she could look into his misty eyes. "You've given me more than everything, darling. My life, my meaning. Our efforts with Josie, the League, exploring my gift, improving life for those in St Giles and Tower Hamlets, my son, my *family*. What more could you give me? What more could I want?"

"Beats me," he whispered, his hot breath skimming her collarbone, "I only know I want to give you more. Give our children more."

"Well, there is one teeny item," she replied, realizing this was the perfect time to introduce the topic. Of course, he would say yes to anything in this mood. "Lucien needs a job. Supervision. Guidance."

Simon's spine stiffened beneath the hand she'd flattened on his lower back. "You wrestle like a street thug, madam. Right for the jugular."

"You could succeed where others have failed. That's a resounding theme in your life. Savior of St Giles, some are calling you." She pressed her lips together to hide a smile that would go over like a lead brick if he witnessed it. "Why not make it a family theme?"

"An Alexander by name *and* combat style, my beloved." Simon scrubbed his fist across his chin with a gently issued curse. "So, Finn kicked my rebellious

THE HELLION IS TAMED

nephew out on his arse. After the boy was dismissed from Rugby. Trust me, I had my fair share of heated discussions with administrators on that campus, too. But they invited me back each fall, much to my surprise." Exhaling, his shoulders slumped. "And to think, Lucien's the *actual* son of a viscount, not a bastardized imposter, and still they expelled him."

Emma reached for a small shipping crate sitting by her desk, intending to drag it over and sit on it so they could talk. Simon was up like a flash, knocking her hands aside, lifting the crate, empty she could've told him, and positioning it before the desk. His hand going out in a flourish as if he'd offered her a seat on a chariot. When she settled, he went to his haunches before her, that slightly terrified look he'd carry until the baby arrived twisting his features.

She trailed her finger down his cheek and watched in delight as his lids fluttered. "He's confused, Simon. Like you were. Everyone in the League is, while managing a mystical talent *and* adolescence. He's eighteen, fighting to find himself, find independence from an overbearing but incredibly loving father. Touching objects and seeing the future, or the past—each and every object you encounter—must be horrendous. Add to that, his father feeling such guilt for *giving* him the gift." She paused, letting her advice sink in. Men often desired to feel *they'd* come to the decision their wives had placed before them. "He needs space. He needs *you.*"

Simon grimaced, his lips twisting. "It must be horrendous. My haunts are nothing like that supernatural burden. I've even come to appreciate them, friends that never, *ever* leave. Henry says he's staying with me until I kick, then we'll walk off into the sunset together."

"Lucien loves you, trusts you. You're closer to his

age. Finn is too soft-hearted to deal with a wayward young man. Julian and Piper should have known better. If only he could meet someone in the League and fall in love, a woman who understands what being gifted is *like*."

Simon rocked back on his heels, his hands going out in surrender. "I give up. Alert Dimitri and have him send the carriage. I'll put Lucien to work at the Blue Moon, maybe even at the Board of Works office. Limit the objects he has to touch, walk him through the uncertainty of our world. An uncertainty he has to accept. And remind him, repeatedly, that there is no true definition for normal." He snagged a half crown from his waistcoat pocket and gave it a reckless spin between his fingers. "What's another child anyway? This will make three."

Emma snorted a laugh through her nose, then clapped her hand over her face to try and call it back, sounding like the undignified Emmaline Breslin of old. "He's 18, not two. You have months before another babe appears to worry over, anxious papa."

Simon's gaze rolled up to hers, so vulnerable she felt hers tear up in response. "I'm thrilled, by the way. Incredibly grateful and happy. I can't believe I'm saying this, but I want as many babies as you'd like to give me." Leaning, he caressed her stomach with a hand that trembled. "I promise to do my best, always. You have my word as a thief."

Rising to her feet, Emma held out her hand in invitation. "I know a wonderful way we can celebrate. Follow me to the bedchamber, and I might be persuaded to show you. As you likely suspect, I'm wearing few layers beneath this gown. We could get to negotiations quickly."

Bracing his hand on his knee, Simon shoved to his feet in a burst of masculine enthusiasm. "I'll follow

you anywhere, my girl. To the past, to the bedchamber, and especially," he said, laughing as he swept her
into his arms and strode toward their bedchamber,
"to our future."

~ END ~

THANKS!

Thank you for reading Simon and Emma's love story! I hope you enjoyed *The Hellion is Tamed* as much as I enjoyed writing it.

Come along for Julian and Piper's tumultuous affair in *The Lady is Trouble* (book 1), for Finn and Victoria's wild ride in *The Rake is Taken* (book 2) and Sebastian and Delaney's love story in *The Duke is Wicked* (book 3).

Have you already read the entire *League of Lords* series? Read on for a sneak-peek into my new Regency romance *The Brazen Bluestocking*, the first installment of the *Duchess Society Series*. A willful bluestocking matches wits with a devilish scoundrel she never expected to desire with every beat of her heart. Banter, scandal and devastating passion.

THE **B**RAZEN
BLUESTOCKING

THE Duchess Society

AWARD WINNING AUTHOR
TRACY SUMNER

ABOUT THE BOOK

A defiant society outcast.
A forbidding rogue who doesn't believe in love.
A passionate wager.

Daughter of an earl, Lady Hildegard Templeton hasn't conformed to what society expects from a woman of her station. Industrious and unique, she's created an emboldened organization for women on the cusp of marriage, The Duchess Society. Called a bluestocking to her face and worse behind closed salon doors, she vows to marry for love. And nothing but. Although the emotion has never shown itself to her. Until she meets him.

Bastard son of a viscount and king of London's sordid streets, Tobias Streeter has spent a lifetime building his empire, and he needs the Duchess Society to find a suitable wife. An asset to expand his worth in society's eyes. But he vows his search will have nothing to do with love and everything to do with vengeance. Until he meets her.

Soon, Tobias and Hildy's plans are in turmoil as they choose between expectation, passion, and love.

CHAPTER ONE

Limehouse Basin, London, 1822

She'd taken this assignment on a dare.

A dare to herself.

Unbridled curiosity had driven her, the kind that killed cats. When it was just another promise-of-rain winter day. Another dismal society marriage the Duchess Society was overseeing.

Another uninspiring man to investigate.

Hildegard Templeton told herself everything was normal. The warehouse had looked perfectly ordinary from the grimy cobblestones her post-chaise deposited her on. A sign swinging fearlessly in the briny gust ripping off the Thames—*Streeter, Macauley & Company*—confirming she'd arrived at the correct location. A standard, salt-wrecked dwelling set amongst tea shops and taverns, silk merchants and ropemakers. Surrounded by shouting children, over-laden carts, horses, dogs, vendors selling sweetmeats and pies, and the slap of sails against ships' masts. A chaotic but essential locality, with cargo headed all over England but landing in this grubby spit of dock-yard first.

When she'd stepped inside, she halted in place, realizing her blunder in assuming anything about Tobias Streeter was *normal*.

Hildy knew nothing about architecture but knew this was not the norm for a refurbished warehouse bordering the Limehouse Basin Lock. A suspect neighborhood her post-boy hadn't been pleased to drive into—or be asked to wait *in* while she conducted her business. Honestly, the building was a marvel of iron joists, girders, and cast-iron columns with ornamental heads. With a splash of elegant color—crimson and black. What she imagined a gentleman's club might look like, a refined yet dodgy sensibility she found utterly… *charming*. And entirely unnecessary for a building housing a naval merchant's headquarters.

Her exhalation left her in a vaporous cloud, and she gazed around with a feeling she didn't like as the piquant scent of a spice she identified as Asian in origin enveloped her.

A feeling she wasn't accustomed to.

Miscalculation.

As she would admit only to her business partner, Georgiana, the newly minted Duchess of Markham: *I fear I've botched the entire project*. She'd taken society's slander as truth—shipping magnate, Romani blood, profligate bounder, and the most noteworthy moniker the *ton* had ever come up with—and made up her mind about the man, concocting a wobbly plan unsupported by proper research. A proposal built on assumptions instead of *fact*. Sloppy dealings were very unlike her. Ambition to secure the agreement to advise the Earl of Hastings's five daughters as they traveled along their matrimonial journey—the eldest currently set on marrying the profligate bounder—had risen above common sense.

Hildy took a breath scented with exotic spice and tidal mud and stepped deeper into the warehouse, locking her apprehension out of sight. She wasn't going to back down now, not when she had *five* delightful but wholly unsupervised women who would make terrific disasters of their marriages without the Duchess Society to guide them.

Marriages much like her parents' were an aberration staining her memories until she wanted none of the institution. They needed her, these girls, and she needed *them*. To prove her life wasn't a tale as ordinary as the building she'd expected to find herself in this morning—society outcast, bluestocking. Spinster. Not that it mattered what they thought of her; she'd rejected the expectations the *ton* had placed on her from the first moment.

"Looking for Streeter, are ya?"

Hildy turned in a swirl of flounces and worsted wool she wished she'd rejected for this visit when a simple day dress would have sufficed. Perhaps one borrowed from her maid.

The man who'd stumbled upon her lingering in the entrance to the warehouse was tall enough to have her arching her neck to view him from beneath her bonnet's lime silk brim. And built like one of those ships moored at the wharf outside. "Tobias Streeter, yes."

The brute gave the tawny hair lying across his brow a swipe, removed the cheroot from his lips, and extinguished it beneath the toe of his muddy boot in a gesture she didn't think the architect of this impressive building would appreciate. "He expecting ya?"

They make them rude in the East End, Hildy decided with a sigh. "Possibly." If he'd been alerted by his future father-in-law, *yes*.

CHAPTER ONE

"Who's calling?" he asked gruffly, digging in his pocket and coming up with another cheroot, even as the bitter aroma from the first still enveloped them. "Apologies for asking, but we don't get many of your kind round here. Some kinds"—he chuckled at his joke and swiped the tapered end of the cheroot across his bottom lip—"just not *your* kind."

Hildy shifted the folio she clutched from one gloved hand to the other. Her palms had started to perspire beneath kid leather. This man was playing with her, and she didn't like participating in games she wasn't sure she could win. "Lady Hildegard Templeton," she supplied, using the honorific when she rarely did. "Of the Duchess Society."

The impolite brute arrested his effort to remove a tinderbox from his tattered coat pocket. "The Mad Matchmaker," he whispered, his cheroot hitting the glossy planks beneath their feet. Horrified, he backed up a step as if she had a contagious disease.

A rush of blood flooded her. *Temper*, she warned herself. *Not here.* The blush lit her cheeks, and she cursed the man standing stunned before her for causing it. "That ridiculous sobriquet is not something I respond—"

"Sobriquet," a voice full of laughter and arrogance intoned from behind her. "Go back to unloading the shipment from Spain, Alton. I have this."

When she turned to face the man she assumed was Tobias Streeter, she wanted to be in control because that was how this day was going to go. Confident. Poised. Looking like a businesswoman, not a lady. Not a *matchmaker*—which she *wasn't*. She longed to tell him what she thought of the rude entry to his establishment when he hadn't known she was coming.

Instead, she felt flushed and damp, unprepared

based on a split-second judgment of the glorious building she stood in. Adding to that, the niggling sense that she'd made a colossal error in calculating her opponent.

And then Hildy merely felt *thunderstruck*.

Because, as he stepped out of the shadows and into the glow cast from the garnet sconce at his side, she realized with a heavy heart that Tobias Streeter, the Rogue King of Limehouse Basin, was the most attractive man she'd ever seen.

Which wasn't an asset. She was considered attractive as well—she surmised with a complete and utter lack of vanity—and she'd only found it to be a *trap*.

"I wondered if you'd actually venture into the abyss, luv," he said idly, tugging a kerchief from his back pocket and across his sweaty brow.

He had a streak of graphite on his left cheek, and his hands were a further mess. Additionally, he'd made no effort to contain the twisted collar of his shirt. The top two bone buttons were undone, and the flash of olive skin drew her gaze when she wished it wouldn't. No coat, no waistcoat. He was unprepared for visitors. However, if she were being fair, she'd given him no notice he was to have one.

"Those feral phaeton rides through Hyde Park I read about in the *Gazette* must be true. They say you're a daredevil at heart, Templeton, a feminine trait the *ton* despises, am I right? Gossip that I'd lay odds you don't welcome any more than that charming nickname your poisonous brethren saddled you with." He tucked the length of stained cloth in his waistband to crudely dangle, drawing her eye to his trim waist. "They can't understand anyone of means who doesn't simply sit back and enjoy it."

"I'm, well..." Hildy fumbled, then wished she'd

waited another moment to gather her thoughts. "I'm here on business. As you know. Or guessed."

His gaze dropped to the folio in her hand, his lips quirking sourly. "My sordid past is bundled up in that tidy file, I'm guessing."

No, actually, she wanted to admit but thankfully didn't. *I've gone into this all wrong.*

She ran through the facts detailed on the sheet in her wafer-thin folio that were not facts at all. Royal Navy hero of some sort, a conflict in India he didn't discuss publicly. Powerful friends in the East India Company, hence his move into trade upon his return to England. Ruthless, having built his empire one brick at a time. Father rumored to be titled, mother of Romani stock, at least a smidgen, which was all it took to be completely ostracized.

Insanely handsome had never factored into her research.

And she'd assumed this would be an uncomplicated assignment.

"Tobias Streeter," he murmured, halting before her. Almost as tall as his brutish gatekeeper, Hildy kept her head tilted to capture his gaze. Which she was going to capture. And *hold*. Hazy light from a careless sun washed over him from windows set at all angles, allowing her to peruse at her leisure.

She didn't fool herself; it was an opportunity he *allowed*.

Skin the color of lightly brewed tea. Eyes the shade of a juicy green apple you shined against your sleeve and then couldn't help but take a quick bite of —the glow from the sconce turning them a deep emerald while she stared. Highlighted by a set of thick lashes any woman would be jealous of. Jaw hard, lips full, breath scented with mint and tea. Not brandy or scotch, another misstep had she presumed it.

When, of course, she'd presumed it.

As he patiently accepted her appraisal, his hand rose, and his index finger, just the calloused tip, trailed her cheek to tuck a stray strand behind her ear.

The hands of a man who worked with them.

Played with them.

She shivered, a shallow exhalation she couldn't contain rushing forth in a steamy puff. Parts of the ground story were open from quay to yard for transit handling, and glacial gusts were whistling through like a train on tracks.

"Alton," he instructed without glancing away from her, though he dropped his hand to his side. "Close the doors at the back, will you? And bring tea to my office."

"Tea," Alton echoed. "*Tea?*"

Streeter's breath fanned her face, warming her to her toes. "Isn't that what ladies drink over business dealings? If ladies even *do* business. Perhaps it's what they drink over spirited discussions about watercolors or their latest gown."

She gripped the folio until her knuckles ached, feeling like a ball of yarn being tossed between two cats. "Make no special accommodations. I'll have whatever it is you guzzle during business dealings, Mr. Streeter."

He laughed, then caught himself with the slightest downward tilt of his lips. She'd surprised them both somehow. It was the first chess move she'd won in this match. "We guzzle malt whiskey then," he murmured and turned, seeming to expect her to follow.

She recorded details as she shadowed him across

the vast space crowded with shipping crates and assorted stacks of rope and tools, to a small room at the back overlooking the pier. His shirt was untucked on one side, the kerchief he'd wiped his face with slapping his thigh. His clothing was finely made but not skillfully enough to hide a muscular build most men used built-in padding to establish. Dark hair, *no*, more than dark. Black as tar, curling over his rumpled shirt collar and around his ears. So pitch dark, she imagined she could see cobalt streaks in it, like a flame gone mad.

Hair that called a woman's fingers to tangle in it, no matter the woman.

The gods had allotted this conceited beast an inequitable share of beauty, that was certain. And for the first time in her *life*, Hildy was caught up in an attraction.

His office was another unsurprising surprise.

A roaring fire in the hearth chasing away the chill. A Carlton House desk flanked by two armchairs roomy enough to fit Streeter or his man of business, Alton. A Hepplewhite desk, or a passable imitation. A colorful Aubusson covering the floor, nothing threadbare and sold because it had lost its value. Her heart skipped as she stepped inside the space, confirmation that she'd indeed misjudged. Shelf upon shelf of leather-bound books bracketed the walls. Walking to a row, she checked the spines with a searching review. Cracked but good, each and every one of them. Architecture, commerce, mathematics, chemistry. Nothing entertaining, nothing playful. The library of a man with a mind.

While Streeter moved to a sideboard that had likely come from the king's castoffs, and poured them a drink from a bottle whose label she didn't recognize, she circled the room, inspecting.

Holding both glasses in one hand, he situated

himself not at his desk but on the edge of an over-turned crate beside it, his long legs stretched before him. Sipping from his while holding hers, his steely gaze tracked her. Fortunately, she realized from the travel-weary Wellington he tapped lightly on the carpet, her examination of his private space was making him uneasy. With an aggrieved grunt, he yanked the kerchief from his waistband and tossed it needlessly to the floor.

Finally, she sighed in relief, a *weakness*. If he didn't like to be studied, he must have *something* to hide. She'd been hired, in part, to find out what.

"This isn't one of your frivolous races through the park." He leaned to place her glass on the corner of his desk. Hers to take, or not, when she passed. The only charitable thing he'd done was pour it for her. "Right now, I have two men guarding your traveling chariot parked outside, lest someone rob you blind. The thing is as yellow as a ripe banana, which catches the eye. They'll slice the velvet from the squabs and resell it two blocks over for fast profit. Your post-boy looked ready to expire when we got to him. Guessing he's never had to sit on his duff while waiting for his mistress to complete business in the East End. A slightly larger *man* might better fit the bill next time."

Post-boys were all she could afford.

Hildy released the satin chin strap and slid her bonnet from her head. Her coiffure, unsteady on a good day as her maid's vision was dreadful, collapsed with the removal, and a wave of hair just a shade darker than the sun fell past her shoulders. Streeter blinked, his fingers tightening around his glass. She noticed the insignificant gesture while wondering if the fevered awareness filling the air was only in *her* mind.

Halting by his desk, she reached for her drink

with a nod in his direction. The scent of soap and spice drifted to her, his unique mix. "This warehouse, it's quite unusual. Magnificent, actually. I've never seen the like."

"I'll be sure to tell the architect the daughter of an earl approves." His gaze cool, giving away absolutely nothing, he dug a bamboo toothpick from his trouser pocket and jammed it between his teeth, working it from side to side between a pair of very firm lips. At her raised brow, he shrugged. "Stopped smoking. It's enough to breathe London's coal-laden air without asking for more trouble."

Hildy dropped the folio, which held little of value aside from her employment contract with the Earl of Hastings, in the armchair and lifted the glass to her lips. The whiskey was smooth, smoky—*good*. "This is excellent," she mused, licking her lips and watching Streeter's hand again tense around his tumbler.

"Thank you. It's my own formula," he said after a charged silence, a dent appearing next to his mouth. Not so much a dimple. Two of which she had herself, a feature people had commented on her entire life.

His was more of an elevated smirk.

"Yours?" Continuing her journey around the room, Hildy paused by a framed blueprint of this warehouse. Beside it was another detailed sketch, a building she didn't recognize. Architectural schematics drawn by someone very talented. She couldn't miss the initials, *TS*, in the lower right corner.

Frowning, she tilted her glass, staring into it as if the amber liquor would provide answers to an increasingly enigmatic puzzle. Aside from disappointing her family and society, she'd never done anything remarkable. *Been* anything remarkable.

When faced with remarkability, she wasn't sure she trusted it.

Streeter stacked his boots one atop the other, the crate creaking beneath him. "A business venture, a distillery going south financially that I found myself uncommonly intrigued by, once I handed over an astounding amount of blunt to keep it afloat *and* demanded I be invited into the process. Usually, I invest, then step away if the enterprise is well-managed, which it often isn't, but this…" Bringing the glass to his lips, he drank around the toothpick. Quite a feat. She couldn't look away from the show of masculine bravado if she'd been ordered to at the end of a pistol. "It's straightforward chemistry, the brewing of malt. But, lud, what a challenge, seeking perfection."

Finessing his glass into an empty spot next to him on the crate, he wiggled the toothpick from his lips and pointed it at her. A crude signal that he was ready to begin negotiations. "Isn't seeking perfection your business too, luv? The *ideal* bloke, without shortcomings. I've yet to see such a man, but the Mad Matchmaker is fabled to work miracles, so maybe there's a chance for me."

Seating herself in the chair absent her paperwork, Hildy set her glass on the desk and worked her gloves free, one deliberate finger at a time. If he believed he could chase her away with his bullying attitude, he hadn't done suitable research into his opponent's background. Last year, the Duchess Society had completed an assignment, confidential in nature but rumored nonetheless, for the royal family. Madness, power, fantastic wealth, love gained, love lost. This handsome scoundrel and his trifling reach for society's acceptance, she could handle.

Although she realized she was silently reminding herself of the fact, not stating it outright.

"Nothing to do with perfection and rarely anything to do with love, Mr. Streeter. The betrothals I support are, like the marriage you're proposing with Lady Matilda Delacour-Baynham, a business agreement. Unless I'm mistaken from the discussions I've had with her and her father, the Earl of Hastings."

He twirled the toothpick between his fingers like a magician. "You have it dead on. Holy hell, I'm not looking for love. Don't fill the chit's head with that rubbish. The words mean nothing to me. They never have. Society only sells the idea to make the necessity of unions such as these more acceptable."

Well, *that* sounded personal. "Lady Matilda—"

"Mattie wants freedom. If you know her, she's told you what she's interested in. The only thing. Medicine." He laughed and sent the toothpick spinning. "An earl's daughter, can you conjure it? When no female can be a physician and certainly not a legitimate lady. To use one of your brethren's expressions, it's beyond the pale."

He winked at her, *winked*, and she was reasonably certain he didn't mean it playfully.

"I have funds, more than she can spend in a lifetime. More than I can. She wants to use a trifling bit to rescue her father, a man currently drowning, and I do mean drowning, in debt? Fine. Finance her hobby of practicing medicine? Also fine. Or her *dream*, if you're the visionary sort. Let her safely prowl these corridors and others on the rookery trail, delivering babes, bandaging wounds, swabbing fevered brows. They have no one else, the desperate souls I live amongst. She'll be an angel in their midst. And me, the one controlling the deliverance. Deliverance for *her* from your upmarket bunch. Who, other than finding ways to creatively lose capital, do nothing but sit around on their arses making up nicknames for those who *prosper*."

"What's in it for you?" Hildy whispered, not sure she knew. Was Tobias Streeter, rookery bandit, shipping titan, this eager to marry into a crowd that indeed sat on their toffs all day dreaming up pointless monikers? When she'd been trying to escape them her entire *life*?

He jabbed the toothpick in her direction, his smile positively savage. "Don't worry about what I need. I don't make deals where I don't profit, luv."

A caged tiger set loose on society. That's what he was. Half of London was secretly fawning over him while refusing him admittance to their sacred drawing rooms.

Not so fussy about admittance to their beds, she'd bet.

He slipped the toothpick home between his stubbornly compressed lips. "Templeton, you of all people should understand her predicament, being somewhat peculiar yourself. Boxed in by society's expectations, unless I'm missing my guess, which I usually don't. I understand, do you see? It's why the girl trusts me. Why, maybe, I trust *her*.

"I know what it's like to be found lacking for elements beyond your control. Where you were born, the color of your skin. Being delivered on the wrong side of some addled viscount's blanket. Think nothing of intelligence or courage, wit or ingenuity, *talent*, only the blue blood, or lack of it, running beneath that no one sees unless you slice them open."

Hildy smoothed her hand down her bodice and laid her gloves in a neat tangle on her knee, Streeter chasing every move with his intense, sea-green gaze. That blasted blue blood he spoke of kept her tangled in a web, day in and day out. He didn't need to enlighten her. Resignedly, she nodded to the folio lying like a spent weapon between them.

"Let's discuss specifics, shall we? Hastings wants you to court his daughter properly. Even if Lady... um, Mattie doesn't require it, *he* does. Flowers, gifts, trinkets. Courtship rituals. The servants gossip, and everyone in London then knows what's what, so this is an essential, seemingly trivial part of the process. I'll assist with the selection. He'd also like certain businesses you're involved with downplayed, so to speak. The unsavory enterprises. At least until the first babe is born. Rogue King of Limehouse Basin isn't exactly what he desired for his darling girl. But you, obviously, got to her first."

"At least I'm not an ivory-turner," he whispered beneath his breath.

She tilted her head in confusion.

"Her father cheats at dice, my naïve hoyden. I do many cursed things, but cheating is not one. Every gaming hell in town is after him." Streeter growled and, snatching up his glass, polished off the contents. Lord, she wished he'd button his collar. The view was becoming a distraction. "There's more to this agreement. I can see from the brutal twist of those comely lips of yours. More edges to be smoothed away like sandpaper to rough timber. Go on, spit it out. I can take a ruthless assessment."

Hildy controlled, through diligence born of her own beatdowns, the urge to raise her hand to cover her lips. *Comely* ones that had begun to sting pleasantly at his backhanded compliment. "Aside from your agreement that my solicitors—in addition to yours and the earl's—will review all contracts to ensure fairness for both parties, there is the matter of Miss Henson."

He whispered a curse against crystal and was un-apologetic when his narrowed gaze met hers. He lowered his glass until it rested on his flat belly. "So, I'm to play the holy man until the ceremony?" Then he muttered something she didn't catch. Or didn't want to. *For a wife who prefers women.*

Hildy made a mental note to investigate that disastrous possibility, although it made no difference. Lady Matilda—Mattie—had to get married to someone. A *male* someone. Why not this beautiful devil who seemed to actually *like* her? Heavens, Hildy thought in despair. The Duchess Society couldn't weather the storm should a scandal of that magnitude come to light. It was illegal, which was absurd, of course, but that was the case. There were whisperings of such goings-on, relationships on the sly.

Rumors with the power to destroy one's *life*.

It was decided at that moment, with dust motes swirling through fading wintry sunlight, in a startlingly elegant office in the middle of a slum. This marriage, between a lady who wanted to be a doctor but couldn't and a tenacious blackguard who wanted high society tucked neatly in his pocket, had to happen. Or Hildy and her enterprise to save the women of London from gross matrimonial injustice was *finished*.

Too, she would go belly up without funds coming in to pay the bills—and coming in *soon*.

Streeter rocked forward, his Wellingtons dusting the floor, upsetting the shipping crate until she feared it would collapse beneath him. "I return the question because it's a valuable one. Besides a hefty fee that Hastings can't afford and will eventually derive from other sources, namely the source sharing this stale malt air with you, what's in it for you? Dealing with me isn't going to be easy. Ask my partners, should you be able to locate them. Mattie isn't much better from what I know of her. Her spirit is part of the reason I believed she'd be the right woman for the job."

Hildy chewed on her bottom lip, an abominable habit, then glanced up to find Streeter's gaze had gone vacant around the edges. The way a man's does when he's *thinking* about things. She wasn't, saints above, imagining the thread of attraction strung between them like ship's netting. He felt it, too. "I'll be candid."

"Please do," he whispered, bringing himself back from his musing, his cheeks slightly tinged. His breathing maybe, *maybe*, churning faster.

"When I arrived, I would've said I was doing it to secure future business with the Earl of Hastings. He has five daughters, as you know, and no wife to guide them. A line of inept governesses, another quitting every week it seems. My proposal?

"I guide him to appropriate men for the remaining four since Mattie has you on the hook. *Decent* men my people have investigated thoroughly. Then assist with the negotiations, so his daughters are protected, pay my coal bill, and we're both happy." Hildy ran her finger over a nap in the chair's velvet, her gaze dropping to record her progress. "Frankly, I need the money as I wasn't left a large inheritance, more a burden. An ever-maturing residence and staff and no funds allocated for preservation.

"And I'm not planning to marry myself, so survival falls directly to me. Likewise, I do this to benefit the young women I work with, if you must know, not simply as a business venture. You have no idea how lacking they are simply from being isolated from any discussions outside the appropriate tea to serve.

They're forced to sign contracts they can't even begin to understand—*lifelong*, binding contracts—with no assistance."

The toothpick bounced in Streeter's mouth as he bit down on it. "What's changed?"

Digging her fingertips into the chair's cushion, she decided to tell him. "I'm *bored* with earls and viscounts in fretful need of an heir to carry on a line that should cease production. In need of capital to salvage a crumbling empire. A rumored Romani bastard who's hiding what he really wants, and I'm the person hired to find out what?" She snapped her fingers, a weight lifting as she spoke the truth. "Now, there's a challenge."

For a breathless second, Streeter's face erased of expression. Like a fist swept across a mirror's vapor. She'd stunned him—and her pulse soared. Foolishly, categorically. Then a broad smile, a *sincere* smile, sent the dent in his cheek pinging. His teeth flashed in wonderfully startling contrast to his olive skin. "Well, damn, I can be surprised." He saluted her with the glass he'd picked up only to find it empty. "A worthy opponent steps out of the mist."

"I'm not an opponent," she murmured, knowing she was.

With a sigh of regret, perhaps because she'd gone back to fibbing, he braced his hand on his thigh and rose to his feet. She watched him cross the room because she couldn't help herself. Tall, broad yet lean, an awe-inspiring physique even in mussed clothing. He moved with an innate grace even a duke wouldn't necessarily have possessed. Natural and unassuming. The stuff one was born with—or without. Elegance that simply was.

He stopped before another of the schematic drawings, an imposing brick structure laid out with mathematical precision she suspected existed only in the sketch. "What if I say no to working with you? Refuse your kind service. Toss it back to Hastings like a flaming ember, pitting his desperation against my ambition."

Hildy understood after a moment's panic that this was part of the negotiation. That the correct response, or non-response, was vital. Retrieving her glass, she took a generous pull, smooth liquor chasing away the chill. "Is it any different than working with your"—she gestured over her shoulder to the warehouse—"bountiful trading partners? We'll be in business together. End of story."

He paused, studying her in a way few men had dared to even while telling her how beautiful she was. Men she'd never wanted to undress her with their eyes, as the saying went. A phrase that until this second had held no meaning.

A peculiar tension, the awareness from earlier, roared between them as if Alton had reopened the doors and let the Thames rush in. As if Tobias Streeter had laid his hands on her. An experience she had no familiarity with which to visualize.

"End of story," he murmured joylessly and turned back to his sketch.

She deposited her folio on his desk, the thump ringing through the room. Outside, a dockworker's shout and the rub and bump of a ship sliding into harbor pierced the hush. He was equally damaged, she could see. And very good at hiding it. They were alike in this regard, a mysterious element only another wounded animal would recognize.

Making the call on instinct alone, Hildy nonetheless made it.

Tobias Streeter wasn't a fiend. He wasn't an abuser like her father.

He was just a man.

A man she was willing to polish until he shone like the crown jewels. "There will be events. Part of your engagement and introduction to the *ton*, as it were. You'll likely need some instruction."

He tapped the sketch three times before shifting to lean his shoulder against the wall in a negligent slump she no longer counted as factual. "I clean up well. Never fear," he said, his voice laced with scorn. Who it was directed at, she wasn't sure. "I'll review the contract in that tasteful folio of yours this evening, then we'll discuss the details tomorrow afternoon. I'll send a carriage with a coachman ready to protect you should the need arise, not those lads just out of the schoolroom you have manning your conveyance."

Glancing to a clock on the mantel that had been cautiously ticking off time, his smile thinned, frigid enough to freeze water. "I'm sorry to rush you out, but I have a meeting in ten minutes that will, if successful, net me close to a thousand pounds. My men will escort you home. Your chariot can follow along for fun." His jaw tensed when she started to argue, and he pushed off the wall with a growl. "Not on my watch, Templeton. Not in my township. Don't even *begin*."

However, stubborn chit that she was, she did begin, opening her mouth to tell him who was managing this campaign to show London how bloody wonderful a husband he would be.

"Tea and some of them lemony biscuits from the baker on the corner, coming right up," Alton proclaimed, stumbling into the room, a silver teapot she wondered where in heaven's name he'd located clutched in a meaty fist and two mismatched china cups balanced in the other. Halting, he took one look at his employer's thunderous expression, slapped the cups on the first available surface, and hustled Hildy from the office.

The teapot was still in his hand as Streeter's coach rolled down the congested lane with her an unwilling captive inside. She suppressed a clumsy laugh to see a coat of arms, painted over but visible, on the carriage's door.

Another aristocrat who'd lost his fortune to the Rogue King.

Hildy collapsed against the plush squabs of the finest transport she'd ever ridden in, realizing she hadn't asked Tobias Streeter how he planned to profit from a marriage he didn't want.

Read on!

ABOUT TRACY

Tracy's story telling career began when she picked up a copy of LaVyrle Spencer's Vows on a college beach trip. A journalism degree and a thousand romance novels later, she decided to try her hand at writing a southern version of the perfect love story. With a great deal of luck and more than a bit of perseverance, she sold her first novel to Kensington Publishing.

When not writing sensual stories featuring complex characters and lush settings, Tracy can be found reading romance, snowboarding, watching college football and figuring out how she can get to 100 countries before she kicks. She lives in the south, but after spending a few years in NYC, considers herself a New Yorker at heart.

Tracy has been awarded the National Reader's Choice, the Write Touch and the Beacon—with finalist nominations in the HOLT Medallion, Heart of Romance, Rising Stars and Reader's Choice. Her books have been translated into German, Dutch, Portuguese and Spanish. She loves hearing from readers about why she tends to pit her hero and heroine against each other from the very first page or that great romance she simply must order in five seconds on her Kindle.

Connect with Tracy on http://www.tracy-sumner.com

Printed in Great Britain
by Amazon